66 Guns and grief haunt this debut novel, linking a shooting on a Calgary train and a hunting trip for caribou at a strange castle in Newfoundland. The book is about grief and loss, yet is oddly funny, the razor-sharp prose like some outport lovechild of DeLillo and Nabokov. HIDES is a little creepy and very impressive. 99

MARK ANTHONY JARMAN, author of *Burn Man: Selected Stories*

66 HIDES is raucous, tender, sly, and as rich and deep as a forest. Helmed by an unforgettable protagonist who knows so much (while hilariously understanding so little), I was gripped from the first page by the unexpected gentleness in this artful and funny novel, and moved by its unexpected turns on grief, and the bonds of family and friendship. An unforgettable work by a superb writer. 99

SUZETTE MAYR, author of the Giller Prize-winning *The Sleeping Car Porter*

66 On the edge of a failing world, four characters come together to see what remains, and what can be salvaged. Rod Moody-Corbett has written a book that seems to simultaneously inhabit our present and our future. The writing in HIDES seethes and crackles with energy— tough, heartfelt, funny, and sarcastic in all the necessary places. 99

TAMAS DOBOZY, author of *Siege 13* and *Stasio*

HIDES

ROD MOODY-CORBETT

All of the characters and events portrayed in this book are fictitious. Any resemblance to actual persons, living or deceased, is purely coincidental.

 BREAKWATER
P.O. Box 2188, St. John's, NL, Canada, A1C 6E6
www.breakwaterbooks.com

A CIP catalogue record for this book is available from Library and Archives Canada.
ISBN 9781778530241 (softcover)
© 2024 Rod Moody-Corbett

We acknowledge the support of the Canada Council for the Arts. We acknowledge the financial support of the Government of Canada through the Department of Heritage and the Government of Newfoundland and Labrador through the Department of Tourism, Culture, Arts and Recreation for our publishing activities.

PRINTED AND BOUND IN CANADA.

Breakwater Books is committed to choosing papers and materials for our books that help to protect our environment. To this end, this book is printed on a recycled paper and other sources that are certified by the Forest Stewardship Council®.

For my brother.

I felt a melting in me.

Herman Melville, *Moby-Dick*

ONE

I THOUGHT COMMEMORATING THE ANNIVERSARY OF TRAVIS'S death with a hunting trip absurd, and I said so. Travis was Willis's boy, the older one, and one of the Holbrook Station dead.

As to the general, and not so general, mechanisms of that tragedy—and I think the word holds in this instance—I am reluctant to speculate. The shooter was dead before the train stopped. That this detail along with its morbid prequel should remain, for however many minutes, unknown (and, what's worse, markedly unimaginable) to those west-going passengers idling up and down the Holbrook Station platform, skimming their phones, texting, shying up the occasional chin to peer, with pristine gloominess, at the arrival board's unblinking red clock, gives rise to a sudden, ungovernable paralysis. Which is to say nothing, of course, for the victims, for all those hapless travellers cowering and clutching each other in the adjoining cars.

I ride buses now, and spurn all subterranean transit. I realize there is little logic in this. No broader blueprint, no rational design. Yet the sight of a train slinking through a cold glassy skyline sets my heart thumping. I experience a similar, arrhythmic twinge, a light but veiny flutter coursing all down the stems of my wrists, on elevators and planes, even on bridges, bounded by river and sky.

All of this happened just over a year ago, in Calgary, where Travis—who, before making his way out west, had distinguished himself in his native (I should say, perhaps, *our* native) Newfoundland as something of a track and cross-country prodigy, decimating many of those decades-old junior and senior records formerly held by Paul McCloy—had obtained an athletics scholarship to run varsity for the Dinos; and where I, a lowly sessional instructor at the University of Calgary, meagerly subsisting on whatever introductory English classes the department, in its penury, might entrust to me, have been eking out a quiet, perfectly inconspicuous existence for nearly fifteen years.

I did not see much of Travis in the months following his initial move, but felt compelled, whether in deference to his father, or else simply to slake some impalpable paternal stirring, to make myself available to him in whatever capacity he should need. I remember one smoky afternoon in late August, I drove him to IKEA and Canadian Tire and Walmart, and helped him cart away what preliminary furnishings my old nickering hatchback might accommodate, stopping at the large wholesale furniture store off Sunridge, which I believe is run by Mennonites, and where Travis, anyway, ended up not buying a chair. Every few months, I'd drop him an email and we'd meet in Kensington for coffee—tea, in his case (typically mint)—or else head into the Oak Tree for a burger and pint. He was a nice kid, attentive and kind, and for an athlete, I thought, not in the least gloating or smug; rather, he projected a dogged, soft-spoken modesty, a philosophical soberness that you sensed almost immediately in his calm, unslumping posture and eagle's gaze.

The last time I talked to him—we'd bumped into each other down by Memorial Park—he mentioned that he'd been seeing a physiotherapist for a minor hip injury, that he was now spending his mornings clocking monotonous, hour-long workouts at the Aquatic Centre, pool running, but that he hoped to be back out on the trails by mid-September, training for fall cross.

For a middle-distance runner his physique struck me as anomalous:

a sharp, knuckly torso, but with the thick calves (bulging through the backs of his jeans like ulcerous gourds or rutabagas) and wide burly hams of a cyclist or speed skater. It seemed inconceivable to me that such legs could be capable of generating much turnover and stride. But then what do I know? He had his father's wavy brown hair, steep, greyish-blue eyes, and hesitant laugh, which sounded almost like a mumble. He kept the beard he wore close, maintaining a scrupulous line along his jaw. The beard was gratuitous but its sloping had the effect of accenting his cheekbones, which were his most striking feature, high and gaunt and gunwale taut; they were his mother's, Caitlin's, exactly.

Caitlin I have known since forever ago, longer than Willis, easy. I'd had a thing for her older sister back in high school, and though the substance of my interest went more or less uncommunicated, its spirit was not lost on the younger sibling, who suffered my wounded overtures, the interminable timidity of my conduct, with commendable indifference and restraint. I remember one winter afternoon during a snowstorm showing up at their house, a thermos of homemade hot chocolate stowed away in my knapsack along with a bag of marsh-mallows, frigid and stale, preparing to confide all.

Climbing the steps two at time, but minding the splintering, faded green slats, now bowed and wincing with the snow, I appeared, in the porch window's bendy glare, eerily laminated. The morning storm had yielded to freezing rain, and behind me the whole city seemed to glisten and twitch. My cheeks were stinging from the walk, my eyelids crusty with frost. I set my pack down under the stoop's boxy black awning and was just taking a minute to gather myself, stomping my boots and peeling away the brittle shivers of ice that had wormed their way under my scarf, clinging to the neck of my sweater like a frieze, when Caitlin popped open the door.

"Go home," was all she said.

She wore sweatpants and a large drooping grey sweater with the sleeves bunched over her fists. She only held the door open a crack. I could just see past her and into the living room, where a stitch of light, far away but dense, like a shred of sulphur, flickered. As I stood there eyeing the foyer and wondering at my next move, the sheer idiocy of my expedition, in all its piteous, lovelorn chivalry, impressed itself upon me with considerable force. I saw myself as Caitlin must have, pathetic and wet.

"Go," she said again. "We're getting sick of this."

———

One run I attended. Just one. The summer of his sophomore year Travis qualified to compete in the Olympic Trials, which were staged at Foothills Athletic Park, not far from campus. Caitlin, who'd flown out for the meet, asked me along. We sat in the packed stands slathered in sunscreen, sipping iced coffee. A greasy reek of French fries and hot dogs wafted off a gleaming white food truck. I don't know why this struck me as odd, but it did. Had I really expected all those in attendance to be quaffing waxy snow cones of Gatorade? Maybe so.

Caitlin, who'd hurled discus in high school, kept me apprised of the finer workings of the sport. As with Noah's birds and beasts and every other kind of creeping thing that slops across this drowning globe, only the top two runners would advance to the national team.

Travis, running the 5000m, finished third.

He ran well (I thought) but was edged out of second place by this gawky wraith of sinew from SFU who overtook him as they came surging through the bell lap—down the backstretch and round the final bend, the stands raucous, shrieking, antic with fans. We stood up from our seats and clapped. Probably I took part in the shrieking. Maybe I even shouted his name.

Now, I don't know much about running, about sports, about what one feels or doesn't feel in the throes of athletic torment, but I believe that I sensed his loss, the inevitability of it, at the sound of that bell, which swung like a giddy toy from its louvered lap counter. The bell clanged, the counter's red numerals revolved to 1, and as the crowd swelled and heaved itself to its feet, I thought I noted, in the slight forward arch of his face, a wincing breath, a faltered thought, a flash of drain.

He flowed through the finish line, stiff bony arms veined and wheeling, then bent quickly and spat.

Caitlin said, "He's not going to be happy with this."

Travis staggered, listing a little, arms akimbo, and knelt down on the gravel berm adjacent the sponged track. He eased off his spikes and massaged his feet. He wasn't wearing any socks.

For a minute he sat there, looking first at his feet, and then at his fellow runners as, one after the other, they streamed to a stop. The kid from SFU jogged over and they shook hands. An older man in a slick black polo with a set of headphones looped low on his neck handed Travis a bottle of water.

"I better go find his tote," Caitlin said. She squeezed my arm and pressed her way down the bleachers.

I waited for the stands to clear—the 5000m had been the last event of the night—before stepping onto the track. The light had ebbed some but the heat had lost none of its radiance. The undersides of my knees were moist and jewels of sweat skittered down my temples.

"Good run," I said. "How you doing?"

Travis shielded his eyes and squinted up at me. "We took it out too fast," he said, lowering his hand. "59, 60, 62." He made a fist and stroked his knuckles across the back of each ankle, digging into their joints.

"You're bleeding," I said.

He'd taken a nick to the calf as the pack jostled for position, elbowing into that inside lane, and a trickle of blood traced a line down his right leg. He tilted his bottle and splashed water onto the wound, which was brief and shallow and curving scythe-like at the top.

"Your mom's gone to find your gear," I said. "Want to stand up?" I offered him a hand and helped him to his feet.

"Thanks," he said.

Beyond the eastern rim of the track stood McMahon Stadium.

Its towered floodlights glowed over the empty football field like the pebbled, incandescent finger bristles of a gecko. Travis leaned on my shoulder and stretched his quads. "You know what's funny?" he said. I shook my head. "Coming into the last lap—" He stopped. Caitlin emerged from behind the food truck carrying his tote bag. The bag was stitched over with old racing bibs. Seeing us, she smiled, and Travis let go of my arm, pivoting his leg and bending down to collect his spikes. "Well, for a second there," he said, and this very quietly, "I was almost relieved."

———

The night of the shooting, I lay in bed with a glass of wine, grading quizzes, refreshing the unfolding story on my phone. Within hours of the attack—it'd happened around rush hour—they'd confirmed that the shooter had acted alone, and that he was dead, but information pertaining to the ages and identities of the nine reported victims remained scant.

A video selfie, posted to social media minutes before the attack, surfaced, along with a lengthy backchannel confession, the most odious excerpts of which were swiftly screen-grabbed and disseminated; our airport code trended (and continued to trend, for days); hashtags blossomed, and with them the usual thoughts and prayers and denouncements; later, we'd learn that the weapon was not an AR-15 but something else, procured illegally, along with the pistol, which the shooter had turned on himself.

Around midnight, I set my phone face down on the nightstand with my stack of quizzes, debated taking half a Xanax, and drifted off into an uneasy, dreamless sleep. When I woke in the morning it was to a call from Willis, who'd been unable to raise Travis on his phone, and who—though he'd told himself not to panic, not to worry, exhorting himself over and over again throughout the night to remain calm, that, however visceral (and, given the circumstances, as a father, even permissible) were his terrors and fears, his anxieties had little utility, no place, no legitimate emotional currency inside of this moment, particularly as one came to consider the real suffering of those who were undeniably dead, for the families and friends of those genuinely and forever gone, and that, in the case of Travis, there had to be some good reason (possibly an eventually somewhat laughable or mundane or even dignified reason) why his son wasn't answering his phone, or responding to texts, or acknowledging receipt of his mother's increasingly frantic emails and Facebook and Instagram messages—had just spoken to a woman, Willis said, that someone from Calgary Police Services had just called him, and that, when he saw the Alberta area code brightening on his phone, his first thought, miserably, wasn't that his son was dead, but that through some horrible bit of happenstance (in which we permit ourselves to feel—despite mounting evidence to the contrary—hope) this was his son calling from a different phone to let him know that he was still alive.

I don't remember what more Willis said after this, nor what words I offered back in stunned, unbelieving condolence. I sat up. An acidic hollowing radiated through my chest. I tried paying attention to the words being spoken to me but could hear only what stood between them, a general drift and brokenness, an interstitial folding away. As my shock dissipated to denial or anger or whatever inscrutable emotional recesses subsist in between all of that, my mind kept turning back to some lines from *Macbeth*, which I was then studying for the seven hundredth time with my ENGL 201s, and how, surprising no one that knew him, Travis had carried himself bravely, how he'd worn, like Young Siward, his wounds on the front.

TWO

BUT A HUNTING TRIP?

The plan, so far as I gleaned, was for the four of us—with the four of us comprising myself, Baker, Willis, and possibly Willis's younger son, Isaac—to rendezvous in St. John's around the middle of October, spend a few nights bumming around the city, finalizing our itinerary and revelling our way up and down George Street in what I foresaw as a wildly prosaic stupor, before making the long drive or, pending finances, short flight up the Great Northern Peninsula. I hadn't spent much time on the west coast, but pictured this expanse as just another bald and gusty bogscape, whose stubbly pine-smudged hills and crags would offer paltry shelter from the elements, and still measlier asylum, I feared, from each other.

It was, of course, Baker who called me, which in itself felt strategic, my every reluctance run aground on his obstinacy.

"But what would we even hunt?"

"Moose," said Baker. "Black bear, grouse."

I've known Baker for too many years. I know there's no talking to him. He's partnered at Hunley's now, one of the oldest plumbing contractors in the city, but for seven years before that he worked as a correctional officer at Her Majesty's Penitentiary—a third-generation guard, tending the same stale, wretched corridors as his uncle and grandfather, the latter of whom, if I'm not mistaken, served as acting warden throughout the sixties. A thick man whose long looming stature and woodsy paunch was offset by a somewhat boyish face, clean and thievish, Baker had been well-liked by the inmates, as far as that went, a reception he credited not (one would have to assume) to his family's disciplinary legacy but to certain permissions and leniencies he accorded the more upwardly mobile murderers and rapists and cut-rate extortionists under his charge. He'd allowed them the use of water weights in their cells, for one: dripping, triple-bagged dumbbells, which, for reasons having to do with cleanliness and waste, were prohibited by the Pen's legislative brass.

But the grimness of the job, its aura of ubiquitous corruptibility (which, to hear it from Baker, manifests on both sides of the bars), combined with the derelict facilities—sections of HMP harken back to *Little Dorrit*, predating Confederation by roughly a decade— had taken its toll. Two months before Baker turned in his papers, a veterinarian on remand for manslaughter (he'd split open some poor junkie's skull with a joiner's mallet who was fixing to burgle him) was stabbed and beaten near to death during an AA meeting. The guys who jumped him, friends of the deceased, I gather, tried hooding the vestibule cameras with t-shirts and towels, but these improvised cloakings only slid off. You can stream a soundless clip of the shivving—track your wounded through a blurry gruel of bodies piling round the instant-coffee station—on CBC.

"So supposing we kill something," I said, "we're just going to— what? Dice up some moose carcass? Parcel it up in our sleeping bags, make tracks for civilization?"

"They take care of the kill site," said Baker.

"Who?"

"The park people," he said, appalled by my ignorance. "You make your tag, they come in, pick you up, run you back out."

Certainly, I am no gun enthusiast. I shot a Beretta at a range one summer and the experience was happily lost on me. I say "happily" as the son of rabid pacifists, under whose prohibitive keep water pistols and cap guns were spurned in equal measure, I've long wondered at what latent obscenities might dorm in me. Of that afternoon I remember mainly the man two cubicles over from me who fired a Colt. The partition walls were made of ballistic grey glass, and streaks of what I assume was probably cordite and the fine brassy nickings left by ejected shells clouded the frame. The man working the Colt wore a pale, saggy blue cap and glasses, and kept turning the pistol around in his fist to admire the cool leathery burnish of its barrel. And I suppose it was beautiful. A length of tattoo traipsed down the man's dominant hand. The outline of a shattered bulb or busted sun. Though he appeared unfazed by the pistol's crisp report, his Adam's apple gulped on recoil, rising in his throat like stuck bread.

Willis's gunmanship went back decades, to plinking paint cans and skeet and nettlesome deer mice with his father's old silver Snake Charmer. Dall sheep, ptarmigan, wild Ontario turkey. His feeds were alive with these exploits.

"Now bear in mind," Baker said, "Willis's been planning on this trip, talking it over with the boys, since before Holbrook."

"And Isaac?"

"I don't know," Baker said. "Last I saw him was at the funeral. Seemed fine, from what I could tell. But I guess there's been some slippage, some concerning behaviour."

"Concerning how?" I asked.

"Withdrawn," Baker said. "The word I keep hearing's withdrawn."

I paced my apartment. It was a stark, ashy morning in late August, with just a touch of sun beginning to insinuate itself in the east, nudging through the bunches of swollen cloud, a sudden, rigid glitch of light. It'd been raining off and on for much of the week, which was good news for the fires roaring to the north and west and sometimes south of me. Magpies wobbled in the dewy sod, pegging up worms. One of these birds, an amputee, I'd seen before: a dim, vermin-cheeked creature with coarse wispy feathers and a mangy throat. The stricken limb looked bitten off in a hurry, the angle of chomp rough and slanted, improbably beaver-hewn. Chickadees darted and flicked in the slack asters, their carolling incessant, electric and thick. The one-legged magpie tacked along my artful clustering of pebbles and stones and fanged cedar chips, over which nefarious, purple-lobed flowers—an invasive species, according to my neighbour, Jerry Toews, a former cabinet minister in the Peter Lougheed government, whose dementedly long flags I could hear through shuttered windows, twirling and clicking on their halyards—drooped in rude pungency.

"So what's your thinking?" Baker asked. "You in?"

"My thinking," I said, "is that this all sounds very expensive. And bleak."

"How so?"

"Insensitive," I clarified. "Grievously ill-conceived."

"You know it's not as glum as that," said Baker.

"No?"

"We wouldn't be gone longer than ten days, tops."

"Well, does it have to be guns?" I asked. "Couldn't it be something else?"

"Like what?"

"Like, I don't know," I said. "Like literally anything."

Though I opposed the plan on moral grounds, I knew—and maybe Baker did too—that my reluctance wasn't so principled as all that. There were practical hesitations at play. I also wondered, but felt at no great liberty to wonder aloud, why our presence was even required in the first place.

"Well what about salmon?" I asked.

I do not claim any greater proficiency with rod and reel, but the thought of camping along the Fraser River Valley—read: a long day's wind through shadowy, fire-scarred Rockies vs. an 8,000 km round trip across five time zones (and god knows how many airports)—appealed. I pictured the three (or four) of us sitting before a large bonfire bordered by wagging alders, drinking strong, syrupy black coffee from those enamel camping mugs with the sparkly white speckles on them, firing up another spliff, the fire reddening and warming our cheeks as we communed and grieved.

"Salmon's out," said Baker. "Haven't you heard? Water's too goddamn warm. Fish won't budge. Nothing bites."

"You know I teach through the fall," I said, my tone blunter than intended. "It's not so easy for me to skip across the country, get the time off work."

"Right," Baker said. "My bad. For a minute there, I forgot you're the only one of us holding down a job in these troubled times."

"Hilarious," I said.

"Don't get snitty," Baker said. "I'm not the one who decamped to Wild Rose Country to pursue a career in—what's it you do again?"

"Point taken," I said.

"I'm serious," Baker said. "Haven't we got an app for you yet?"

I stepped into the kitchen, flipped open the blinds. Dark, briny flickings of bygone curries and sauces mottled the slats. I could see Jerry out in his backyard now, posing in front of our property line with push mower and pruning shears, his perennial, Band-Aid–brown cargos hitched high over hips, shaving back deadish-looking foliage in anticipation of fall, a tidy foraging of sticks and tough, greenish-red twigs massing in the centre of his lawn off the firepit (a vast, brick-ringed affair, at whose highest, northernmost fringe there protruded a long runic pedestal or plinth, on top of which were arranged a chorus of horrific wooden sculptures and figurines, which Jerry, in his untiring retirement, had apparently whittled himself).

"You still there?" Baker asked. "Hello?"

"I'm here, I'm here. It's just—Jerry," I said.

"Which one's Jerry again?"

"My neighbour." I sniffled. The rain had driven away most of the smoke but the air, passing through my poorly sealed windows, still smelled of dampened campfires and broiled plastic. "He's got all these little, like, ghouls scattered across his lawn."

"This is the flag guy?" Baker asked. "Your patriot?"

"That's the one," I said.

My relationship with Jerry is genial but not effusive. We exchange a minimum of pleasantries while binning compost or recycling. I know that he considers my bachelordom—my inconstant solitude—odd, as, indeed, I remain ambivalent about his woodworking. All these hideous orcs and dwarves brandishing acorn halberds and scathing grins. I find it concerning. And I say this as a teacher, as one constitutionally accustomed to parsing the cryptic, artistic wanderings of unsettled youths. That Jerry, a man who—to go by the bumps and smears and Rorschach varicosities—must be toeing eighty, varies the positioning of these figurines atop the abacus of his unmarked plinth with such anguished deliberation—all of these pieces, I should say, rarely facing each other, but pivoted, this entire wooden multitude oriented in the direction of my kitchen window—suggests a kind of game or idle derangement, which, if the latter, I am loath to interrogate. Some depths are best left unplumbed.

"Anyway, so look," I said, backing out of the kitchen. "Like I was saying, about this trip, my fall term, it's—"

"Let me stop you right there," Baker said. "I'm forgetting the best part."

"Sorry?"

"We'd miss the election," he said. "In October."

"Well what difference does that make?"

"If we plan it right," he said, "if we're strategic about our days, we'll be completely off-grid. No Wi-Fi, no cell reception. Imagine that. We'd miss everything. All of it."

I told Baker that I'd have to think this over, that I wasn't so sure I'd be able to wangle the time off work. What with the current political clime—hinting, here, not at the forthcoming federal election (about which, true, the prospects were once again looking pretty shitty) but at a rash of recent budget cuts—it wasn't necessarily in my best interest to leave anyone around here in the lurch; but that, yes, sure, I'd mull it over for a few days and get back to him.

"And remember," he said, "because I know money's an issue, all you're having to worry about here's the flight. Willis's taking care of the rest."

"What are you saying?"

"It's taken care of," he said.

I shook my head. "You couldn't have led with this?" More annoyed than incredulous.

"The Castle," Baker said. "That's what the place is called. I'll send you the details."

We said our goodbyes and I cancelled the call—pressed end. Then I did some Googling.

THREE

IN A WORD, THE LINK BAKER FORWARDED ME WAS FUCKED.

Dull, seagull-grey background across whose lustreless palette there emerged, jerkily, in fluted streaks and swirls, an amateurish rendering of a molten skull and antlers. Menu options made to look like petroglyphs—scruffy, cave-marred drawings of coyotes and crows, a stencilling of carrion or click beetles—floated cursorily, wordlessly, over the antlers' beakier knots and dells. Depressing a crow prompted a gusty implosion. The skull (and skull's nimbusing foragers) retreated and dissolved, were whisked away, *Matrix*-style, in a sweep of weeping pixels.

I sat in the hallway off my bedroom office, on my fold-up stationary bike, facing a bare ochre wall upon which disparate swatches of scorched orange had been tested, my bike's gears demoted to their quietest, unclicking decibel. I am a good tenant, a grateful tenant, a respectful one. About six years ago, I lucked into a cramped basement apartment whose accents include an uncovered junction box my landlord has warned me not to fuck with under any circumstances; a porous, low-ceilinged living room with a mean-looking gouge rising off a dysfunctional wall sconce; an ever-humming fridge that often snarls and thrums in the night; and a short leaky toilet with a rickety rose seat whose slow-filling bowl I've overflowed more times than I care to remember. And yet—and we can always count on another "yet"—I remain reasonably contented here. I'm willing to bet that I conduct my best, boldest, most nuanced research in this hallway, my phone slanted over the bike's digital interface, supporting my weight on the crossbar with one arm, unmindful of posture—my poor twingy shoulders, my slalomed spine—scooping a thumb along the bar's soft, squishy plastic, where I've worried a pleasing blister, a fret.

The Castle.

I'm not sure what I expected. A few grainy, low-res shots? Pictures of dead things and the people who'd deadened them?

Well, the feel here wasn't that, exactly. There was money about. Lots of it.

About an hour west of St. Anthony, the Castle's territory, as distinguished from the Castle's central facility or "keep"—which seemed, from the looks of things, a destination in itself—spanned some two hundred square kilometres of legitimate wilderness, eroded mountain vistas, and unsheltered shorelines of nubbly tundra and tuck.

The area boasted an assortment of camps, which were accessible by float plane, boat, and ATV. Eastern Canadian moose, woodland caribou, black bear: these were the big-game tickets on offer. I perused a list of allowable weapons, marvelling at the raw eroticism of break and bolt action rimfires, semi-autos, shotguns. The language was gorgeous and terrifying. Buttplate and checkering. Fore-end, spacer, pleated palm swell. Why all the specificity? Sling stud. Barrel nut. Blowback. Why here?

I tried to picture myself stooped athwart a woody blind, camo-clad, tear troughs shadowed in lampblack, levelling my muzzle at some gullible ungulate busily munching on whatever it is moose or deer or woodland caribou like to munch on—oats, I speculated, acorns, abject grasses—but found myself balking at the pivotal moment, averting my gaze, snapping a twig, going shaky, unable to make a clean shot. As undergrads, milling in Willis's apartment after a night of fruitless boozing, gorging ourselves on hasty eats—no-name calzones nuked to bursting, chips, ramen, tater tots painted in queso—I'd always envied the ease with which Willis, in the midst of some gore-porn slasher/ shoot 'em up, his breath tangy with nacho dust, differentiated among calibers and gauges. SIG Sauer, Ingram, Franchi SPAS-12. I envied him his rude fluency, the berserk schooling.

And the money. These days I envied the money. Willis could afford this? And would willingly comp my admission?

Your basic package ran $9,500 per, which was madness. I wasn't confident that I had $1,000 in my chequing account.

This included chaperoned hunting, lodging, warm meals, tags, snacks, equipment and weapons rental, float plane support to and from camp, boats, motors, butchering, field cleaning and quartering, caping, game bags, and curing salts. Shuttle buses from the St. Anthony Airport could be booked online, while mandatory certifications, firearms safety courses, and hunting licences were obtainable through the Castle's certified Fisheries, Forestry and Agriculture liaison, Esme.

A bolded subscript on the FAQ page informed me that the Castle was apparently warren to an overpopulation of coyotes whose unlicensed harvesting was "highly encouraged" and gratis.

When Baker told me we'd be hunting black bear, I assumed, or half assumed, he was full of shit. But sure enough, snout slumped over a scant, withery white log, eyes closed, paws cupped, those broad shaggy arms crossed, punitively, one over the other, as if awaiting shackles, there sprawled a deflated bear carcass, attended to by a short grey-haired woman in reflective overalls and beige boonie. You could see, through the folds of this woman's jacket, the tough, mellow curves of her biceps—they looked like dinner rolls. Blood pooled on one side of the log. The blood had a slightly tentative, or superficial, tint to it. Like something out of a Mary Pratt. Jellied dogberries, I thought, trapped in glass. There were many images of antlers and skulls, whole galleries of heads, cratered and seamed and provokingly eyeless. Those belonging to the moose I found most compelling: long and lobed, the palms and finely serrated tines, if I can call them that, flush with growing bone.

If all of this seemed fairly standard fare, then the Castle's central compound or base of operations was something else entirely. Here, the pervading aesthetic seemed to be one of sterile estrangement. Less hunting lodge than bougie mediation retreat. Nestled right along the coast, on the western banks of the Castle's peninsular wall, this area comprised a panoptic flange of clover-leafing hunting studios: stilted, Nordic-style dorms sided in bright metal and wood.

Here, amenities abounded. There was a fitness centre, complete with saltwater pool, 250-metre green-on-blue polyurethane indoor track, squash and badminton and "collapsible" basketball courts, cardio equipment, nautilus gym, sauna, steam room, and hot tubs; there were a pair of shooting galleries (one indoor, one out); bookable eateries, vaulted, sea-fronting dining rooms, firepits, "roasting stalls," and kitchens; they had a bar, a library, a movie theatre, a tea room, multiple observatories, and a pavilion where, weather pending, Castle staff staged concerts and plays throughout the summer (by October, we'd just miss their last Ibsen). Maybe I'd forgo the feral theatrics, opt in for a steam, a tea, a deep tissue massage.

Niceties notwithstanding, I noted a number of odd stringencies. Wi-Fi was available but its use "absolutely prohibited except for emergencies"; at management's discretion access could be granted on a "case-by-case basis." Guests relinquished their phones and wireless devices upon arrival. In return, for an extra charge, the Castle provided you with a wiped burner and tablet which admitted you to a private network allowing guests access to a limited array of digital services; meaning, I guess, we could chat with each other but not the outside world. The Castle was also—and this I liked very much—adult only. Persons under the age of eighteen were strictly forbidden from entering the premises.

A testimonials page featured clips and blurbs from celebrity patrons. Catherine O'Hara, Meghan Markle, Peter Mansbridge, and the disgraced author of that neural net tell-all. Werner Herzog had visited, multiple times. There was a picture of him up on the site, in greenish fatigues, binoculars dangling, his long fleshy cheeks pinkened in the wind.

"We are deranged beggars exploring the hallowed bounds of the Holocene," his blurb began. "Thank you to Dr. Judith Muir and to her esteemed colleagues for sponsoring my journeys throughout these peculiar and futile lands. I look forward to returning soon."

The further I scrolled, the faster I pedalled and clicked; and, I confess, for a minute I entirely forgot about our quest's graver incitement.

The Castle's founder and CEO gave her name as Dr. Judith Muir (her husband, Doug, was listed as resident sommelier). A profile pic showed a small sturdy woman in her early sixties with thick silver hair—the woman with the bear?—centrally parted over an abrupt unwrinkled brow. Her eyeglass frames were clear and stylish. You could see into their machinery, the metal of them, through the plastic, as into the limbs of a prehistoric insect, bulbed in amber sap. She was, or had at one time been, an ornithologist of significant distinction, tracing the migratory patterns of northern gannets relative to their exposure to certain "extra-environmental" stressors along the Gulf Coast. There were links to a number of her books and articles, a *Globe and Mail* profile, and another one done up in *Canadian Geographic*. A lengthy list of the Castle's corporate sponsors followed.

I stepped groggily off the fold-up, my left heel totally numb. There was much to consider.

My fitness, for one. Though I biked, or positioned myself languidly over my fold-up, nearly daily, my body kept evolving new cricks. Mornings I woke to fickle limbs, coughs, shiny red rashes and zits, both knees popping like fresh kindling as, seizing the sleep from my eyes, I muddled my way out of bed and into the bathroom, disdaining the mirror which showed, amid the specks of toothpaste and spit and snarls of frosted shaving cream, everything—everything.

Work was another problem. Though, if Baker was right and we'd only be gone a week or so, I could probably cancel class last minute, fire away some postdated emails, pleading flu or—better yet—flu-like symptoms. Then came the money. The money, the money. Even if Willis footed the bill, a trip to NL, my second in as many autumns, would set me back. And then, too, I'd have to think about accommodations on either end of the hunt. Would I stay with my father? Would the old paterfamilias have me? Would I even bother letting him know I was coming home?

I hadn't been back to St. John's since Travis's funeral, where I'd made the mistake of staying with my father and my father's girlfriend, Beth, for the few days I was home. I liked Beth fine, and had in fact met her a handful of times before. She'd worked at the recovery centre in East Meadows for a number of years as an outpatient addictions counsellor, and appeared to exude a soothing, countervailing force over my father, whose myriad irritabilities—what manifested, to my mind, as a general hardening of old prejudices and insularities—I found, as the decade succeeding my mother's rapid decline (to the cervical cancer that killed her) narrowed to a close, unnavigable. It is not my intention to paint my father as a hard-hearted satyr. My parents had been separated for just about fifteen years when a slight swelling in my mother's legs, accompanied by a dull, hazy ache flowering queerly over her shoulders, which my mother once described to me as feeling almost like how—no. Let's hold that thought. Let's shelve that metaphor for a rainy day.

As for my father? Well, I suppose that as a son, as his son, I wanted more from him; not for my mother, I mean, but for me.

Still.

It is the case that we comport ourselves with too much emotional symmetry, my father and I, to endure one another's company for very long; and I'll admit that my mood, through the duration of this last visit, in which I kept chiefly to the basement, retreating to its fusty, unfinished quarters as into some surly adolescence, was not good. To our credit, or in deference to Beth's reigning patience, an amount of civility was attempted: longstanding aspersions regarding my precarities (financial, spousal) were passed over in silence, a quiet, candlelit stroganoff withstood.

SON

Pass the asparagus.

FATHER

The imperative mood is ill-suited to this, our most lavish repast.

SON *reaches across the table.* FATIIER *whaps* SON's *hand with spoon.*

FATHER

Say please.

SON

What is wrong with you?

BETH

(*To herself.*)

Can we *please* just try to enjoy our food?

Tiptoeing through the kitchen by the glow of my phone, I inoculated myself—a man of forty-six years—like some kind of inviable ingrate with nightly raids on the liquor cabinet, availing myself of vodka and bourbon, but never the good Scotch. No one said anything to me about this, but I suspect that my crimes were registered, if not by my father then by Beth, who, though she exhibited few scruples in matters of consumption (and appeared, anyway, to enjoy her wine), seemed, on occasion, puritanically alert to the speed and frequency with which my father, who has never been much of drinker, imbibed.

The bed that I slept in, the bed I grew up in, still bore, along the top rail of its footboard, the glow-in-the-dark stickers of wayward comets and stars, whose lambency, though markedly diminished, hadn't quite lapsed. Tossing in bed with my phone and my vodka, my thimble of dessert bourbon, I listened to the sounds of that house, that haggard old house, which someone should've sold years ago, torn up the property and sold while the asking was good, the familiar jeers of its furnace, those aquatic, tuba-like gulps, with one earbud out.

The memorial service, which Willis and Caitlin had decided to keep private (a loftier remembrance, complete with readings, music, a commemorative—but, so the Facebook page insisted, uncompetitive—run, was scheduled for Bannerman Park), had taken place at Caul's on LeMarchant, just up the block from Harrington, my old elementary school. It was there, while waiting for my parents to pick me up one afternoon, that a pair of older kids from one of the other schools (faceless assailants to me now) knocked me to the ground and made off with my book bag, overturning its meagre contents into the gutters as they fled. I was uninjured but badly dazed by the incident. I remember feeling a special dismalness for the objects themselves, for the scattered pencils and strips of flung paper, for the translucent blue sharpener with the one shallow hole and one thicker, for the slivers of sooty pencil shavings whose fine, flaky wooden coils resembled the inner ear of some elaborate mollusc or conch, and for the small grubby red eraser in which I'd engraved my initials with a bend of roughened paperclip, and maybe, too, for the paperclip; as if the purpose of this assault were not to hurt me but to visit a private humiliation upon these things, these innocuous items I'd made the mistake of cherishing.

Needless to say that my father, who thought nothing of binning my childhood toys, of rounding up all my doe-eyed teddy bears and *Star Wars* figurines and consigning these pallid plastics and allergens to the trash, misunderstood the precise status of my sorrow that day. He thought I was hurt because I was hurt, that the tears that came welling to my eyes were tears of embarrassment, or of minor physical pain. But that wasn't it, that wasn't the language of my sadness—not at all.

The school is something else now; or, rather, a series of some-things. Daycare, insurance agency, Domino's. The ground-floor window out of which my fourth-grade doldrums sought idle release now houses a barbershop with a giant stencil of a moustache, imperially orientated, if memory serves, obscuring its central pane.

Isaac, three years his brother's junior, delivered the eulogy. He was joined at the podium by his sister, Penelope, solemn and bored and very much the youngest of the bunch, her attention shifting from her brother to the mourners, whose gazes she met and somewhat insanely, I thought, held, to the large funeral wreath adjacent the closed casket (under whose dark stainless steel hood I can still imagine him, refrigerated and prim) to the lilies and orchids and stout white petals ribboned in whiskery spruce. Isaac wore a sharp charcoal suit and slender tie. He was scrawnier than his brother, and funnier. The pages he'd prepared and occasionally abandoned, in lieu of some subtler musing, were tousled and creased, and though he read with unshaking hands his voice sounded a wheezy, somewhat fevered note, mildly ravelled in phlegm. At one point near the eulogy's end, Willis's mom, sitting in the front row, swaying, broke out into sobs, and Penelope, pawing through her dress pocket, unearthed a wad of tissues and toddled these over to her grandmother.

I didn't cry at the funeral. I sat to the side of the family, two rows back, next to a gaunt older woman in a suspenseful black hat. She was a friend of Caitlin's or of Caitlin's mother and sucked clear liquorice candies throughout. These came in curious abundance from a green gingham clutch she kept on her lap. Each time she reached into her purse for another candy, which action she performed blindly, with admirable deftness, shucking open these flat, golden-foiled wrappings with her thumb, I kept thinking that she might offer me one, and I wondered, hunkered down in our pew, at the propriety of this offering, which I intended to refuse (with small silent smile and halting palm), but she never did.

Willis was a wreck, and looked it, the large blue expressive eyes gone stony with gloom. The slopes of his cheeks, which were frazzled with stubble, hung, shrunken and chewed, like dry dented fruit. Also, he'd done something unfortunate and new with his hair, slicking it tight to the side in a shiny wet part, a rowdy cowlick sparking off the crown where the coverage thinned pinkly to reddish-grey scalp. Standing, post-eulogy and slide show, in front of Caitlin and kids, he struck an unreliable pose, unsure, I imagined, where exactly to place his hands.

And later, round back of Caul's, Baker, tucking into a smoke, saying, "Sure, you're right; he's off. But then when hasn't he always looked like some big old fucking bag of milk?"

Now, as I wiped down the bars of my fold-up with a ratty dish towel, I wondered at the dimensions (and density) of my reluctance. Probably it's putting this business a little too morbidly if I admit that I'd come, in recent years, to associate St. John's exclusively with death.

My mother, Travis.

Then again, it was also true, and also vaguely muddling in its truth, that while I viewed this hunting trip as morally asinine, with the felling of stately cervids sounding to me like nothing so much as a deplorable dumbshow of the very massacre that'd left Willis sonless, something about this place, the Castle, genuinely intrigued me. In a weird way, in a way I could not yet wholly assimilate, I'll admit I was curious, and— what's more—I didn't want to be left out.

I took a long slow gulp of water, picked up my phone, belched.

"Okay," I texted Baker. "Fuck it. I'm in."

FOUR

IN THE WEEKS THAT FOLLOWED, I DITHERED AND PREPPED.
I booked a cheap flight that would see me milk-running through
Toronto and Halifax, arriving in St. John's just after dinner on the first
Wednesday of October, with a still meatier sequence of layovers (St.
John's–Halifax; Halifax–Montreal; Montreal–Edmonton; Edmonton–
home) awaiting me on my return leg.

Willis forwarded me an itemized receipt confirming my admission
to the Castle; and, since we'd be leaving for St. Anthony "early-early" on
the Friday, he suggested I spend Thursday night with him. This left me
one unaccommodated (non-hunting) night in St. John's on either end
of my trip. Though I was fairly certain Willis and Caitlin wouldn't mind
me staying on an extra couple days, given what I knew (or didn't know)
about Isaac's well-being, I was unwilling to impose.

I debated messaging Baker—Baker, who's been renting the same
bright, bay-windowed walk-up off Gower for nearly two decades—but
I wasn't so keen on his futon, which I was even less inclined to share with
his dog, a sinewy, ill-tempered boxer named Brad, whom Baker cherished
and coddled and doted upon with an ardency I thought diagnostically
compulsive and which made you a little sick to witness, the servility of it.

Hotels were out of the question. I couldn't quite afford (or justify affording) them—fun fact: I make less as a sessional instructor than I did as a TA—and then, too, it's always struck me as deceitful, as somehow municipally seditious, spending a night in a hotel room in your own hometown. I did find a nice enough Airbnb on Prescott, which offered a decent view of the harbour, but weighing autonomy against cost (and admitting such hours as I intended to spend prostrate, sleeping or feigning sleep), I decided, finally, to email my father to alert him about my trip. He texted me back a few days later from what he persisted in calling his "work Android," asking if I needed a place to stay.

"That would be great," I texted. "Thank you."

"thumbs-up emoji," he wrote back.

My classes that term clustered on Tuesdays and Thursdays, which, barring office hours, kept me off campus most of the week. This was my preference. I'd inherited a tenth-floor, west-facing corner office from my former supervisor, Marit, lately retired, and though my name now adorns the acrylic plate stamped to the door—which discount plate I'd printed and plaqued at my own expense—I've always had a hard time accepting this space as my own. Partly this comes down to Marit, whose books still litter the shelves. These are books of theory, mainly, shrink-wrapped anthologies, chapbooks, old, unopened galleys and proofs. I pocketed the good stuff ages ago (first edition of Davenport's *A Balthus Notebook*, hardback of Malcolm Lowry's final novel, *October Ferry to Gabriola*) and dragged the rest of what I deemed sellable down to Pages Books in Kensington for dispersal.

Apart from my immediate teaching materials, uncollected exams and essays, the odd library book, my apples and aspirins, my drawered hand sanitizers and masks, I tend to keep things pretty spartan. Saying this, I'm not looking to score any Thoreauvian brownie points. Such scantiness as I inhabit owes to a definite pragmatism. I'm wallowing on borrowed time up here. My neighbours know this. Know that my long unbroken view of campus (Swann Mall below with the Rockies beyond) far exceeds the premium of my contractual appointments.

Which, fair enough. I would only add that the classes I teach, subordinate, low-level snorers geared at non-English majors, are not in much demand among senior faculty, particularly since with each passing year we keep seeing a precipitous rise in enrolment (my sections now cap at 130 per); which—all griping aside—if anything can be said to justify my geographical longevity, it's this: I teach the classes no one else wants to teach (the only classes, perhaps, the department, which earns its bread and butter on the backs of my refried PowerPoints, really needs to teach), and I do so reasonably well and largely ungrudgingly, without any genuine aspiration to improve my lot. This makes for a strange admission, but here goes: I am well suited to a certain quiet complacency, a professional torpor; call it what you will. It is still possible, I suppose—I remain a youngish enough cis white male for now—that one day I might jump ship, forsake the academy and seek gainful (if not gleeful) employment as a technical writer in government or (what amounts to the same thing) oil and gas. But who am I kidding? I am resigned to my modest grind. Resigned like all but a few of my former classmates to the systemic futility of the academic job market.

Of course, this wasn't always the case.

Under Marit I'd written my dissertation on Beckett. Or rather on some lines Beckett purportedly lifted from Spinoza's *Ethics* and re-employed as an epigraph in chapter six of *Murphy*. I promise not to start us down a whole Geoff Dyer novel about what I uncovered (or failed to uncover) here—feel free to look me up on ProQuest—but reading my way around in the second volume of Beckett's correspondence, which (at the time about which I'm digressing) had just come out from Cambridge UP, I spotted some striking discrepancies in his philosophical readings, which begat this meandering examination of his letters and diaries and German notebooks, through the course of which research I set out to prove that Beckett had cribbed his sources from an obscure German primer. I nailed my defence (I don't mind saying), but about a year later, as I was readying the manuscript for submission to various academic presses, I uncovered Matthew Feldman's *Beckett's Books: A Cultural History of Samuel Beckett's 'Interwar Notes'*, which effectively rendered my thesis kaput. I ended up reviewing the Feldman—Feldman, who's moved on to the study of contemporary fascism—for *MFS* (my loftiest publication to date).

Back then I was teaching only one section—an early, overweening facsimile of the courses I do now: Intro Literature; Intro Literature and Society; Intro Theory; Intro Poetry; Intro Novel—applying for post-docs, fellowships, and such tenure- and non-tenure-track jobs as (once upon a time, and a very good time it was) bled through the pipes, reviewing and editing at any journal that'd have me, rehashing the usual takes and lists, churning out my share of hasty pop-culture silage, all while trying to manoeuvre my Beckett thing into an amorphous Flann O'Brien project, in the hopes that I'd land something, anything. Well?

Well, there were some bites, some furtive nibbling (I interviewed at U of T Mississauga but I'm still waiting on that callback!), what my father, the playwright—in whose GG-winning *Baleen* there figures a heroically unemployable philosophy prof: BENJAMIN (*Thirty-seven; bald, thick-set; curler's body*), whose academic travails loosely mirror my own—called, with real cynicism, "near misses." I kept, as Beckett did with the dozens of rejection slips he received on *Murphy*, a running tab of my efforts, until—also like Beckett—I didn't. Some months passed, a year, another; you get the picture.

Obviously I wanted, I pined, I thirsted and yearned. Oh, yes. But what did I want? Grad students, for one. Grad classes, for two. I envisioned my Beckett project as part of a much broader sequence of investigations charting a whole host of artistic misreadings and thefts. My books (plural) would emerge regularly from reputable presses, line the departmental vitrine, the first a thing a prospective student or janitor or lost philosopher might encounter when stepping off the elevator. Maybe I'd live near enough to campus that I could bike to work and carry my seat through the halls, the legs of my trousers stuffed deep in my socks, a beloved oddity. Maybe the department head would know my name and not grudgingly remember it while chewing his bottom lip and squinting (the difference, let me tell you, is striking). Fellow colleagues would gather round my timbered kitchen island and feast upon whatever it is fellow colleagues feast upon, cured meats and pickles, I speculated, but good ones, sweet ones, pimpled with dense warty nubbins. Over great wines and bad, we'd jaw and imbibe, malign tannins, explore our communal rue.

But, no.

In place of grad students, a plague of bros, a purgatory of terfs and tin-hatted incels. Gone were the days when the papers I returned to my students bloomed ardent with ink. Whatever happened to the man who attended to his students' sentences with more care than he gleaned in their making? Where once I agonized over every "utilizes effectively" and "in conclusion" and "persuasively demonstrated," I now found that a simple "awkward" or "AWK" sufficed. I unwed wacky run-ons, harmonized tenses, tightened theses, and rewrote entire sentences in the interest of suppressing an "is to be found." Paragraphs of scrupulous editorial feedback appended the thinnest submissions. I responded to emails. I held office hours. I prepped. Yes, let the record show: I even read my own assigned readings.

But then something coarsened or bleakened in me. I disengaged; I dialled out.

My books went unwritten, my essays unpitched. I'd committed to memory my top three RateMyProfessors reviews:

1. **Kinda out to lunch.**
2. **An easy marker but I probably wouldn't recommend him to first years.**
3. **one of the worst prof's i've had. He is not helpful at all and often ignores students with hands. Paper feedback took to long and was not useful. Lecturers were very borring and i hate be the one to saying it but the shirt with the stripes are not doing him any favors.**

The feedback I received on my USRIs offered a more measured perspective—praise be the 60 per cent of non-respondents who, for the price of a B-minus, couldn't be bothered to fill out the form. But look, those reviews made for unhappy reads. I tried not to take them too personally. To this end, it helped to pity my students, most of whom needed a decent mark in my class in order to pursue careers in business and kinesiology and nursing and whatever else. Tuition was insane, student housing in crisis. Many of my students were holding down part-time jobs on top of a full course load. Who was I to remind them that, in conclusion, and possibly throughout history, the passive voice is to be avoided? Wouldn't I hate my guts too?

Not that my students exhibited any shame when it came to enlisting the latest AI, carpet bombing my inbox with all that impenetrable averageness. Write me a five-paragraph essay in the present tense with a debatable thesis statement about the use of eyes, seeing, sight, and eye imagery in William Shakespeare's *King Lear*. Now add an introduction and conclusion. Include three secondary sources. Generate an MLA works-cited page. Include some typos.

Who was going to stop them? Ward them away from such summary seductions? Me? Don't kid yourself.

My colleagues looked upon me with plaintive acquaintance. I took to declining the elevator, marching up the ten flights of stairs to my office—or Marit's office—just to avoid their avoidance.

Sweaty and wheezing, then, I sat at my desk, reading sentences like "Since the beginning of time, the men of this universe has often sought to keep the civilian in chains" or "August was concerned with weather or not men could be taught and the ways that texts and words function as signifiers in this process," and wondered, vaguely, how I might've fared in law school.

Anyway. Part of me thought maybe I'd better notify the department, let the interim head—a halitotic cog on loan from (checks phone) Classics—know I'd be absent a few days (and possibly, pending the seriousness of the Castle's digital restrictions, incommunicado, too), but I didn't feel up to entrusting my classes to some incorruptible grad student, which I was sure they'd recommend I do.

So, in the end—to usher us back to our seats, back into narrative time—I left it so long that indecision and apathy won the day, and I resolved to go with my original plan (zero-hour sick emails) and tell no one in the city where I was going. Which suited me fine. The truth is I've always felt this nagging impermanence in Calgary. In many ways it amazes me that I've lived here this long. I have few friends in Calgary, and pride myself on this reclusiveness, which has always seemed to me a marker of an indomitable, monastic-like seriousness (or something). I often go days where the only people I engage in conversation are the more sycophantic (job-bent and grade-haggling) of my students, maybe the grocery store clerks who coordinate curbside pickups, or the woman who cinches my shawarmas, slips me warm fatayers on the sly. This is not to say that St. John's vies with any more paternity for that title: home. It doesn't. Though there are times when I miss the island, the people, the sea, the scoured skies and whittled inlets aburst with bawling gulls, I know that to live there again, even contentedly, would be to invite, or court, a kind of sickness.

By which admittedly freighted proclamation I intend only this: I wouldn't want to see my failures further reflected in the eyes of family and friends.

Living away, and staying away, keeps me—or to press the matter with a degree of finitude: the idea of me—safe. Neither Baker nor Willis knows anything about my life, really. The tidal degradations of my works and days. To them, I remain as I've always seemed: pretentious and vexed. My father knows the depths of my despair more than most, and so naturally it follows that I fear him most of all. Fear is maybe laying it on a little thick. Let's call it what it is and shuffle on: resentment. I resent him who knows my depths so well.

———

The weekend before I was scheduled to fly out, I sat down at the kitchen table with a notepad and pen and took stock of what outdoorsy equipment I owned. This didn't take long. I had a too-warm yellow raincoat with metal snaps that I'd hardly ever worn and which I thought might stand up okay in the wind, so figured I was good for a shell, but otherwise I was completely without tackle. All my socks were thin, slack-banded, and tattered. I had no decent undergarments, no thermals. My gloves were fingerless smoker's mitts, my one toque pilled and ravelling. It wasn't entirely clear to me what sort of gear we'd be expected to bring. Binoculars? Headlamp? Gaiters? Bug spray? The closest I could scare up in the way of a pocket knife—not that I intended to pack anything that would require my checking a bag—was a winged corkscrew with a retractable foil-cutter whose ridging was sealed over in rust. At minimum, I figured I needed boots, socks, a good pair of gloves, and possibly a whistle.

So I decided to shop, to let myself spend. I stopped in for lunch at Donna Mac—gin and tonics (plural), tuna crudo, with an order of za'atar fries—and then onto MEC, where an older attendant with a spiky red beard like the spine of a venomous sea urchin helped me into a pair of rugged hiking boots with a breathable, waterproof membrane and orange laces. I picked up a pair of merino wool socks (expensive), a tube of sunscreen, a wooden toothbrush, thermals, headlamp, a thing of handwarmers, insulated gloves, toque, whistle, a box of chocolate almond PowerBars, and a trowel. I'm not sure why I bought the trowel. They had stacks of them on sale in the metal bins by the cash—2 for 1 trowels (so two trowels)—and it just seemed like something I needed to have.

The price of all this roughly equalled a two-night stay at the Delta. Not including lunch.

I had no idea what to bring for a book, but wanted to read, or—let's face it—be seen reading, a work of sufficient obscurity. Marlen Haushofer, the latest Cărtărescu, maybe Gerald Murnane's *The Plains*? I managed to squish all of my gear into one backpack and one carry-on-friendly suitcase. I set the timers on the living room and bedroom lights, adjusted blinds, checked outlets and elements, booked a car for my morning ride to the airport, made a pot of lemon ginger tea, hopped onto my fold-up, sent my father my flight information, queued up an episode of *Seinfeld* on my phone—the one with the dermatologist and the meat slicer, where Kramer tumbles into a room full of potatoes—took two Robax Platinum (regular strength; I know my limits), and decided, in breach of the no-smoking clause in my lease agreement, to crack a window and get lightly stoned.

The next morning, as my driver heaped my suitcase and backpack into the trunk, Jerry stepped onto his front porch. He stood barefoot in a scummy powder-blue robe with what looked like tiny embroidered chickens plastered across the chest. He held a short coring knife and one of his gruesome wooden progeny. If I had to guess, I'd say the ghoul he'd been chiselling was about half done.

"Morning," I said, smiling.

Jerry didn't say anything. He placed his sculpture on our porch's shared beam, angled it so that its scowling features met my own, and recapped his knife. Then he stepped back inside the house.

FIVE

A DAWNING AUTONOMY, PERCOLATING IN THE SUBURBS of my bowels, overtook me as our plane, banking over the Atlantic, unfolded its landing gear. I upped my seat and thumped my armrest, hoping to revive the catatonic sawyer snoozing next to me. "Look alive, old fellow," I wanted to say. "Time for supper." I squeezed my nose and popped my ears against the pressure, gazing out the window. There, tilting up at me through a slim gristle of fog, were the South Side Hills, an expanse of sheer, fir-capped cliffs, encircling the city's harbour like a claw.

In our younger (more invulnerable) years, Willis and I would often drive down to Fort Amherst, park our car in the thin gravelly close near where they've chained off the old barracks, and trudge up the streambed. The trail, originally intended as a waterline and munitions conduit during the Second World War, proceeding through a slight, muggy copse in whose peaty, low-lying scrub there abounded blueberries and goldenrod and bunches of pillowy bog laurel, crested onto a wide rocky outcropping rounded in folded conifers. We'd linger for hours up there, cracking beers and halving smokes, which the woman who worked the Tucker's off Empire most weekdays sold singly, fifty cents a dart, parcelling them away for you, your Player's or Export A Golds, in the brown paper bags more typically reserved for Fuzzy Peaches, Sour Patch Kids, and Cherry Blasters. Some days we'd drag up a duffel of thieved golf balls (gathered, under cover of night, from the pollarded fringes of the Clovelly driving range) and a few of my father's clubs—like his persimmon driver, which he'd kill me to know how I treated it, chipping its plated wooden sole right down to the dirt—casting purblind drives into the greyish below.

Our plane cruised out over the harbour and continued on its northern course. The last light was draining from the day, and as the city centre faded to boxed commerce, untillable fields, and farmland, streaks of rain started across my window, beading right along the wing, over spoilers and flaps and pinches of blurred cowling. The overhead lights blinked and our flight attendant made a final duck through the cabin, righting seats, snatching plastic. My guts were a mess, an apocalypse of candied cashews and vodka, but I felt none of the panic, none of the broad, euphoric hatred, that typically grips me during a flight. Cubes of rain mobilized like Tetris tiles on my window, and I watched them fall, stumbling in a slow glide.

I regretted accepting my father's invitation from the moment I unbuckled my seatbelt. The way an accident, some minor household calamity, grafts itself onto your mind's eye before it happens, I saw it all—the jumped mug's shards of buoyant porcelain—quite clearly, and too late.

It was just after seven. A faint rain pattered on the tarmac, and the yellow chevrons stirred in the puddled light. I fetched my suitcase from the overhead compartment, retreating to my seat to make way for a weary mother and child. We filtered down the emptying aisle, passing from plane to carpeted jet bridge, a sudsy whiff of disinfectant mingling in the concourse's cold and coppery air.

The terminals were empty, all the gates and glinting kiosks closed. I set my bags down on a slatted, teal-cushioned bench and retied my shoes, squinting over the gaudily patterned tiles, which were done up in slivers of what looked like gold and cherry nougat, seamed in rivery grout. My fingers tingled and itched. Clearly I'd overcommitted on the cashews. There were patches of mangled nut snuggled all down inside the gaps between my teeth (which are in terrible shape, let me tell you, crooked and sore and brown as milked tea). I cupped a hand over my lips and nose, and considered my breath. Sour, buttery. I forced a cough, emitting a tidy dry burp, and proceeded through a set of frosted glass doors, my eyes dimming over as I stepped onto the escalator, my backpack and carry-on settled on the next treaded step.

My father was there, waiting but not looking for me, thinner than I remembered him, a sluggish scowl fixed to his cheeks. The car rental booths before which he stood with folded arms drawn fast in his pits, appraising travellers, were shuttered. Seeing me, he scrunched up his face, disappearing his philtrum in a sneer of white stubble—this constituted a smile—released an arm, and waved. His hands looked sunburned, anointed in rash, and the left one, the waving hand, wore a strict band of cotton.

"It's good to see you," I said.

"You look drunk."

"What happened to your hand?"

"Cat."

"Cat," I said. "What cat?"

We embraced. Dark blood showed on the bandaged hand, sparing one digit but coating the tips of two fingers, a knuckle, and the flat, veiny trail of his thumb.

"It's nothing to worry about," he said. "With cats the main thing you're wanting to keep in mind are your tendons. Because a cat's teeth," he said, parting his lips, giving me the teeth, spit, a livery sash of gum, "they're sharp, sharper than a dog's, anyway, and coated in bacteria. And I guarantee you don't want any of that creeping into your system."

"Where's Beth?" I asked.

"Who?"

It was my turn to scowl. The black puffer he wore with vented collar and arms was zipped up all the way to his chin. I waited for him to speak, tracked his gaze as it took in the crowd assembling before the unmoving carousel, a slant of blood, no thicker, maybe, than the brain of an ant, tightening on the white of his canthus—the eye closest mine.

"I'm fucking with you," he said. "I drove. You got bags?"

"Just these," I said.

"Okay." He readjusted one of his knuckles. "Follow me."

We took Higgins Line to Allandale as far as Confederation. Across the street were the steeper, bumpier knolls leading off Pippy Park where I used to go tobogganing. Election placards dotted both hills: reds, blues, a skimpy stippling of purple. On the backs of the broader foam boards, which stood on thick plywood struts, some anonymous wag had stencilled anarchic cartoons and phalli. One of these boards showed a pretty capable rendering of Charlie Brown in a red MAGA hat whose thought bubble exhorted the reader, or possibly just Charlie, to "fuck i."

The hills levelled out on a fold of addled grassland knobbed in hoary goose shit. The perpetrators, beaks bent up along the pleats of their breasts such that they resembled tumbled wasp nests, slept, amid the cattails and reeds and shoots of ticklish milfoil, at a little distance from their excrement. Rounding Long Pond, I noted the intersection where many summers ago Baker had totalled his sister's Subaru gunning an advanced green. He'd come out of the wreck shaken but unscathed. And unmarried, too. His fiancé, an up-and-coming civil litigator at Lindsay and Scott (Chicago Justice, we called her, for reasons I can no longer corroborate), riding shotgun on belated airbags, had, according to Baker, rescinded things on the spot.

"You been to see Mom lately?" I asked. I waited for my father to speak, searched inside his face for an answer, but none came. I hadn't intended this question unkindly, but I wanted to know. She'd hoped for a plot at Mount Carmel but the Catholics weren't accepting submissions. Hers was a simple stone, upright granite on square stage, lodged in Bannerman Park.

My father shrunk down in his seat, reached into his pocket, and handed me a pack of gum. "For your breath," he said. "Which smells god awful, by the way."

I accepted his gum, popped the foil cell, and slipped the the firm minty oblong onto my tongue, letting that first wild rush of menthol fill my throat while I chewed.

At the corner of Elizabeth, we idled behind a navy pickup with stacks of brown lattice fencing heaped in its bed. A Pepe the Frog decal and three white runic thorns adorned the rear panel window.

"How's it been here?" I asked. "With like everything that's been going on."

My father cocked his head, swished his jaw from side to side, and yawned. "Same as anywhere, I guess. You heard about the statue?"

I had. Someone—the right blamed an oil-loathing left; the left, perceiving a setup, fingered a self-sabotaging right—had shot up the Ocean Ranger Memorial with pink and green paintballs, and splashed vats of what authorities later identified as Karo syrup and red food colouring (the same cocktail John Travolta doused Sissy Spacek with on prom night) across the statue's commemorative plaque and gardens. Turns out, the culprits were just a bunch of disenchanted hellions from Gonzaga, spoiling for trouble, for clicks; politically unaffiliated, or so their parents attested, as yet.

"Has anyone decided what they're going to do with them?" I asked.

"You mean in terms of punishment?" My father snorted. "Community service seems to be the going consensus. Department of Justice and Public Safety, together with the school board, the Provincial School District or whatever, they've got this idea where—" The light changed to green, but the pickup wasn't budging. My father hovered his palm over the horn. "Guy's probably on his phone."

"Just be patient," I said. The pickup lurched into gear, a plume of black smoke sputtering from its exhaust as it sped across Elizabeth, lattices rattling. "You were saying? Community service?"

"Right. So the idea, get this: it's part of this new program, this safety initiative, to track wildlife on the highways, keep the herds from straying onto the TCH."

"And so the kids do what?"

"Don't know yet. But I guess the idea here is they want to instill a sense of responsibility, of historical, provincial respect—one kid per moose."

I pictured a fleet of mutinous teens, my own students, me, warding roaming herds off the road. "I can think of worse ideas," I said.

As we pulled onto Newtown, my father drifted into second, occasioning a costly-sounding lurch and wheeze in the transmission, which appeared now to be clicking or knocking also—the hysterical pulse of a downed helicopter, whoop-whoop-whoop-whoop-whoop, closing over flattened fronds—as we bumped up over the curb and came to a heavy stop. I stepped out of the warm, still-pinging car, and took a deep breath. The air had that strong syrupy smell of leaked coolant.

"What's with the sound coming off the car?" I asked.

"What sound?"

My childhood home bore no political affiliations, and this was a relief. There were no placards, no flags, no suggestive stickers or outré iconography. I'd never been so bold as to broach the subject, but I despaired at Beth's politics—or perceived politics—and at my father's nascent heresies. An avowed socialist—his second and, after *Baleen*, most successful play, *A Supermarket in Clarenville*, chronicles the utopian travails of a band of luckless fox farmers in the 1890s—he'd lately taken to upbraiding all comers.

I started up the driveway for the steps, whose wide concrete slabs were glossily charred. Had no one told me about a fire? The shade was of an old cast iron cauldron with splotches of inky-black scum clinging to the risers like tar. Or maybe it *was* tar?

"What's happened here?"

"Don't get him started," said Beth, emerging from behind the screen door for a hug. "We had some work done on the steps, which, as you see—"

I shouldered my pack and we hugged. The arms of her shirt were of peach chiffon, smelled vaguely of jasmine, and made a sound like a dragonfly's wing when I brushed them.

"How was the flight? Did you eat? Here," she said, grabbing my carry-on, "let me take this."

"He's not going to want to eat," my father said. He was hunched over the driveway now, his back partly turned to us, inspecting a mauve, berry-shaped rock.

"I snacked on the plane," I said. "But thank you. I might pick at something."

"Well there's a leftover rice thing with leeks and a piece of salmon if you change your mind. Whatever you need, really. Just make yourself at home."

"Thanks, but I'm meeting Baker downtown for a drink in about an hour."

"Leaving us already?" my father said, dusting himself off. "Well, it's been nice having you."

"Ignore him," said Beth. "What he means is he's happy to give you a ride."

The steps worsened as you walked up them—like a portico opening on Mount Doom—and, in places where I was registering an onyx-like shine to the blackness, you could almost see what had been attempted in the way of an artful texture or weave.

"Is this texturing deliberate?" I asked.

"What's that?"

"These lines," I said, pointing. "All these bumps. Are they supposed to be here?"

"I don't know," my father said. "I guess so. One thing I'm definitely starting to realize is that you just can't get good work done around here anymore. Not in this city. Should've been a simple re-sealing job, but—"

"Speaking of which," Beth said, "I should warn you that the carpet downstairs where they tracked everything in looks a little dirty, but it's not."

"We had to get it deep cleaned."

"But there's still streaks."

"There's a lot of streaks," my father said.

We followed Beth into the kitchen. The recessed light fixture above the sink looked new, so new, in fact, that a tab of neon-red tape dangled from its copper faceplate. There were dirty bowls and pots stacked on the counter and dishes and spatulas brining in the sink and a trail of crumbs crunched underfoot and I worried for Beth's feet, which were bare. To the side of the sink a quartered lime sat on a short wooden cutting board, a handsome paring knife with a Pepto-pink hilt resting on the board's bevelled edge. Beth offered me a beer. My father accepted one, too.

"You talk to Willis?" my father asked.

"Not yet."

"So let me get this straight. He pays your way. Sponsors this entire trip. And what, you haven't even let him know you touched down?"

"I'll call him," I said.

"Where were we, we were out the other day, we saw them down to the store?" asked Beth.

My father scratched his chin, went to the counter, picked up the cutting board and, wincing, sucked a wedge of lime.

"He was with his kid," said Beth. "What's the youngest one's name again?"

"Penelope," I said.

"No, sorry. The middle one. The son."

"Isaac," my father said. He flipped one rind into the sink where it splashed and bobbed in the sudsless water and grabbed another. The lofted lime, buoyed by unknown currents, wobbled once and, flaunting its chewed grooves, disappeared beneath the brine.

Beth said, "Isaac, right. Yeah, he doesn't look so good. He seems to have gotten all kind of skinny." Beth shook her shoulders. This was what skinniness looked like. "And stern. He was wearing shorts."

"Shorts?" I asked.

"It's been freezing and—"

"Really cold," my father said. "All my peppers—just completely covered in frost."

"And he had on these big long flappy safari shorts which—with the—you know, the pockets?"

"I might make a jelly with them," my father said.

"Did you say hi?" I faced Beth, and tried to ignore my father.

"I don't think they saw us," Beth said. "In my opinion they should've taken both those kids right out of school and—"

"They're still edible," my father said. "I brought them inside to let them ripen. Though what you want, what you really need for a good jelly is cider."

With that, he lobbed his second rind into the sink and missed. It banked off the rim and skittered across the counter. I flinched. Beer foam sloshed from my startled bottle. The lime rind pinwheeled along its western course, bearing floorward, and there I stopped it, catching the unruly fruit in my palm, while my father laughed and laughed.

The basement was exactly as I'd left it after Travis's funeral, draughty and rank. The slate coaster was still crummy with coffee stains, the rings sticky and seared and quilted in dust. I doubted they'd had anyone down here after me, and I wondered if my father had bothered changing the sheets. I propped open the window and drew back the comforter, the faded, beachy-blue fabric dappled in lint. I laid my suitcase out on the floor and chucked my backpack in the closet.

At the thump of this weight, something inside the closet stirred, and a small, three-legged tabby emerged, stretching out a front paw as it hopped—managing a sort of pogo-stick-like stagger—over to me, purring and scrubbing its cheeks across my shins. I sat down on the bed and scrolled through my phone. The cat hopped up onto the mattress and continued rubbing against me, making heavy open-mouthed purrs as I scratched its chin and nuzzled a pinky along the bald silken felt of its ears. First the magpie and now the cat. What was with all of these amputees?

I had two student emails, neither urgent. One requested an extension on the first close reading assignment, which I granted—I will always grant an extension—while the second, from a former student, concerned a missing reference letter for a travel abroad program, which baffled me.

"sorry hey," it began. "I didn't get into the program like you hoped and I hoped because they said my application was incomplete even though when I technically checked online it said it was complete so I emailed people in charge again who they said you said they were missing a letter from one of my references and that's why I wasn't able for it to be able to be completed on time. I have emailed my other reference letter person just in case so sorry if you've already did this. It is just really important to be me because part of my future is I wanted to get in. This is Donald by the way of ENGELS 274.05."

I couldn't tell if Donald—or, as I sometimes preferred, *the* Donald—intended "Engels" as a joke or if the word had surfaced unbidden from the recesses of some fouled algorithm, and honestly— honestly—it didn't matter. I had no idea what he was talking about. What program? What letter?

Few students loom long in my memory, but the Donald lived there rent free. A solid, unswervingly mediocre student (C–/C), always with a question, a contentious comment, or complaint, I'd first encountered him in ENGL 201, and then again in ENGL 362, the British Literature (1900–1945) class I inherited from our resident modernist the semester she went on mat leave (thank you, Lena!). ENGL 274.05 was Pre-Confederation Narratives of Upper Canada, a wintry slog of imperilled sonnets and racist travelogues I'd taken on last January from the late Lochlin Bruce (bison burger, pulmonary embolism); it had been my third tour with the Donald, and I badly needed a furlough, an armistice, an epoch of Donald-free R&R.

Somehow, the email ambled on for another two paragraphs, but as I was skimming (and rehearsing, mid-skim, my response: *Dear Donald, Thanks for your email, but I have no idea what you're talking about. Are you certain that you solicited a reference letter from me?*), a text from Baker flashed over my screen, "We doing this?" so, thumbing "en route," I ignored it.

SIX

I TOOK WHITEWAY AS FAR AS LION'S PARK, ARCING MY WAY
across the old blighted softball pitch where, for a bit of candy or
a can of pop, I used to retrieve fly balls and grounders in one of the
splintery, chip-wood baskets with the braided wicker handles you
never see anymore; and on past the playground—the domed climber
and slides and laddered parapet opening on a row of swings, the
chains twisted and gnarled and eerily seatless (like a fetishist's arcane
manacles); past the sandboxes and teeter-totters and curling rink and
low shake-shingle cabin with its honeycomb-grated windows plated in
sun-bronzed foil; and up onto Bonaventure, slipping the square silver
key Beth had lent me and my own keys, office and home, through the
tabs of my knuckles as I rounded the Belvedere Cemetery, passing
no one.

It felt good to be up on my feet and moving. The rain had abated to
mist and the air had that slick unmenacing crispness to it, and probably,
too, I needed the walk. I never walked, never thought of St. John's
as a walking city, as conducive to a soft October stroll, until I moved
away from home. There were too many hills and tilted avenues,
sidewalks thinning to gravel and silt as the dinky streets dumped onto
the busier ones. Also, I'd decided to break in my hiking boots, which

I had not worn except to strut and bend purposefully around the carpeted arteries of the MEC. They were bulkier than I remembered. And taller. The orange laces twinkled and flamed; my soles clunked.

Coming up on Military, past St. Bon's, I kept to the side of the Basilica, opposite the Rooms, whose façade, bathed in gaseous, mast-lit halides, shone damp and beige and bland. I'd forgotten how abrupt, how jagged and joltingly segregated, were the steps leading down Garrison, which I took in a hurry, feeling the pinch of loose cobbles all the way up in my shins, as I came clopping across Queen at a tormented gallop, steadying myself on a canted crosswalk bollard whose cold yellow casing shifted and winced in my grip.

"Jesus Christ, guy. Easy," said a young woman in a faded jean jacket and Keds. Taking me in with a grin (sidelong, toothy), her eyes, I thought, contained more amusement than affront. Her companion, shuffling into the light, had on a high sleazy blue beanie and drank from a bottle of beer he kept stowed in his parka.

"I got all night," this man said. "I just need to know where I'm going."

I muttered an apology, my phone open, professing obscure urgencies, as I hastened past them, continuing across Duckworth, descending on McMurdo's Lane.

The Duke was unchanged but, to my eyes, shrunken and needy. I posted up at the bar just after ten. Baker had texted again saying he was running a few minutes late, would I mind ordering him a cider, preferably a Strongbow, and in a can if they had it, with a glass of ice, cubed not crushed, on the side. "k," I wrote back. My bartender was in her forties, bottle-blonde and brusque, with a glossy black stud spotting her labrum. I ordered Baker his cider and, for myself, a pint of Black Horse and double Jameson neat, just a little something, I figured, to reconceptualize my buzz.

"Let's see," said a man standing behind me.

"It's not her," a second man said, cupping his phone.

"Fuck off. Just let me see. I can't tell if I can't see."

Peering into the mirrored bar backing, I saw, beyond the shamrock garlands and scarves and fifths of refracted whiskey, a good showing for a Wednesday, the booths bodied and sloshed, the whaps (i.e., VLTs) happy. Though I love the Duke, love its whole warm wooden feel, I've always felt at a volatile remove from its kin, either too young or just too fucking old, and that night, as I took down the foam on my Horse and ministered to my whiskey—who orders Jamies by the finger in here and not a shot?—I felt my years, the untidy effort of my drunkenness, acutely.

There were a few faces I recognized, or half-recognized, but only Paul Fowler I knew by name. He stood at the opposite end of the bar by the grilled, neon-chafed windows talking to an older man with a steep rangy face, pitted and scarred, with the beginnings of a mullet feathering off his ears and down over his collar, a man in his sixties maybe, a man with a moustache.

I knew Paul enough to nod hello, but doubted whether he remembered me, and that was fine. Everyone knew Paul. His shrunken smiles, his freckled brawn. We'd ended up taking some of the same classes together back at MUN: History of Espionage, O'Connor's European Armies and the Conduct of War; boyish, enticingly puerile electives, to be sure, in satisfaction of our respective degrees. O'Connor was a force unlike any I've encountered in the academy. He had the body of a Scottish long-swordsman, the reach of a Potsdam tallboy, and the beard of a French sapper. His classes were riveting, noteless soliloquies orated on high. He was peppy on Austerlitz, Ulm, on Napoleon's *manoeuvre sur les derrières*, the perforated music stand he retained as a pulpit wobbling in one fist. The university was then in the process of ridding the Arts and Administration building of asbestos, and I seem to recall they had us, that term, lodged in the cramped, carpet-walled basements of Statistics and Math. Crossing back to class from the library, I'd spot O'Connor sitting outside Henrietta Harvey, admiring the courtyard's bronze armillary, smoking, going his Styrofoam coffee alone. God knows what sort of impression he left on Paul—Paul, who'd deployed to Kandahar in '06 or '07, where he'd run forcible disruption ops against insurgent strongholds north of Zharey, obtaining medals, a wound, renown.

"How's your beer?" my bartender asked. My glass—I hadn't even noticed—was nearing empty.

"I'd do more of the same," I said. "Thanks."

She idled a moment, biding my dregs. Her cheeks were rosy, puttied in blush, and the crests of them, along their hollows, pink as lobster flesh.

I finished my whiskey and edged the glass to the side of the taps. The dimpled, tin-plated counter smelled of fish, smeared mayo, and fries. Pushed up against the napkin dispenser was a red sandwich basket with two large uneaten wings in it. I nudged the thicker wing, gooey and broiled and woolly with salt, debated eating it, and did. I set the basket aside and scrubbed my fingers with an arid Wet-Nap. When I looked up, staring into or at me, in the bar mirror, was my old crush, Caitlin's sister, Megan, and her husband, whose name, though I'd had it told to me countless times—as recently, perhaps, as Travis's funeral—I'd never quite bothered to remember, which ambivalence caused me no small amount of social dread, fearful as I was for the day when, emboldened by some beery intermission of decorum, he might call me on it. I dabbed my lips with another stitch of napkin and smiled hazily into the mirror, as they stepped out of their booth and collected their coats, skirting the tall pillared counters for the door.

"We still working on these?" my bartender asked, sliding my drinks down in front of me, indicating the wings.

"Sorry," I said. "No."

I looked back to the door but Megan and her husband were gone. Had they not seen me? Had they seen me and preferred not to? She works, Megan does, in pediatrics now, a much-sought-after physician up at the Janeway. Mother of two, lover of huskies, Whole30, vintage typewriters and lamps—I go by the feeds here, a willing subscriber. And the husband—the intended, we'd called him—figuring in all these pixels, too. Ideally stubbled, hirsute, wisps of the stuff snaking off triceps, edgy and honed, flourishing through the sheer of the steeply pitched V-necks he favoured.

He and Megan had been married for well over a decade, I guessed—he was, strictly speaking, an intended no longer—but his doting was notorious, a known quantity among many generations of family, fringe suitors, and friends. In fairness, the man's adoration outweighed my earlier avidities by a power exponentially unthinkable to me. I mean that he registered every anticipated—and unanticipated—request with an acuity that seemed freakishly algorithmic. He materialized and popped up, a constant, unlowerable ad. Equally understood, in the face of this unceasing devotion, was Megan's prickliness, an unreciprocated, public reluctance for affection. Here, I'll admit that my eligibility as objective, unbiased arbitrator is plainly wanting, but, fuck it, the whole thing struck me as possibly hugely sexual, somehow. Not in any perceivably adulterous or cuckoldy-type way (though maybe), but there was some sort of dynamic at work here, a matrimonial dialectic whose precise moral superstructure (or economy) exceeded my scant stores of empathy and understanding.

"Buddy," said Baker.

I felt hands, padded and thick, on my shoulders, and I dropped down from my stool to greet him.

"Digging the hat," I said, and let go of his shoulders.

"Gotta stay warm," he said. "Your boy's starting to lose it up here."

Baker palmed off his hat, and hooped it over the arm of his chair. A stout ginger feather, vanes paling to fawn, adorned the brim.

"Pictures don't do it justice," I said, sizing up his skull, which was zitless and sheeny.

"Go Bic or go home," he said. "What're we drinking?"

"Jameson," I said. "Horse. I ordered you a cider."

"You wanting a shot?" our bartender asked.

Baker faced me. He suffered, or claimed to suffer, from an undiagnosed (or self-diagnosed) gluten sensitivity, preferring clear liquors and ciders, but quirked up his brow in gentle ascension. "Sure," he said.

"Neat?" our bartender asked.

"Let's try a cube."

Baker undid his coat, his scarf, his cardigan, eyeing his pour, leaving his Henley, which nearly matched mine, intact. "What's this? Doubles?"

"Always," I said, and I drank.

Baker brought the drink to his lips, sipped once, and set the glass to the side of his beer coaster. He tented his hands under his chin and flicked his pinkies up and down. "You see Megan?" he asked.

"I did."

"She looks good," he said.

"She does," I said, and she did.

"You talk to her?"

"We said hi," I lied.

"I feel sorry for what's-his-face."

"The intended," I said. "It's a lot."

"The most," said Baker. "Christ. All these omelettes. Every goddamn morning on my phone. I've never seen so many eggs. Tarragon and feta and whatever else. I can't understand what you two ever saw in each other."

"Technically, we didn't."

"That's right," Baker said. "In my mind, I always imagined you two as a couple, but then, in reality—"

"Reality was a whole other story."

"You were so hung up on her."

"I was a different man."

"Were you?" Baker asked.

We were quiet, and an unwelcome silence ensued. We sipped our drinks, resisted checking our phones, and I caught myself wondering, idly, at the probable longevity of this friendship.

Doubtless, I'd become stilted and odd, a shadowy, slow-witted conversationalist. But then maybe there was more to it than that, more than my prized asceticism at play. It occurred to me, and not without a certain arrogance or aloofness, that I had nothing in particular I wanted to know about Baker, that any question I might put to him, be it about family, work, love life, our forthcoming trip, etc., would ring false, and that, what's worse, I would not be able to hide (or distort) this falseness, this resounding ambivalence, if that's what it was, and that Baker would see in these inquiries, in me, simply the rude labour of my efforts, my expired interest laid bare.

Baker circled his cider's rim with a pinky and rested a thumb on the glass. His nails were not long but their moons were serrated and inset with dirt. He swirled his whiskey, dancing the cube and steering its legs.

No, we weren't so dissimilar, he and I. Our work was contractual, our homes rented. No siblings, no wives, no children. We'd each lost a parent and long ago othered any budding significants. For my part, I wanted to think that these vacancies were voluntary. I had no interest in extending myself, in—wait for it—transmitting the boredom and the ignominies of existence, to borrow from Flaubert, happy Frenchman; but Baker, I knew, desired these things, a family, fatherhood; and I suspect he saw in me, in my easy abdication of these totemic trappings, everything he feared and detested about himself.

"And so how's Isaac?" is what I finally managed. "He's still coming?"

"So far as I know," Baker said.

"My dad said he and Beth ran into him. Beth said he looked pretty off."

Baker took a small sip of his whiskey, fished out the cube, crunched it. "He's big into gaming."

"Gambling?"

"Gaming, as in computers. PC stuff. Dragons and dwarves and like that," Baker said. "Apparently he doesn't leave his room except to shit. Stays up all night, sleeps most of the day. They found bottles under his desk. Of piss," Baker clarified, taking a deeper sip of whiskey and motioning for another round. "They've got him seeing someone now. Some therapist or counsellor. I think they're all doing a once-a-week thing as a group, which, I guess that's helping. But for a while there it was pretty touch-and-go. Wouldn't even speak to Pen for the longest time. Not a word."

"I had no idea it was that bad," I said.

"No?"

"Willis never said anything to me. No dwarves. No piss bottles."

"You ever ask?"

I considered lying. Debated painting myself as a benevolent simpleton, inquiring, well-intentioned, but woefully out of the loop. Instead, I opted for some version of the truth. "Aren't we getting a little old for that?" I asked.

"Meaning what?"

"Meaning nothing," I said. "This incessant checking in. Can't we just dispense with the questions, assume a baseline worst-case scenario across the board, accept that we're all just barely keeping it together, and move on?"

Baker studied me. The whites of his eyes were bulgy and raw. You noticed the black rings circling his irises before you quite registered their depth of colour, that faraway green, a shaded sage. "And how are *you*?" Baker asked.

"I can't tell if you're fucking with me," I said. He sounded sincere, sober. I tried, but couldn't hold his gaze.

"I'm not. Or maybe I am. Either way," he said, the eyes steering off, releasing me, "you look like shit."

"I'm wearing the same shirt as you."

"Exactly," Baker said. "That's exactly my point."

Our bartender slinked an arm past our stools and piled our empties onto a cork tray. "How we doing here, boys?"

"Two waters," Baker said.

"Whiskey back," I said.

"Doubles?"

Baker shuddered. "I'm going to take a leak."

I waited for him to disappear before gesturing to our bartender. "A shot of Goose in those waters, please." I opened my wallet and sat a twenty atop the bar's gridded black matting.

The bartender studied my money. Her lips were soft and full

and a blur of pub light muddied her stud. "You're sure your friend won't mind?"

"He's fine with it." I passed the bill onto the glass rail. "Trust me," I said.

She picked up my twenty and tilted it, gauging authenticity, before slipping it into her apron. "I'll take your money," she said. "But I'm not spiking your buddy's water." She returned to the taps. I smiled but caught sight of myself in the mirror, and good god. Baker was right. Not that I doubted him, my indelible wreckage. The hair, the flush, the craggy teeth. I really did look like shit.

The bartender respawned with our waters, our well whiskeys back, and set all four glasses before me. "I wasn't sure if you still wanted these," she said, meaning the whiskeys.

"We did," I said, spacing everything out. "Please and thank you."

I drank greedily of my ice water. It tasted good, like water. I couldn't say for sure if there was vodka in it.

"Don't look now," Baker said, assembling himself back in his seat, "but I know that guy."

"Who?"

"By the ATM."

"A former tenant of Her Majesty's?"

"Something like that."

I raised my water and made a quick scan of the bar. A gangly man in a baggy fleece hoodie and jeans stood at the ATM, thumbing twenties.

"A guy like that," Baker said, "and you almost always wonder what he didn't go in for. Nice enough fella, though. Good hand-eye. They used to keep him in net."

"Sorry—what are we talking about here?"

"I never tell you about that? Yeah, we used to let these fuckers play ball hockey in the gyms. Back before I started, guys be playing inmates on guards, and once in a while—look, this is insane, you think about it, but we'd get other teams, guys coming in from the outside."

"Civilians?"

"Stevedores. Firemen."

I had no trouble picturing Baker in this role, but I wondered at our youthful truancies. Blundering aboard foreign trawlers late of a Friday night, slinking around those echoey cabins and hulls, pilfering what little loose oddities were ours for the taking. I include myself in these transgressions. We nabbed tins of soup, biscuits, ArVids—stunted video cassettes that reminded me of the Betamax tapes James Woods feeds the fleshy cavity thriving on his gut in Cronenberg's *Videodrome*—sacks of hard, lumpy bread. I liked to park myself off the front railings, on what I believe might be called the flying bridge, and consider the play of lights on the water, the ribbons of moon, the riffling seaweed and kelp. And then there was the night we found the doors to the Kirk unlocked, forded its stone portico, stumbled down the arcaded aisles and into a narrow vestibule where we took turns riding the chiming rope, sounding off a last call to worshippers worming their way home from the pubs.

Paul Fowler approached us, leading with the hurt leg, plucking himself forward by the heel.

"Hey, big man," he said, draping an arm over Baker. "How's life?"

"Surviving," Baker said. "You?"

Paul giggled and his face, the pale and dotted skin—these freckles stood out on the undersides of his eyes like the tiny black stabs you find in a bite of dragon fruit—wrinkled with him. He gave me a quick upward nod but it was pretty clear he had no idea who I was.

"I'm here trying to get Bishop back in gear," he said, letting go of Baker, and scanning a finger down the bar. "That's right, I'm talking about you, you weird, old, crotchety-looking fuck."

The man with the moustache wallowed off his stool and careered past us, beelining for the head.

"His wife left him," Paul said. "Nobody really gives a shit and honestly I don't even think I really give a shit but tonight I'm just trying to get through to him. I think we might be dropping down to Republic next. You guys should stop by," he concluded, buoyant, popping an arm back over Baker's shoulder, regarding our matching shirts. "Unless I'm intruding."

"Paul." Our bartender held a debit machine in her hand and waggled it. "Settling up?"

"Gentlemen," said Paul. "Maybe we see you."

We ordered another round and another one, on top of that, minus the cider and Horse, a fortifying toast for the road.

"Should we bounce?" Baker asked.

"Deoc an dorius," I said, raising a cheers, and bottoming my last in one go.

"What'd you just call me?"

"Door drink," I said. "It's either Irish or Gaelic or—"

"No, that's enough. I'm sorry I asked."

Baker paid our tab and we steadied our way down Water, weighing the Grape (dead), the Rose (cover), Erin's (never), and Bar None (too sober by a half), before stopping into RBC to haul out some cash. Outside the bank a man in a navy trench coat with lank mealy white hair asked if he could bum a smoke.

"Sorry," I said. "Don't smoke."

"How 'bout a light then?" He searched inside his coat pockets and fished out a bag of rollies, loose tobacco, frayed business card peelings, and butts. The cigarette he placed between his lips wasn't much broader than a grilling skewer.

"Don't have one of those either," I lied.

Baker reached into his own jacket, producing a green Bic. The man puckered his lips to the flame Baker sheltered for him, admiring the windy lean of fire as he dragged. "You want to buy my sword?" this man asked, sniffling. He drew a tab of loose paper from his tongue.

"I'm sorry?"

"What kind of sword?" Baker asked. He had a cigarette of his own started now, too.

"It's like a sport sword," the man said. He opened up his arms. "I don't know. About this big. Sort of thing you'd see in the Olympics.

But like ages ago, in olden times. It's got a really good handle. I've hardly used it."

"I'm intrigued," said Baker. "But I think I'd want to see it first."

"That figures," the man said. "I'll bring it over. What we'll do, we'll go right down to the water where you can really swing it. See if it doesn't fit."

"That's exactly what I wanted to hear," said Baker. "We'll be there."

The man went quiet. A crease of skin, which I'd mistaken for a scar, stole down the length of his right cheek, like the strap of a monocle. He pulled on his cigarette, which he'd managed, somehow, to extinguish. A crooked beak of ash obscured most of his ember. He turned away from Baker and looked down at my boots. "So what's your fucking problem?" he asked.

Coming up on George Street, we lost our friend to a hot dog stand, and dipped into Lottie's for a round of White Russians, the dance floor barren and poorly. We thought about maybe heading into Christian's for bitters and popcorn, or O'Reilly's, Bridie Molloy's, Trappers, but neither of us could remember what night Wednesday was, which bars boasted what specials when. And we felt old, or I did. Vomit shone on the cobblestones, pulpy and glossed. The thoroughfare teemed with children, pastel polos, plaids, sequinned bottoms and tops. These were bodies and minds younger than most of my students, and I wanted—idiotically—to save them. A single man in possession of an empty pint glass emerged on the Green Sleeves patio, perving.

"Look at this guy."

"Stop pointing at people," said Baker. "You're going to get both our asses kicked."

Baker shuffled and tipped, listed against my shoulder.

"You okay there?"

"Just keep walking," he said.

We steered off George Street and onto Water, past the Murray Premises buildings, whose stooped scarlet dormers brooded over us like owls. The Port Authority had installed fences and much prohibitive signage along the harbour wall, but these energies seemed more gestural than not. The air smelled of diesel, soaked pilings. Gulls bullied the mounded sewage and salt heaps, turning in the night sky like magnetic stirrers on a hot plate. Their occasional cries carried a plaintive, striving quality. Baker lit another cigarette, offering me one, which I declined. Before us were tankers and smaller, blunter vessels, roofless dinghies and motorboats with outboard engines leashed to their backs, skegs thistly with scum.

I followed Baker along the length of the docks, downwind of the smoke curling over the brim of his hat. The road was striped in bright oily puddles. A gap in the fence presented itself and Baker passed through it. "You coming?" I ducked under the sagging chain-link fence and joined Baker on the other side. The hull of the tanker closest to us held some of the water's wiggle and shine. A set of stairs, cordoned in mesh netting, proceeded up the boat. There was a time when we might've clambered over the gate and up those stairs, the corrugated steps creasing underfoot like foam.

A friend of my father's from way back, a sound technician on loan from Ukraine or Belarus somewhere, had once, one drunken night, found himself aboard an old Soviet trawler (a Pushkin, these were called, though the derivation of this name eludes me). He'd bumped into a few of the crew at a newsstand, and helped the beleaguered seamen procure *Playboys*, cigarettes, and booze. Impressed by his Russian, and thankful for his help, they invited him back onto their ship, where they plied him with black bread and vodka. They drank all afternoon and well into the evening, and around midnight the boat left the harbour with my father's friend onboard. When it was discovered they were carrying unwanted cargo, the trawler was well shut of the breakwaters. They put down an anchor off the South Head, lowered a lifeboat, and sped my father's friend ashore.

Baker snapped his cigarette off with forefinger and thumb, a trail of sparks dimming out over a puddle with a sizzle. He hurdled the gate and started up the gangway. "Come on," he said.

I shook my head.

"Seriously?"

He was about halfway up the steps.

"I'm not going," I said.

I backed away from the boats and along the edge of the pier. I could feel the weight of his gaze, or—more likely—its absence, as I ducked back under the chain-link fence and crossed the street. Then it started to pour. Baker's shape wove around the boat, bumbling and hunched. I waved but it seemed unlikely he could see me. Down past the wharves, by the box eateries, a set of headlights flicked on. At first I thought the car was on my side of the fence but, as it crept closer, I realized it was patrolling the harbour's inner wall. "Baker," I chirped. I couldn't see him. The car stopped at the base of the ship, and a man with a flashlight stepped out, fanning his beam up the steps. He unhooked a radio from his belt and spoke some words into his device.

I thought I saw Baker shimmying up the bridge, but the shadow slipped from view. I debated texting him. I had my phone out and was writing "they're here," but then I thought better of it. A siren whooped and a second patrol car pulled up beside the first. Another officer stepped out, shielding his neck from the rain. They consulted, panning their flashlights across the deck. The first officer proceeded up the gangplank. I put my phone back in my pocket, perked up my own hood, and fled.

SEVEN

I AWOKE THE FOLLOWING MORNING (OR WAS IT NOW
afternoon?) to small mercies. My wallet and phone stacked neatly on the
bedside table next to a tall glass of water and a large uneaten bowl of rice.
The water was a nice touch, evidence of unremembered cunning, but
I didn't know what to make of the rice, this heap of plain old barren
basmati with its meaningful kinks of soya sauce like larky urine in
snow—where had this come from? I had no memory of cooking,
cleaning. I recalled a lonely walk in the rain pursuant of cabs, but could
not say for sure whether I'd snagged one. Had I walked? Crawled? Crawled
and then rolled? I sat up and managed a sip of water. My phone was dead,
my wallet still brimming twenties. Rain pattered on the grass, rapping
on the bowed window screen; and, further off, flicking in the trees,
the plaintive jape of crows. My temples fizzed. The whole inside of
my mouth was of the coarsest sandpaper. You could strike a match off
my lower incisor, obtain flame; flop me down on all fours, soften
splinters with my tongue. I wore pants, socks, most of one boot.
I scratched my chest. I am allergic to cat dander and the front of
my sweater was bibbed in hard glaucous snot. I drank more water.
There was a knock at the door, a staticky shuffle of fabric, creasing feet.

I opened my bedside drawer and—let's not dwell on my motives here—inserted the bowl of rice.

"And may one inquire," my father said, inching into the room, handing me a mug of coffee, "where His Highness spent the night?"

I thanked him and sipped, snapped up my charger, and plugged in my phone.

"I couldn't remember how you took it," he said.

"This is perfect," I said.

"God. It smells awful in here." My father had on his standard daytime fare. Snap-button (salmon-pink) polo over beltless black jeans and Crocs. Fresh bandages adorned his wounded hand. "Did you puke?" he asked.

"No," I said. "I don't think so."

"Forty-eight years old." My father wagged his head.

"Forty-seven," I said. "Forty-eight in December."

He studied the bed—me, my one boot—judged the corner closest him reasonably unpolluted, and sat. "I've been up for hours," he said. "Went into the Y early this morning for a workout. They've got this new machine where you sit up next to it with your thigh and press your arms down like this and then bring them back up again *really* slowly. So that was nice. Then Beth and I came down to see if you were awake. Brought you some water. It'd stopped raining for a little while and we were thinking we might all go for a walk, and—" And here he stopped, peered around the room, sniffed. "What happened to the rice?"

"What rice?"

The cat hopped up onto the bed and crawled across my legs, settling itself down, finally, between my jagged shins.

"When I came in here this morning to bring you water there was a gigantic bowl of rice on the table."

"I have no idea what you're talking about," I said.

My father soothed the end of his nose and studied his fingers. It seemed like he wanted to smell them. "You been talking to Willis?" he asked.

"I haven't talked to anyone."

I folded one of the thinner pillows behind my neck and tried straightening myself up: a mistake.

"Did you sleep in your pants?"

"Yes."

"In your socks?"

"Yes."

"Did you ejaculate on your shirt?"

"My shirt. No."

"It looks like someone ejaculated on your shirt."

"It's not—it's snot."

"What?"

"Snot," I said. "Mucous. Sneezes. The cat."

My father stood up from the bed and went to the window, parted the blinds and breathed deeply of the moist and muddy air. "'So wither'd, and so wild in their attire—'"

"'That look not like the inhabitants of the earth,' yes, I know. High bard marks. We're all very impressed."

"You should call Willis," my father said.

"Why do you keep talking about Willis?"

"He called me."

"You?"

My phone buzzed. Charged enough that I could turn the thing on. I had many missed calls. Two unknowns, six from Willis, and one text: "Call me."

"What'd he want?"

"They threw Baker in the drunk tank last night."

"Jesus."

"Caught him running around one of the boats. Guess he shot his mouth off, or I don't know." My father smoothed his stubble, and appeared also to flex his right forearm, wriggling his wrist while he preened. "It's a good thing he's still got friends down at the lockup, is all I'll say. They might've charged him."

"Is he okay?" A sour stab whirled in my chest. I toed the back of my boot, and the cat hopped off my legs.

"He's fine, I think. I don't know. Embarrassed," my father said. "I would be."

"But they didn't charge him? Drunk and disorderly or whatever?"

"No charges that Willis knew of."

"But what did he say exactly?" I sat up. I was tiring of our knuckle-headed palaver. "He called your cell? Your work phone?"

"He called the house. Beth answered."

"How is he?"

"Willis?"

"Baker," I said.

"Well, so he says Baker's bailed on this trip which—and that's partly what he was calling about. Says he sounds a bit of mess, Willis said. So he's out."

"Well, fuck," I said.

"Yeah, that's what he said. Said it sounds like whatever this was, was bad."

"I should call him—I should get dressed."

"Willis?" my father asked.

"Baker," I said. "And Willis. Both." I opened up the bedside drawer and reached down for a shirt. The bowl of rice wobbled on the drawer's bottom.

"What've you got in there?"

I didn't say anything.

"What've you got the rice hid in your drawers for?" my father asked.

"I don't know," I said. "It doesn't matter. I just need a shirt."

"That was perfectly good rice."

I opened the next drawer and pulled out a T-shirt, shying my body away from my father, as I unstitched my sweater.

"Your back's looking stronger," he said. "You know you've always had such nice sturdy shoulders. Like your mother."

"Fine," I said, slipping the T-shirt over my chest, "I'm going to call Willis and then I'll come up. Do you mind just giving me some privacy?"

"Yes, of course. I'm sorry."

I led him to the door. I tried to smile but I felt terribly ill.

"Wait," he said. From somewhere down the hall, beyond a chugging dryer, I could hear Beth calling my father's name. "I'll be there in a minute," he boomed. The sound, the liberal nearness of it, throttled me. "Look, there's something else. Willis—he's still got this other ticket."

"Baker's? He paid Baker's way, too?"

"It's a lot of money to just piss away."

I shook my head. How much money was Willis hemorrhaging on all this?

"And so here's the thing. He asked me if I might want to come along. I wouldn't necessarily hunt. I don't know that I could, actually, that I would ever want to kill something, but I thought it might be fun to see this place, see what it's all about. I heard from Kevin they do productions out there, that they've got their own little troupe or theatre company. Could be interesting."

"I'm sorry, but—"

"Obviously with your permission."

I gulped, or tried to. My throat felt like a homespun Christmas bauble, a childish pinecone, glittered in seed. I downed the last of my coffee.

"So what did you tell him?"

"I said that I'd have to check with you, that I didn't want to cramp your style."

"What style?"

"That's exactly what Willis said." My father laughed. "But seriously. I talked to Beth, who's fine with it. And I gave it a little thought and—I don't know. Maybe it'd be nice for us. The two of us, a sort of father-son thing. And Willis and Isaac—"

"Could be," I said.

"So what do you think? He called about an hour ago. Willis. I told him I'd get you up."

"Health-wise," I said. "You're sure you're up to this?"

My father considered me, my tits. The word he was probably

looking for was gynecomastic—from the Latin or Greek, but meaning basically man boob.

"Beg pardon," he said, "but I'm probably in better shape than you."

EIGHT

MY HANGOVER HAD NOT MUCH ABATED BY MID-AFTERNOON.
If anything, it'd hardened and steeled, obtained tenure. There was no
talking to it. I could feel its unwanted leer pressing down on me like a
wet tent. The coffee had stopped doing whatever coffee does midway
through my second cup. It'd switched teams, partnered up with my
hangover, and was playing for keeps. I showered and shaved and opened
my neck up with a disposable razor I'd found in the bathroom cabinet
alongside a bottle of antibacterial hand soap, which I'd engaged as a
lather. Blood beaded and pilled under my sutures of toilet paper. Now
everything itched: my face, small talk, reading, unwinding a vaporous
tangerine. I managed two ibuprofen and, hunkering under the steps, the
better half of a joint. (I'd packed away an armada of Rugaby Moon pre-
rolls in an empty Altoids tin along with my Xanax, the Rugaby being a
good dry hybrid that agreed with me.)

With Baker AWOL and apparently ignoring my calls, and my
father keening around the basement closets for his gaiters and blue
long johns and "graphite lubricant" ("Where's that pouch with the tube
we used to use? Did we get rid of that?"), I half-hoped Willis might
cancel the trip.

The unvarying maleness of our expedition, oppressive from the first, had grown even more unsettling in light of this latest *Lear*-like charade. There was too much nature in this, altogether too many fathers and sons. I did not want to go hunting with my father. Or rather, I did not want to go tramping around the woods with him, swatting mosquitoes (Would there still be mosquitoes in October?) atop some foggy knoll, while Willis and Isaac rambled their way through the baser elements, performing their obscure ceremonies, slant rain rising edgewise off the ground. I wanted to go back to sleep, or back to Calgary, perhaps, to my apartment, to re-enwomb myself in the predictable, mundane depression I'd hollowed out for myself—call it a life.

Willis and I talked briefly on the phone, commiserated over Baker, who, Willis assured me, was incommunicado but home. We agreed that I'd pop by late afternoon/early evening for dinner and drinks—"Be good for you to see the family."—but now that my father was tagging along, Willis figured we could probably dispense with the pre-flight sleepover and rendezvous early Friday morning at the airport.

"Can I bring anything? Dessert? Wine?"

"Naw," he said. "We've got all kinds of that shit over here. Feel free to invite your dad and Beth though. Forgot to mention it when I was talking to him earlier."

"Sure," I said. "I'll ask."

I didn't ask. I showered a second time, attended my nicked neck, tried calling Baker, desisted, composed and deleted texts whose syntax tracked insensitive (or brazenly irreverent), attempted to vomit, failed, located in the downstairs pantry one can of Day Boil (4.5% abv), snuck this away to my quarters, imbibed, felt better, didn't, set my clothes and gear out for morning, brushed my teeth, applied a generous dosing of odorous moisturizer to cheeks, nose, neck, and nape, while slowly ignoring face in mirror, joined my father and Beth for tea and biscuits, apologized for my late-night repast (and for such noises and messes conceived in these energies), assuring all present parties as to the unlikely occurrence of further alimentary excursions, with advance apologies for any lapses of same.

"And remember we've got to be at the airport for five," I said.

"Don't look at me," my father said. "I'm not the one you need to worry about."

I arrived at Willis's empty-handed shortly after four. The sky had cleared and a wan light passed through the lacy choke cherries and pines that enveloped their lot. Built in 1892—same as the beer and same as the Great Fire after which the former acquired its name—theirs was a three-storey semi-detached Second Empire home that backed onto Rennie's River. With its arched dormers and high mansard roof topped in cast iron cresting (complete with avian weather vane) and two great glazy bay windows facing out on the street, you half expected to find these embellishments reappearing from within: ivory-stemmed silverware and claret-coloured armchairs shingled in gilt tassels, rococo scrollwork, cabinets of coffined black lacquer; though I knew Willis's interiors inclined clean-edged and modern.

A slate junco alighted on the paved walkway and jabbed at a crimson smoosh of fruit. I stood on their stoop, scrubbed my boots on an expensive-looking mat set in an aluminum frame with teak inlays, rang the doorbell, and waited. The weathervane's fin eddied and creaked, its beak and sun-smeared wattles aiming east. I cupped my hands to one of the side windows and peered into their home. The foyer was overrun with shoes and ruptured bankers boxes. Neurotically well-barbered shrubbery wavered in the glazed windowpane. Even the glass, greeting the blank pudge of my palms, remitted an exorbitant sum.

No matter the money, the umpteen titles and jobs, I couldn't think of Willis as anything other than a weatherman. For years he'd worked as a consultant at CBC, but when Ed Ogilvy arrived on the scene, ridgy and suave and oozing an easy amiability Willis couldn't hope to feign—"The fuck am I supposed to do? Take it personally?"— Willis left broadcasting and became an operational meteorologist for an independent forecasting concern off Freshwater. He clocked monotonous overnight shifts in a modest loft, servicing all the major offshore accounts: Hibernia, Husky, Exxon, Suncor. Bunkered away in his tiny tube-lit carrel, he generated daily weather reports and wave predictions, tracking periodicity and duration, depths of closure, surf zones, seismic surges and swells. "Mainly what we're after here are wave heights. Any kind of ugly-ass-looking combined seas and you've got to haul up your drills. I'm talking millions of dollars on the hour lost—gone."

The company subsisted on oil, oil and—before Pelmorex snapped them up—Ontario, for whom Willis provided short-term winter storm reports (snowplow and highway de-icing consultations); as well as atmospheric readings for the IESO, who runs the electrical end of Ontario's nuclear program. "Same as oil," Willis said, really dumbing it down. "Only instead of waves it's lightning. But lightning's touchy, and pretty fucking hard to call. Basically what we're tracking here is atmospheric instability. CAPE, lifted index, Showalter. Mostly it's models doing most of the work. Me, I'm just sitting at these three computers jogging numbers around."

Then came his Marches, Marches 8 and 11, our Ides, Willis called them. "What can I tell you? Sunday you've got Saudi Arabia dropping oil $6 to $8 per barrel. Global stock market crashes and crude futures go into a total freefall. Three days later and it's travel bans coming out of the States and the WHO declaring a global pandemic. You do the math."

Willis rode out the downswing for as long as he could, and when the bottom finally dropped out of fossil fuels, he left weather for wind. He now worked as a site manager for a Danish energy investor, Østlig, overseeing the installation and maintenance of turbines and wind farms across the southern shore. The money was still good—really good, in fact—yet Willis despaired at the flak tendered him on behalf of his former oil buddies (guys who'd cast him as a latter-day Brutus). Willis's sites proved a frequent mark for such newfangled advocacy groups as Meet the Frackers and the Republic of Diesel, ragtag factions of disaffected unionists and militant yellow-vesters who regarded as dubious and ideologically derogatory science, global warming, vaccines, masks, BIPOCs, BLM, 2SLGBTQIA+, Libs, and white people from Denmark. They picketed project sites; they swatted and doxed. The Republic's front man, William "Little Old Fat Billy" Oldes, made international headlines when the IED he'd intended for a set of turbines detonated prematurely in his car, martyring him from the knees down.

As for Willis, I know the mania weighed on him. How could it not? But it was the pigeonholing that grated. "I just don't get why they keep calling me a socialist. I'm like, guys, hello, what do you think I'm doing over here? Writing tree poetry? I fucking love capitalism."

And lately, from the looks of things, capitalism—late capitalism—loved Willis.

I rang the doorbell a second time, and knocked. Theirs was the sort of bell whose music reported indoors but not out. Or else it was broken, though nothing around here looked off. I took out my phone, and saw that I had a text from Willis: "we're out back asshole. I can see you pacing on the Nest. What's with the boots?"

"where?" I wrote back. "should I go around?"

A burst of footfalls came dashing down the hall, and Penelope swung open the door, two small chubby hands gripping the knob, my admittance a matter of ample uncertainty.

"Hey," I said. "I like your costume."

I at first thought she was maybe a spider or ant, an octopus. Foam fingerlings, tentacles, issued from a harness strapped to her back.

"Your parents in the yard?" I asked.

Penelope didn't say anything. Her hair was wild, spiked out on the sides in stiff flaxen knots.

"Look who it is," said Caitlin, crossing the long hallway in socks. "The silent accomplice."

"Guilty until presumed innocent," which wasn't what I meant to say.

Penelope retreated from the entrance. I stepped inside. The air felt cool and fresh. I took off my coat and folded it over a narrow wooden bench fetid with running gear. The doormat was smudged with damp yellow leaves and an acropolis of boxes and bubble packing lined the foyer. I despise wealth and mistrust disorder but find especially derisory the disorderly rich. I smiled.

"Sorry," Caitlin said. "Doorbell's on the fritz. It's—" We hugged. "Don't mind the mess. We've got—I don't know—*things* everywhere."

"Research?" I asked.

"I wish," she said.

For the past however long Caitlin has worked as Assistant Dean of Libraries at MUN, a title that I've always thought sounded astonishingly fictitious, like Ring Bearer or Master of Coin. Lord knows what this assistant deanship entails. Policies of digitization and privacy, enforcing stricter return mandates, outlining vogue budgetary amendments. Easy enough for me to make fun. The truth is I envy her. Her full-time academic job. Her gaudy title. Where's my gaudy title? My local stability? The MUN campus houses six locations, and Caitlin still operates out of an office at the Centre for Newfoundland Studies, where she cut her teeth on Cassie Brown's archives, preparing a detailed registry of the sources Brown used for *Death on the Ice* (which account, for the uninitiated, details the great sealing disaster of 1914).

Penelope scooted behind Caitlin, her spikes ducked, gripping at her mother's trim denimed legs.

"I was just saying how much I like her costume."

"Say hi, Pen."

"Hi Pen," said Penelope.

"Are you an octopus?" I asked.

"Ostrogoth," she said, sighing, and placing a pinky directly in her ear.

"Did you say Ostrogoth?"

Penelope inched forward, raised her left foot, and extended her arms wide, her right knee bent and wobbling. She studied my boots.

"You mean like the Roman Empire?" I asked. "Like Theodoric the Bede or whatever?"

Penelope didn't answer. She lowered her leg and stepped herself fully behind her mother, a flossy length of tentacle (spear?), beaded in mirrory shingles, bobbing off Caitlin's knee.

"Cod," said Caitlin. "Ostracod. She's our little seed shrimp, aren't you, sweetie? See," she said, strafing, "these are her antennae and over here—come here, Pen—these chewy parts, these are her mandibles."

"Or, as we like to call them," said a voice, presumably Isaac's, "home to the world's oldest fossilized penis."

Caitlin closed her eyes and took in a shuddering breath. "You don't even know if that's true," she said, releasing the breath, and muttering something else I didn't quite catch. "And I think many people might question the credibility of your sources."

"425-million-year-old fossil, preserved in ash. Said David Siveter, paleontologist at the University of Leicester, the copulatory organ is, and I quote, large and stout."

"Don't listen to him, sweetie. You look beautiful. Anyway," said Caitlin, freeing a leg, "come in. Come in. Don't worry about those boots. Willis's out back."

I followed Caitlin down the broad, vine-patterned hallway and into a kitchen of seamless white cabinetry. Hanging on the wall across from a coved breakfast nook was a framed stencilling of the old racing bibs that'd once coated Travis's tote bag.

"This is awesome," I said.

"Isn't it?" Caitlin said; and then, guiding Pen by the antennae, "Why don't you go get your colouring?"

7375. 2132. 8346. 602. The bibs retained their crumple and fade, their splotches of jumped mud.

"One of Travis's friends from school, Emily. I think she's in design. She gave that to us."

"I love it," I said, taking a seat on one of the swivelled bar stools.

"So I hear you guys had a big night," Caitlin said.

"It was something," I said.

"Wine? We've got red open."

"Sure," I said. "Red's great."

The room smelled of curry and onions. She poured us some glasses, stemless and fat, set them down on the countertop bar, and returned to the fridge.

"Can I help with anything? Smells great in here."

"That's just leftovers Isaac's reheating. We thought we'd make little pizzas."

"Works for me," I said.

"Hey, hey. Look who it is," said Willis, schlumping in from the hallway. I came to my feet and we embraced. All this hugging, gripping, touching. Sensing muscle and bone. I didn't love it. I missed the old rules, our clinical distances. Willis's skin—I had my hand on the back of his arm—felt ragged and hairy. He'd put on more weight; his cheeks and short, swollen nose were bloated with rosacea, he'd abandoned the slicked-back prohibition-era coif for a new cut that tracked a little less fascist, and he seemed to be trying to grow (or culture) a beard.

"Are you flexing?" he asked, relinquishing me.

"It's possible," I admitted.

"That's weird. Why would you do that?"

The microwave didn't ding but advanced a series of shrill chirps like a nuclear siren in the throes of a radioactive episode and now Isaac slithered into the kitchen, wearing earbuds, tapered grey jogging pants, and a white T-shirt with an image of the *Jaws* movie poster (ascending shark on unsuspecting beach bum) scrawled on the front of it. He opened the door and lifted a steaming splatter tray off a round Tupperware container impastoed in a soupy bronze sludge. He gave this a stir, tried a bite, popped it back in the microwave, and licked his spoon clean.

"Guest," said Caitlin.

Isaac started, removing one bud. "What's that?"

"Could you acknowledge our guest?"

Isaac dumped his spoon in the sink, clicked off his phone and removed his second bud. He turned to me and smiled, making eye contact with me for the first time.

"Hey," he said, tensing his arms over the counter so that the joints of his inner-elbows winged out. Blue veins that made my own veins quiver to look at spanned the length of his forearms, bolting over tendons, which were themselves unnervingly pronounced.

"What're you listening to?"

"Wallace-Wells," he said.

"Never heard of them."

"His climate guy," said Willis.

"*The Uninhabitable Earth*," said Isaac. "It's a good book."

"Maybe you should try reading something happy," said Caitlin.

"Or reading." Willis smiled. "We all packed, Greta?"

"Willis." Caitlin held open her palm. "Not. Helpful."

"Sorry. I'm sorry." Willis pressed his own hands together and bowed, his grin nowhere near gone. "You packed?"

Isaac pulled open a drawer and selected a fork. "What's it look like I'm doing?"

"Reheating a meal?" Willis asked.

Penelope dawdled back into the kitchen and handed her mother a vast purple sketchbook.

"I'll take a look after dinner, sweetheart," Caitlin said. "You take this. Why don't you go sit on your stool and practice your drawings?"

"He's off on this whole doomsday tangent," Willis said, facing me.

"Aren't we all?"

"I try telling him it's not that bad. That you got to learn to look at the positives."

I smelled my wine. "And how's that going?" I asked.

"Here we go," said Caitlin.

"What?" said Willis. He walked over to the fridge and cracked open a can of Coke. "All I'm saying is that, look, when it comes to this Wallace-Wells guy or, you know, McKibben, Naomi Wolf or whoever, these people are activists, okay, they're writers, they're—what I'm saying is, is if it's warm, and I'm not denying anything, I'm just saying if it's warm and extraction's dead, then what have we got?" Willis poured some Coke into a thick, square-bottomed tumbler, sousing his cocktail with a generous belt of Lamb's. "Don't get me wrong," he said, speaking just to me now, "it's good to stay informed. You've got to read and you've got to pay attention but you've also got to pay attention to what you read." He sipped. "Could use some ice," he said.

Isaac, eyeing the microwave, stopped his dinner, and set his vulcanized chickpeas down on the counter. He looked into his food, its rivulets of reddish grease seeping through the sludge, and said, "Three-quarters of Somali families are currently without access to water."

"Too bad for Somalia."

Caitlin opened a cabinet and passed Willis a cutting board. He placed it on the counter beside a tilted wooden knife block.

"In Siberia—"

"I don't want to talk about Siberia. You see, this is the problem. This is exactly what I'm getting at. It's your thinking. Our thinking, I should say. We're never thinking about the here and now. The concrete. You look at *our* data, not Somalia's, not the *New York Times* or fucking Siberia's, I'm sorry, Pen, daddy shouldn't swear, and see what stressors we're facing in the immediate—and I mean the immediate of the right here and right now—and which ones of these systems crises, these 'cascades,' as you call them, are impacting the island you inhabit? Bad weather. Okay. Well, when hasn't that been the case? More hurricanes. Maybe. But those are more likely to damage the Maritimes. So what else?"

The fridge door beeped and Isaac nudged it closed.

"More wind and rain," Willis said. "Got it. Coastal erosions and coastal flooding. Warm weather salinizing the water, which, okay, might impact crabbing, soften the shells or whatever, but, in the meantime, in the intervening, interim or whatever, if it's warm—and I'm not denying anything, undermining the severity of things, or even really saying that we shouldn't be doing everything in our collective power to turn things around, though, of course, we can never turn things around, and that's part of it, part of our whatever, our global predicament—but if it's warm, why not make a buck off the Americans and Europeans and Japanese or whoever else's got money to spend but can't go scuba-diving anymore with those vandalized manatees because of cyclones and volcanoes blowing up all over I want to say Fiji?"

"Okay," said Caitlin. "Maybe we can skip ahead to the part where we're all in cooldown mode now."

"In Tokyo," said Isaac, "the cherry blossoms are in full bloom."

He transferred the contents of his dinner into a stoneware bowl and left the room.

"He keeps this up," said Willis, and stopped. "It's a total Ponzi scheme, I get that, and I feel bad for his generation, I do—sort of—but you just can't go on thinking like this."

"Starting to sound a little blue about the gills," I said.

"Blue? I work on a fucking wind farm."

"And I take it you're not voting," I said.

"Are you?"

———

Caitlin and I decorated pizzas while Willis and Penelope tended the outdoor oven.

"I don't think he knew how to crack an egg before we got that thing," Caitlin said.

Hooded in rockwool, the oven rested atop a concrete hearth bedded in ceramic fibreboard and insulating brick; and all of this—oven, hearth, stand—nested in a four-foot-deep hole Willis had trenched out with a backhoe and filled in with one ton of washed draining rock. The oven's dome and arch—two hundred squares of buff-yellow firebrick Willis had chiselled all by himself with a rented diamond blade set in a fifty-five-year-old wet saw—got up to 550°C but could withstand heat nearly twice that.

"Somehow this doesn't strike me as an everyday appliance," I said.

"You'd be surprised," Caitlin said. "I hate that we have it but now that we do? It's got its perks. I'll give him that much. That thing will stay hot for days. You take out the fire and keep the door shut, and it'll still be about four hundred degrees in there. Good for bread, bagels. Slow-roasted chickens, moose, beef. You name it. The fire usually peters out by about day four. Perfect for rusks."

"Rusks?" I asked.

"They're like a hard dry biscuit," Caitlin said, holding up her hand. "Willis calls them his lembas bread."

"Of course he does," I said.

"Likes to dip them in tea."

I examined our ingredients. There was a homemade pesto Caitlin had mortared up with basil grown on a sill, a spicy bhuna curry Willis had saved from the last time they'd ordered India Gate, canned tomato paste, peppers, pineapples, diced mushrooms, zucchini, black and green olives, arugula, spinach, chilied mango, prosciutto, thin slices of moose—"Chewy," said Caitlin, "and sometimes you get pieces that are a little bloody, but really good"—cheese.

"So how are things with you guys?" I asked. "How've you been holding up?"

Caitlin mopped her brow. "With me? Look, I'm not going to lie, there are good days and bad. Pen's a delight, an utter joy, and Isaac, I don't know. He and his dad are more or less as you see."

"I'm sure the trip will help."

"I hope so."

I refilled our wine, and went to the window. Penelope cantered around the lawn with a tasseled wand. Willis watched her from the oven, smoke surging off his shoulders like two misty horns. I took a deep breath. The cinders smelled sweetly of alder.

"It's funny," she said. "You know, we weren't even supposed to be here."

"Who?"

"Me. Or Willis. One of us, anyway." Caitlin swished her wine,

grimaced and sipped. "We were supposed to split up. That's what—"
She held her glass to her lips but didn't drink. There were lines on her
chin, thinnish twists.

"I'm sorry," I said. "You really don't have to say anything.
I just—"

"You know that initially that's what this whole trip was supposed to
be about, right? Willis was going to take Travis and Isaac out west, and—
I don't know—let them know what was what with us. The whole idea
sounds so totally idiotic to me now. I'm not sure we really had a plan."

Caitlin rested her glass on the counter, picked up a sliver of
green pepper, pared away a clef of clinging white pith, and slipped the
pepper into her mouth. "I'm sorry," she said, munching. "I'm not sure
why I'm telling you all this. It's okay. Honestly. I mean, the irony is
that—it's ridiculous to say—but the irony's that the second we heard
what'd happened, the moment we knew about Travis, everything else,
everything that was wrong, just sort of dissolved. It was almost like,
through him—it was like somehow he gave us a second chance."

I didn't know whether to say sorry or not. I wasn't sure what the
moment needed here but when Caitlin looked up from her glass our
eyes met and I thought I could see, in their corners, tears. I placed
a hand on hers and held it firmly, squeezing her fingers, pressing on
the bones of her thumb. And then I hugged her. The hug, judging from
Caitlin's face, surprised both of us. Its suddenness and want of feeling.
It was a good hug. A long one.

"I'm really glad you're here," Caitlin said. "For Willis. And
for Isaac."

"Me too," I said, though I wasn't sure how to interpret this.
I hadn't felt important in years.

———

We ate and we drank. I liked the pesto but didn't care for the moose.
We switched off wine and onto flat yeasty bitters Willis had brewed in

his basement. I preferred the wine. We joked about Baker but, to my relief, avoided diagnosing the night's crack-up in any detail. And what more was there to say, anyway? The talk revolved around our hunt. Apparently the site's owner, Judith Muir, would be joining us.

"A chaperone?" I asked. "Seriously?"

"More like a guide," Willis said.

"I used to see her around MUN when I was an undergrad," said Caitlin. "Strange woman. Sort of unconventional. She wore these long flowing black gowns like a judge or a cleric, and kept birds, all kinds of taxidermies, in her office. Crows, ravens, these big ugly gulls. She was weird about privacy. Didn't want anyone recording her lectures, which didn't fly then and certainly wouldn't now." Caitlin reached across the table and plucked an olive from Penelope's hair. "I remember she tried to get one class to sign an NDA, which, let me tell you how much the administration loved that. She also had some sort of weird dietary thing. Ate a lot of popcorn. Her husband used to bring her these big clear garbage bags full of plain unsalted popcorn. No butter or margarine or anything like that. She had theories about fibre, gut flora, and roughage. There was a rumour going around that she mixed shredded printer paper with the popcorn, as well as linseed and flax meal. One time I remember seeing her in the tunnels, and—"

"Can we have an ice cream now?" Penelope wanted to know.

"Did you finish your supper?" Willis asked, examining her uneaten slices, her mesas of peeled cheese.

"I tried finishing most of it."

"What's this big part right over here doing? You're not going to finish this part?"

"That's for your supper."

"No, I don't think so. I already had mine," said Willis.

"Why don't we get you cleaned up and into your PJs," said Caitlin, "and then we can see about an ice cream."

"Promise?"

"Promise," I said.

Caitlin scooted Penelope off her stool and Willis reached over and took a bite of her pizza. He sat back in his chair, thrusting out his chest as he chewed.

"You excited to hunt moose again?"

"I am," Willis said. He rested his knuckles against his lips, and released a soft, florid burp. "My last time out wasn't so good."

"When was this?"

"This, it would've been what, three years ago, maybe. Christ. Travis and I and Pat—you remember Pat—and Pat's weirdo nephew with the teeth?"

"I think so," I said. Pat harkened back to Willis's Suncor days, a consummate angler and bowman.

"We flew into a spot up off the Gander River a ways. Something a little like what we're gearing up for now, minus the amenities, I guess. No serious commercial outfit, is what I'm saying. Just some guy Pat knows who's licensed to fly this beat-to-shit bush plane. Worst flight of my life, probably. And I've flown in Cougars where we got big old gobs of ice growing on the rotors. But anyway. With Pat we had it all squared away with his buddy in Gander so he'd drop us into camp early. Hunt, sleep. Cook up a few feeds. Signal him when we shot something. This was deep woods. GPS but no cell reception. He gave us this large white linen flag and showed us on a laminate map whereabouts he'd installed a pulley and hoist. So that was okay. Told us he'd fly over every morning we were out, see if we needed anything, told us if there was any kind of issue or emergency, just to crank up that flag, and he'd put down and come get us. We also had a 12-gauge twin basic flare gun and a box of extra cartridges, so I wasn't too worried. Plus the walk out was maybe like twelve, thirteen klicks. Tops. Not a fun walk, mind you. Up to your shoulders in tuck. Black flies big as your thumbs gnawing at you."

Willis stopped and listened. Water rumbled above us, a fluent deluge. "Bath time," Willis said. He raked up the last of Penelope's abandoned cheese and dropped it down his throat like a pelican. There was no chewing going on here.

"And Travis," I said, "he must've been an old hand."

Willis winced. Old hand. This expression didn't come easily to me, and we both knew it.

"It wasn't his best hunt," Willis said. "This was just after he crapped out at the trials."

"I thought he ran well," I said.

"Sure. Of course. He did. He always ran well. It's just—he was so bent out of shape. Beating himself up. Finally, I said to him, said: Look, this is not sustainable. I'm buying you a ticket, you're coming home, that's that. I expected him to put up a fight. This would've been right in the thick of cross-country. Not that he'd been planning to do much racing that fall. Because of the trials. But I still assumed he'd start in on some bullshit, lay on some elaborate excuse as to why right now just wasn't workable. But he didn't. Sure, he said. So I bought him a ticket. And I've got to say I was beyond excited. I can't tell you. Forget the hunting for a minute but just to have him home for a few days, all of us together. It was something.

"Anyway," Willis said, belching again. "So where was I?"

"You were saying Pat—Pat's friend."

"Pat's friend, right. Fucking guy. So he sets us down on the water and we unload all our gear and it's just the four of us and we've got the camp set up, all our tents and gear squared away, and we decide to take a wander of the area, case everything out, and Pat, I swear his buddy hasn't got the plane off the water yet, and Pat spots this big old lumbering bull on the beach, dipping its head in a stream, lapping, and Pat raises up and just drops him—BANG!"

Willis panned his open arms across the table, squinting his left eye, ghosting recoil.

"Pat's got this old British .303, supposedly belonged to his dad, and these jacketed rounds he uses. The gun's Boer War ancient and chancy as all hell potting anything deeper than 250 yards, say, but this was a close shot. Took him clean in the head. Bang. So we're excited but pissed—even Pat's pissed, a little. Here we're just after getting our tents set up, our ride's gone, and Pat's bagged his quota.

"We dressed him right there on the beach. I send Pat's weirdo nephew back over to where we pitched the tents to bring us some tarps and knives and cheesecloth bags that we'd be needing for the meat, and I sent Travis along too, and I told him, Trav, I said, why don't you do us a real solid and bring us on back a nip of that Lamb's.

"So we got the moose broken down and parcelled away as best we could—going quickly, since we wouldn't be saving the hide—and the rest of the afternoon and night we kicked back by the fire and shot the shit. We stowed some of the moose in the coolers we'd brought with our other food and the rest we hung up high in the trees, keep the critters away. That night we drank, sang songs, ate potatoes, rice, backstraps and tenderloin, and the heart. We rinsed the heart out in the stream and hollowed it out, junked all the icky valves and things, and then we packed that thing up with a nice bit of dressing Pat had made. Celery, onion, parsley, a spot of rosemary and oregano. Some of that good savoury. Nothing fancy.

"Next morning we raise up the white flag just like Pat's friend said to, and we break down our tents, pack up all our shit, and get everything loaded on down to the beach and ready to go. And then we waited. And waited. And no plane passed. We waited all afternoon. We were all getting a little antsy. Not angry. Or not real angry. Not yet. We waited down to the beach until late in the afternoon, fired off a flare, but still no plane. Pat's nephew kept asking to shoot the flare on the other side of the beach but I didn't want him wasting the cartridges. Then it got late enough, the sky darkening, and we decided to trek back to where we'd camped the night before and laid most everything out again. We rejiggered the meat in the trees and cooked up more steaks.

"All our moods were souring some, but Travis was sitting in one of his sooks. Kinda rude, surly. Keeping away from everyone. I asked him what's the matter and he just shook his head. It's nothing, he said. Doesn't look like nothing, I said, thinking to myself kid's probably pissed as I am about Pat's buddy and the plane, but no. That's not what he meant. Said he didn't give a shit about the plane. I'm talking about

ROD MOODY-CORBETT   89

all of this, he said. All of what? I asked. I hadn't a clue what he meant. So he looks at me. Gives me that hard look he gets right before a race. You wouldn't understand, he said. Well that helps, I said. That clears everything right up!

"Now I feel bad saying this but Travis had this way of putting a puss on that just completely stopped a conversation in its tracks. Used to make me so mad I could hardly stand it. Only tactic I ever come up with was to leave him be. So that's what I did. I just shook my head, chalked it up to the general sullenness that seemed to be weighing down on him all summer long, and I let him mope. Okay, I told him. Real glad you came out!

"We slept fitfully, or I did. I was very worried about the meat.

"Anyway, so here we are, next day, up at the crack of dawn, doing all the same shit we done the day before, exactly like Pat's friend's asked. Broke everything down, cranked up the flag, unhooked some of the meat, which was starting to smell, not badly, but just a little on your fingers, and got everything down to the beach. We'd emptied our coolers and stowed all the meat we could fit in there and weighted these down in the water for what good that might do.

"Pat's nephew kept firing off his rifle into the sky, saying maybe someone'd hear us, but no one could hear us. When he got tired of shooting the sky, he took aim at a crow that'd perched itself on a tree down near the water and killed it. Blew its head off all over the rocks. I didn't even know what to say. After a while some other birds came down and picked at it. Now it was late afternoon and getting dark again. Travis and I went back to camp to set things up but right away we knew something was off. The meat that we'd left up in the trees had turned and there, in the clearing, everywhere in the trees, were birds. Crows, ravens, goshawks, jays. Seemed like hundreds and hundreds of them. It was amazing to see all these birds at one time. There was nothing we could do. We abandoned camp and the rest of our meat in the trees and we pitched our tents down by the beach. That night we didn't even bother cooking. I ate a few slices of bread with mustard and tuna and drank my last beers. We didn't bother starting a fire. All night all you could hear was the birds. I thought they slept at night, went away to their nests or rookeries or wherever and slept, but these noises, of meat getting eaten and hoarded, it was something else, I mean it was unceasing. Next morning after we shot off our flares, I went back to sneak a look at our camp and there was nothing there. Some feathers and torn scraps of bag strewn around the clearing, but nothing, not a trace of meat to be found.

"Pat's friend glided in later that day. He made some excuses. Fucked if I remember them now. I was ready to kill him but first I wanted him to fly us back home. We got everything loaded in the plane but the coolers of meat. We couldn't really tell the difference anymore but Pat's friend said the smell coming off them was unconscionable. Smells like fucking death out here, he said. We opened the coolers and looked inside. It was terrible. Slithery white crawlers and maggots like chunks of wriggly cream and blowflies or maybe gadflies with that greenish tint coming off their bristles flicking around in the cheesecloth, crawling all over where the meat's gone puffy with bloat. We dumped the coolers, unloaded all that meat on the shore, and tried rinsing the coolers in the lake. But that smell. Travis nearly puked. Ethanethiol's the chemical of purification most mortifying to humans, I told him. Same as ethanol basically. But instead of oxygen you've got your sulphur. I told him vultures love this shit. That's why we add it to butane and propane. You know it was an oil company in California was the first ones to put two and two together? Just before the Second World War. It was because vultures kept hovering over their site every time there'd be a leak. Turns out there were traces of ethanethiol and that's how eventually they knew. Was the birds told them.

"Then Travis told me to shut up. He did. Said it so fast I don't even think he knew he was saying it. Just shut up, he said."

Willis trailed off. He pulled at the stubble on his chin and thinned his lips. "I chalk it up to the hunt, to Pat's fuck-up of a friend. That, and the whole business with the trials. Which like I say. He was in a

real state. Whole reason why I asked him on the trip in the first place." Willis left off with his primping. "I was only trying to help. Guess you could say all of us going off tomorrow is my way of maybe making that up to him. I don't know—"

I studied Travis's collage, the waxy red and black numerals, the punched-out holes through which silver pins had passed. 7375. 2132. 8346. 602.

Willis strummed the table. "But that smell." He sniffed. "The cling of it, how I felt walking around with it, living on my skin, stinking deep in my pores, for days. It was just like Pat's buddy said. Like death, he said. And it was."

NINE

IT WAS JUST AFTER TEN WHEN I LET MYSELF IN THROUGH THE front door, slipped out of my shoes, and found my father strewn over the living room couch, snoring, a buoyant loop of content beaming mutely from the tablet whose soft plastic stand he'd draped over an empty box of Kleenex, a stack of old floral coasters engaged as a brace. I sat down on the stool opposite him and unzipped my coat. He was all set for tomorrow, his backpacks and Cold War–era Timberlands with the natty yellow-brown laces doubling down their solid brass D-rings and eyelets tucked away by the hall closet.

Cabbing home—up Carpasian, down Pine Bud, and back over Bonaventure, left onto Whiteway, your first right, second left etc. (blue door by the light, thanks, don't need the machine, I've got cash)—I'd been looking forward to scouring the fridge for leftovers (I hadn't had anything but pizza to eat all day), downing a few cold rubbery potatoes drizzled in hot sauce and dusted in salt, maybe wreaking a quiet raid or two on the liquor cabinet, a bourbony digestif, before retreating to the basement, my earldom, my lair.

My father's body, such as it was, didn't figure in much of this. Wadded up against a pillow with a stich of blanket drawn over the base of his knees, one limp bandaged hand cresting the fraying hem of his pocket, he slept with his mouth slanted open, a strip of spittle tanning his chin. It was chilly; the fireplace's chainmail screen was parted, and a dry, dusty wind rattled down the flue. I tugged the blanket off my father's knees and drew it up over my own. His presence, or what, in my aborted bacchanal, I read into his presence—the implication being that he'd waited up just for me—rankled. I wanted no part of it.

My parents divorced in my last year as an undergrad at MUN, a mutual and, you might say, amicable parting. My father kept the house. I can't remember when he and Beth started dating, or when they moved in together, but it was long before my mother died.

Since my last visit, the living room had taken on a distinctly curatorial aspect, an accumulation I attributed to Beth, what with my father's sense of décor seldom exceeding a frat boy's beggarly furnishings. His beloved flat screen defrocked, expelled to the coldest, narrowest spit of real estate in the house (what used to be my bedroom), the orientation of the entire living room had pivoted, as if in grudging accommodation of the front window, over which a stiff rattan basket displaying three diminutive, stained-glass terrariums featuring a variety of spiky green succulents, lustreless gemstones, and sand, dangled.

There were framed photographs—a single black-and-white shot of yours truly, warily approaching a petting zoo fence—lining the sill proper, along with some other items: soapstone mortar (less pestle), rusty rail spike and bolt. There were cookbooks and photo albums and frumpy art atlases and a turquoise storage bin bursting with cat toys and brushes on a shelf below the window. Pushed up against the basket was a bound copy of my dissertation. *Amor Intellectualis quo Beckett se Windelband Amat: Samuel Beckett*, Murphy, *Baruch Spinoza, and the Problem of Philosophical Influence*. My god, what a title. Had I given this to them? I must've. And they'd kept it? And, what's more, my father was willingly showcasing this in the house?

A regiment of fine, teacup-feeble cherubs in postures of serene supplication dominated the fireplace mantel. Were these spiritual ornaments? The seraph closest me sported a skirt of tense shaggy fronds. Cicada wings pouted from her spine. She knelt sleepily in a diorama of steroidal mushrooms, but did not appear to be praying or entreating the courtesies of any deity that I knew of. Her head resting on the tallest, broadest mushroom, a plush scaly cap, her fine, creamy fingers gingerly plucking its gills, she looked bored and horny, and, in my father's company, I felt a terrible onrush of shame.

I grew up in a secular household. Shorn of Catholicism, my mother might attend midnight mass for the music and middling pageantry, but there were to be no doughy cherubs nor ornery angels stitched to our tree, if we had a tree. While my mother maintained a more broad-minded attitude toward what religious education I received in high school (this is Judaism and these others, over here, are the world religions), my father was another matter. From him I inherited a singularly religious impatience, a quiet but brutal atheism, and though I never cornered him on the origins of this cynicism, as a child, I suspected some foul (and formative) incident.

Sitting on the stool, watching him sleep, I wondered at the devotional provenance of these objects, and at my father's apparent slackening of scruples. Of all the ways he might've softened—and all the ways he hadn't—now this? I listened for his lungs, their softest scuffle and flap, following the tired, childish rise of his chest. My own breathing, I noticed, had quickened. The air was coming in heavy and fast, faster, in fact, than I could reasonably manage. A ferric swell murmured in the back of my throat. I laid my hands flat on my knees. Had my fingers always looked so wide and red? I sensed their heaviness, yes, the weird weight of them, across my knuckles, there where the skin stood wrinkled and pruned. I closed my eyes, cracked a big toe, and raked my heels across the rug's worn, yarn-like tract.

There, on the windowsill, was a single picture of my mother, the evening's wind marring the frame's cheap styrene with stark branchy shadows, engulfing her in a boreal fume. Fiery and sudden. The picture, taken on their honeymoon at Basin Head—they'd gone for the beach, for the silica-rich soil renowned for its song—showed my mother, bare-shouldered and slim, trying the water with an outstretched foot. Sandals, which she held by the straps in her right hand, depended at her knee. A scum of cirrus stood off the edges, with a breeze rumpling her (then) long (then mostly) auburn hair. I liked how the waves looked in the picture, and always had, stilled in a splintered ripple. In the bottom right-hand corner of the frame, a small shirtless boy sat before a grubby castle, a serious, almost studious expression on his face, knees squat in his trench, nursing a sagging summit in sand.

The child is not me. I've never been to Basin Head, but we often travelled, the three of us, to Nova Scotia, to Windsor, where my mother was born. She'd inherited an old farmhouse southwest of the Avon, a tilted house—peeling, whitewashed clapboard, long ago sold and destroyed. And, watching my father, I remembered a story my mother would sometimes tell me about this home, which had belonged to her grandparents, and where, as a young girl, she spent entire summers, and how, this one afternoon, she'd witnessed, or claims to have witnessed (I've heard a few versions in my time and god knows what's first-folio these days), her dog getting struck down by a car. The accident was nobody's fault, or—and here, perhaps, was the moral—nobody's fault but her own. A little-used access road ran perpendicular to her grandparents' lot and I guess the dog had slipped off its leash, if it had a leash, and off the property. By the time my mother arrived on the scene, the offending Camry had sped away, leaving (in a daze of gusted gravel) this crumpled, rasping shape in a culvert, hind legs kicked and twisted. There wasn't much blood that my mother could see, which seemed to her like a good thing, and the tiny rasping sounds appeared slight and trivial, comical even, like the rickety, seesawing yawns of a cat. She knelt down and scooped the dog up into her arms, cradling its head, careful to avoid touching the legs. It was some type of mutt, I think, a Jack Russell–Westie cross—January or June, I can't remember its name, but suspect it contained or sought to root itself in a month. Walking the length of the driveway back to the farmhouse, not rushing, but covering the distance, nevertheless significant, at a measured pace, my mother, whispering the dog's name over and over again, January or June or Juniper maybe, felt something inside the dog slump, and, drawing up short of the porch, she set the dog down on the grass, and, kneeling again beside the wounded animal, listened deep inside its chest, feeling at its nostrils, worming a finger inside its gums to waken it, applying the soft, hollow stalk of a plucked dandelion across each unopening eye.

There was no one else home and she didn't know who to call. For me, I imagine a sky the low mineral blue before a storm, offset by a wild, blinding sway of grass. And this is how I choose to see my mother, or remember her, hands sticky with stalk sap, as a child I would never know, stooped amid a palate of fall colours, the golds and reds of dying corn.

My father's hand fell from his pocket and dangled from the couch. His lips were closed. When I was a boy, my mother often said how much we looked alike. "It's uncanny," she'd say. "Just my tiny little him." I stood up from the stool, returned the blanket to my father's lap, and kissed him very gently on the head.

TEN

WERNER HERZOG WAS COMING.

The Muirs, in the hopes of inducing a celebrity endorsement, had comped his first visit, and Herzog, or simply Werner, as the Muirs called him, with grating insouciance, had fallen completely in love. Last summer he'd installed his own private studio, a spherical, many-windowed observatory or dorm, at the edge of camp. It stood back a ways from the communal firepits and fenestrated shooting gallery, on broad iron stilts, a vast, lunar orb of glass. He wasn't much into hunting, Werner; baser fowl—the joke went—exempted.

As for us, our party was slated to arrive at the Castle shortly before lunch. The trip left me feeling thirsty and ill, with a dim, murky soreness—as attributable to the flight (we'd coasted in on one of those puny taupe-panelled Caribous) as to the pilfered bourbons and bitters I'd knocked back the night before—reeling over my eyes. I looked forward to checking in, surrendering my devices, downing a Xanax, a straightener, if I could muster one, before bunking down in my cabin for a long, mindless nap. My father's ebullience ran in excess of these energies. *Be tired*, I willed him from the back seat.

He rode shotgun, his backpack and depleted hydration bladder hugged to his chest like a joey, and engaged our driver, a squat, pursy man with three sparse slashes of hair stitched to his scalp, in a tireless Q & A. I'd missed the guy's name but had, thanks to my father, the makings of a CV down pat. He'd worked on a number of rigs, Hibernia, Hebron; he'd fit pipe at Muskrat Falls, but lost everything when the project tanked. These days he served as a part-time gofer—"I do groceries and tourists and sometimes, I don't know, all sorts of other little side missions"—for the Muirs, and operated a medical courier service out of Stephenville with his sisters. He managed a steady income through the summer months, which saw an influx of Americans, Germans, some French, but the winters were desolate, sclerotic and grim.

As we merged off the highway and began our winding descent into camp, the road tilted down a close, gauntly wooded path, studded with birches, firs, and tangles of dying pine. These last were badly abscessed, the limbs twisted and mauled and limply mating. The road's surface was of rutted macadam, and our driver seemed intent on absorbing every callus and puddle. Barn swallows startled off the gnarlier willows and shrubs, unamused, though maybe more bored than frightened. I felt unwell. My seatbelt lacked a shoulder strap and the buckle clutched coldly across my gut. I closed my fingers over the handrail, weighed the shading of our driver's hairs with renewed animus, charted freckles and fiery liver spots, divining constellations across this celestial swirl. Ours was a species of driving in which the positioning (and general jostling) of organs in your ribcage revealed itself at every turn, and I marvelled at Willis, who remained fast asleep, and at Isaac, who, donning wireless earbuds, appeared to be listening to another audiobook, and possibly following along in a thick battle-scarred paperback he held open on his lap, underlining sentences and blocking out snippets of text with a yellow highlighter, but turning the pages at what I judged a somewhat listless or inattentive rate, his eyes, I thought, skimming just a little too far off the page.

My father's inquisition, meanwhile, remained unceasing. "I guess you don't get many visitors out here in the winter?" "It's okay if I roll down my window?" "Does this charger still work?" "Now, in your experience, do you find that Germans tend to be pretty shitty tippers?" "How many kids you say you got?"

"Children?" our driver said. "There are no children here."

The forested road turned over to smooth jointed concrete and sloped onto a narrow causeway margined in clean granite cobbles and grass. The grass was overgrown and abundant with colour. Hawkweed, clover, withered yarrow or vetch. On either side of us was the ocean, swollen and turbid. A current, folding in from the east, tossed its spume over the rubble-stone levee, where the waves crashed and rescinded, peeling away from the shore with a shy, almost metrical languor. To our left was a gravel parking lot and picnic area. A stout, waffly cairn, whose structural integrity seemed both dubious and brazen—why stack the smallest rocks bottom to top?—pointed away from the parking lot toward a row of shacks fronting on a clanky metal wharf segmented in plywood jetties. There were no boats here, but a woman in a billowy, caper-green poncho stood beside one of the open-air fishing stages or dogtrots untangling a sweep of snarled silver netting. Facing us, she shifted her garments and seemed about to wave, but merely brushed aside a tress of hair.

Up ahead, you could see, way off, rising over a wide open ridge of stone, a dingy lozenge of sun, and a few greyish buildings plotted along the coast like runes. A serrated wooden fence with four high rounded lookouts, picketed in flags, spanned the length of this ridge.

"Had a friend back at Suncor who swore the best buck hunting was ones drawn from a height," Willis said, eyeing the lookouts. "Never could see the sport in it myself. Sitting your ass down in some dumb tree all day. Tell me, where's the toil and honour in that?"

My father gaped. "Shit," he said, pressing a finger to the window, blood flushing on his nail. "They've even got a whatcha call it, with the clocks?"

"A belfry," our driver said.

Cattle loitered in the long flat boggy meadows below these escarpments, and I felt my spirits lift as we sped across the causeway, passed under a gated arch, and drifted back into some semblance of civilization.

Before us, the eponymous Castle loomed, a tall, turreted structure whose predominant masonry reminded me of those old Macintosh computers, the 128K and glorious SE my parents had kept in their respective home offices, platforms upon which, in the absence of structured childcare, I'd hemorrhaged days, weeks, if not months, of my life. *Shufflepuck, Cosmic Osmo, SkiFree.* The main building was about as wide as a good-sized sports complex or Costco, and maybe twice or three times as high. A moat of miry black water defined these exterior fortifications—which comprised, according to our driver, a curtain wall and crenelated trim just like the gapped ramparts of the Great Wall of China. Defunct arrow-slits fitted in cobalt glass were niched above a bowed entrance which featured an actual winch-operated portcullis and drawbridge. The drawbridge was lowered and joined onto a duckboard trail that fed into a gardened courtyard, what our driver kept calling "the bailey," and which did not appear traversable by car, the bailey.

The driver pulled up under an awninged tollbooth adjacent the bridge's front gate. You could hear waves smashing somewhere beyond us and what sounded like racquetball or the sharp nifty clap of rifle fire.

"Unreal," my father said.

We arrived to some fanfare. A phalanx of about a dozen or so guests and what looked like Castle staff had corralled outside the tollbooth. The staff were distinguishable by their ribbed vests and russet turtlenecks, which they wore over shimmery, spandex-backed pants with neon-green stripes. The guests' ensembles, like our own, tended toward muted blues and beige. As we stepped down from the van to unload our gear, the group began to disperse.

Two of the well-wishers lingered by the entrance.

"We thought you might be Werner," the woman said to me as I dropped my suitcase from the trunk.

"He's supposed to be here now," her companion said. He was much younger than his partner—a slim, scrappy-looking guy, with a terse nose and inky black hair stiffened up at the front in a Tintin-like quiff. "It's all so sad," he said. "We just keep waiting and waiting for him. All we want right now is some good news."

A second woman coasted toward us on a fat-tired bike. She pulled up short of the couple and shook off her helmet. The helmet was one of those with a sweep of spikes running up its centre like a stegosaurus. She whispered something to the first woman, her eyes trained on my father.

"It's not him," the first woman said, snappish.

My father, for his part, had never heard of Herzog.

"How is that possible?" Willis asked.

My father shrugged. "I don't get it. He's some kind of actor?"

"He makes documentaries," I explained. "Or, I don't know, I guess he acts. He did this one movie about a bear, *Grizzly Man*, about a guy who he and his girlfriend get eaten by a bear, and another one about a pilot shot down over Laos in the sixties who later goes back to Vietnam to re-enact traumas he experienced as a POW."

"Didn't I see somewhere he was in one of the new *Star Wars* movies?" Willis wanted to know.

"*The Mandalorian*," said Isaac. "That was ages ago. And technically it was a series."

My father considered Herzog's orb, ovoid, twinkling. Certainly its dimensions suggested something intergalactic and alien. "Well, that all sounds very insane," he said. "Still, I'm impressed with the architecture."

Back past the orb, submerged in a cool brackish valley, blanketed in neoprene tarpaulin and penned in behind a gated chain-link fence over whose bubbly splay of razor wire a pair of sleek, Kevlar-plated drones kept a constant, twitchy vigil, lay some kind of *objet d'art*, the much anticipated unveiling of which would presumably occur before Christmas.

Rumours around camp (we'd soon learn) abounded as to the

precise species of this art. The gabbier of our fellow guests volunteered many hypotheses, with the growing consensus among them inclining toward a slab of outlandish movie memorabilia. I'd seen my share of Herzog's movies, but I couldn't imagine what sort of memorabilia these people had in mind. Busted, arrow-pocked hull from the steamboat in *Fitzcarraldo*? Gigantic soapstone statue of the boiled leather shoe Herzog consumed in 1979 to remunerate fellow documentarian Errol Morris's completion of *Gates of Heaven* (q.v., *Werner Herzog Eats His Shoe*)? A grizzly seemed too on the nose.

Herzog had conscripted a pair of lapsed grad students from the Earth Sciences department at MUN to keep an eye on his fence and service his drones, which local raptors tended to mistake for prey. These students, who'd come up to the Castle on a fully funded work term—something to do with crustal subsidies and tectonic regimes—slept in shifts in a thick azure pup tent at the base of the orb. "It's nothing," one of these sentries would later tell us. "People need to seriously just chill the fuck out. Like, honestly, there's nothing to see back here. I'm telling you, it's just where he keeps his canoes."

My father sneezed. Corn nuts flaked the bib of his fleecy, which he picked at, mindlessly, stuffing the clear errant kernels in his mouth.

"Bruce," he said, reaching an arm through the window to shake our driver's hand. "Thank you. I've never seen anything like this."

My father wiped his palms on his jeans and rested his one scabby hand on the hood of our van. He drew back a leg, stretched one hamstring and then the other, giving each of his heels a ginger little kick at the conclusion of these exertions. Stepping away from the van, he clicked his fingers in front of Isaac's eyes, pointed at his own ears, mouthing "headphones."

"What?" said Isaac, resigning a bud.

"Imagine what it must've felt like to be a Viking," my father said. "Coming up on all this."

Isaac made a pan of the castle, the moat, the bailey, the grassy knoll where the land dipped down to rocks and measureless grey waves over which gulls nattered and moaned, milling in a lurid helix. "Must've been pretty fucking cold," he said.

I helped Willis unload the rest of the trunk and wheeled my things toward the drawbridge, pausing to lower my case's telescopic handle, which seemed a dainty, inflated extravagance, unsuited to our medieval milieu.

"I guess this is where we're supposed to be going?" I asked.

The attendants had dispersed along with our welcome party, which struck me as odd. Had they been expecting someone else, too?

Willis shrugged. "Only one way to find out."

The moat was shallow and, up close, its blackness took on a starker viscosity. Plump, yam-tummied fish with slender whiskers (barbels, I think these are called) waggling off their chins turned in the molasses-like murk. I hurried over the bridge and under the gate's sharp latticed pikes, worried that the door might give way and skewer me.

"Are we in the wrong place?" Willis asked.

The inner walls reminded me of one of Escher's lithographs, tiered steps zigzagging down stoops of dodgy scaffolding.

"You'd think someone would've told us," my father said.

"There's some guy over there," said Isaac, lifting his suitcase.

A man in a safari pith descended a set of steps and disappeared entirely from view. He materialized, moments later, absent pith, on a platform still higher than the one he'd walked down, and, ducking back down another set of stairs, was gone again.

"This place is wild," my father said. "But I think I'm into it."

We followed a firm wooden footbridge across the courtyard toward the entrance, where the trail, bending over a lightly purling brook, funneled us on through a stand of pillared hedges. The green of these thickets glittered in surreal silhouette. I brushed a leaf with my thumb. Its short, feathered petals gave off a sweet citric smell, of dried cedar and gin.

"Come on," Willis said. "There's a door up ahead."

Above us swooped some kind of tercel or hawk, a lean, sable-winged creature, with loose leather straps arching from its talons like prey.

"Should we knock?" my father asked.

It seemed to me that we'd been walking for many minutes, but when I turned back to face the bridge, I could see we'd come hardly any distance at all.

The round wooden door was painted a sickly lemon yellow with a cast iron knocker moulded in the shape of a roaring bear. Isaac reached up and rapped it. A sound scanter than tickertape snowing on a trading room floor. Between the waves and awkward applause of what I was now registering as gunfire, I could hardly hear it. The hawk scudded and plunged, whooping hoarsely.

"Should we call?" my father asked. "I've really, really got to take a leak."

"I don't think they gave me a number," Willis said.

Isaac went to knock again but Willis stopped his hand. A bolt lifted and the door swept open.

"Sorry, sorry," said a voice, a woman's.

"Are we too early?" This was my father's formulation.

"No," the voice said. "Or I don't know. Maybe?"

A young woman in a drowsy green dress and Birkenstocks stood before us, her hair swept back in a high bouncy ponytail, a single bulb of toe (and partly painted nail) protruding from a hole in her right sock. "You guys the hunting?" she asked, cupping a yawn. "Party of four?"

"That's us," said Willis.

"Was it Doug sent you?"

"Doug?"

"Never mind. Look, I'm Esme. It's—just follow me."

We scooched inside a dark sconce-lit vestibule and followed our guide down a winding flight of stairs. The walls were damp and smelled strongly of moss. There were no handrails, few treads, and what candles and torches we passed cast abbreviated flames. At the base of the staircase stood a thick steel door. Esme stopped and fished inside her gowns for a lanyard, flattening a fob on the door's digital reader. The reader emitted a tender chirp and the door parted along its medial seam.

"Okay," she said. "This way."

Esme led us down a hallway and through another set of doors and we entered a vast and vaulted atrium. Broad lighted tiles blanketed the length of this room, which terminated on a wall of floor-to-ceiling windows overlooking the sea.

"Please have a seat," she said, indicating a reception area at the mouth of the atrium. "I'll find someone."

Esme disappeared through a set of swinging glass doors and we set down our packs and suitcases and positioned ourselves around a table of polished driftwood. My father took off his hat and fiddled with its brim. We yawned in tandem, exchanging a look of mutual incredulity. Moments later Esme returned in the company of a short blotchy man in a turtleneck.

"Sorry for the confusion," this man said. "I understand you guys are with Doug?"

"Who's this Doug guy?" my father asked.

"That's funny," the man said. "I'll have to use that one."

Our reservation was under Willis's name. Esme directed my father to a washroom, and while Willis sorted out our cabins and equipment rentals, Isaac and I strolled through the atrium. The garden presented an odd horticultual amalgam, with your indigenous flora cheek by jowl with a more equatorial fare. I browsed the display tickets, square wooden plates stamped in gilt script. Rhodora and coltsfoot, anthuriums, bromeliads, some seriously poisonous-looking bush vines. I breathed. The room smelled wonderfully of sprinkled soil.

Pausing before a hump of spotted violets, a ladybug hopped onto the edge of my thumb. It fidgeted its wings and a grey light gleamed through its ruddy carapace. I shook my hand, and continued to the windows, where Isaac stood, eyeing a gluey pleat of sky.

"How you doing?"

He leaned his head on the glass. "How much do you think this all cost?" he asked me.

"Our rooms?"

"Sure," Isaac said. "We can start there. How much do you think it cost to build a single room?" He looked away. It didn't seem as though he needed an answer.

We appeared to be near a kitchen or dining hall. Waiters in white button-downs and maroon, Dorset-bib aprons, rolling trolleys of foiled dishes, came and went through a set of saloon doors, behind which I could hear a clatter of pans and clacking porcelain, a voice yelling "Runners? Runners?"

I peered into the window, at Isaac's reflection, and noticed something funny on his chin, just below his lips, a greenish-blue fleck.

"Is that toothpaste?" I asked.

"It's for my pimples," said Isaac, facing me. "You're supposed to leave it on overnight. But I like to wear it through the day, too. It helps reduce the swelling. The redness."

"Don't they have toners for that kind of thing? Clearasil. Oxy. Something a little less conspicuous, maybe. Something a little less green?"

"Oh sure," said Isaac, and carefully daubed his chin with his thumb. "But you never know what you're getting with that stuff."

"No?"

"Ever hear of inflammatory bowel disease? Ulcerative colitis?"

I nodded.

"Don't get me wrong, I know it looks weird. I'm extremely aware of how weird it looks."

"Well, don't beat yourself up about it," I said. "If you think it'll reduce your chances of getting IBS, then more power to you."

"IBD."

"Sorry?"

"Inflammatory bowel disease. There's a difference."

My father sauntered toward us, a conspiratorial smirk forming on his face.

"They've got penises inside the bathroom," he confessed. "Like, a lot of penises."

"Isn't that where they're supposed to be?" Isaac asked.

"No, I don't mean real penises," he said. "These are more like art penises. Hanging on the walls above the urinals."

"Art penises," I said. "As distinguished from—"

"It's true. You don't believe me, come see."

"Hey guys, guys," Willis called out. "Over here. Bring your shit."

We came together in a huddle, a stench of corn nuts and almondy soap wafting off my father. "So we're all set," said Willis, handing out envelopes and keys. "Our rooms are good to go, and we're booked into the armoury for after lunch. Esme—where'd she go? She'll be the one running us through our paces."

"Don't they want our phones?" said Isaac.

"Yeah, and they want our phones." Willis flipped open a brochure and began studying a map.

"Is there food somewhere?" my father asked.

"The cabins have all got their own little kitchenettes or whatever, but there's an eatery in here." Willis turned the map around in his hands. "I can't tell which way this goes."

"I'm starving," my father said.

"Why don't we dump our shit, reconvene back here for lunch before heading off to the armoury."

"That works," I said.

At the front desk we signed some forms, took a minute, and prepared to say goodbye to our devices. Polling stations wouldn't close for hours yet, but I scrolled anyway, inuring myself to the news's consoling rhythms.

Let it be said now (and said quickly) that I cared who won but it didn't matter. Winning didn't matter. Winning, it seemed, was no longer the point. Divisiveness, turmoil, fracture, a panoramic apprehension reigned supreme. Already protests and counterprotests had erupted across the country.

"God," my father said, his face wan. "Any of you seen this?"

"What?"

"Last night," my father said. "In Montreal." He passed me his phone.

I expanded the clip and rotated the screen as Isaac and Willis drew near.

The short video showed Dorchester Square smoked over in gas, a wide line of police kitted out in full paramilitary regalia pressing on a horde of protestors. The low-angle shot fluttered and thrust, but the focus soon resolved on the shape of a single protestor, a jean-jacketed man in gas mask and goggles, shaking a sign near the front of the pack. I couldn't make out what his sign said and wondered if I might hit pause.

"I don't need to see this," Isaac said. He backed away, sniffling, just as two officers broke through the howl and surge and grabbed the masked man by the shoulders and, knocking his sign to the ground, secreted him behind their ranks. My father sighed.

It seemed clear to me what was going to happen next, and I wanted to look away, felt that it was, in effect, morally necessary to cease participating in this terrible, placid spectation, but I couldn't. And neither could Willis. The camera tilted and jerked and seemed to pass to a higher hand, ascending to ampler vantage. Below all was a flurry of clubs and shields and crushing knees. The camera tightened on the writhing man, on the hands he held up before his face to congest the unbroken gale of blows. The violence was incredible. There was so much delight in it. So much precision and speed. Gloved hands stood the man upright and brought him back down again. Blood flowed from a gash expanding across the top of his head like an oil slick. He was no longer wearing a mask. His lips were shaking and split. He looked very afraid, and he looked very young. Now the brocade of cops paused and seemed to brace themselves for a surge unseen as the camera jolted and cut bumpily away.

I gave the phone back to my father. Willis put an arm over Isaac's shoulders. Isaac wiped his nose on his sleeve.

"Gentlemen," a voice said. "I'm sorry, but if you please." On the check-in counter a flat fireproof box—it looked like a miniature tomb—appeared before us. "Your phones."

ELEVEN

"SO FIRST UP, SHOW OF HANDS," ESME SAID. "HOW MANY
newbies we working with today?"

My father inclined his chin in my direction, the grey of his stubble
flashing under the quartz lamp's icy white light.

"What?" I asked. "I've shot a pistol."

"One time you did that," my father said.

"Well wasn't that the question?" I asked.

Esme made a note on her pad. She'd changed into cargos,
mica-black steel toes, and what I want to call combat suspenders.
She wore a sandy-grey T-shirt with the sleeves doubled over her
shoulders, and sashes of sweat and smooth auburn hair furled from
her pits. She paced. Her cargos' pattern resembled swirls of tubed
cookie dough.

We were gathered in a too-bright classroom adjacent the shooting
range, an antiseptically bleached space columned on the wall nearest us
with aluminum drawers and heavy foam baffles.

"Like what you'd get at a morgue," my father said. "Way they glide
right back in through the wall."

Stacked in the corner, opposite a set of double doors leading out to the range, were two broad, padded tables, resplendent with weapons. Rifles, shotguns, shells, rounds, bipods, noise-cancelling headphones, packets of burgundy ear gummies, goggles, smart scopes, and sights.

The floor was pebbly with slip-resistant matting. The matting appeared both spongy and sloped, listing toward an open storm drain at the room's centre, from which a length of pink rubber hose, encased in green mesh, extended.

"And what about you?" Esme asked, tilting her pad at Isaac. "You've done some shooting?"

"Grouse and rabbit," said Willis. "Had him out last fall on my Bobwhite."

Esme reached into a bin and handed each of us a tablet. "Okay," she said. "Now, before we get started, few things. First up. Safety. When you boys are on my range, whether you're discharging a firearm or just standing around picking your nose, you've got to be wearing the right gear. That means boots, goggles, and ear protection. No exceptions. I see you're all wearing collared shirts and that's good. That's what we like to see. We won't be engaging secondaries this afternoon but God loves a collar. So that's first thing. Next up. When you're in here, or out there, on the field, all firearms must be unloaded. Unloaded and held up in your arms like this. What we call a two hander or ready carry. Once you're all squared away at your station, you can set your rifle down on one of the little tables we got laid out for you. What I'm wanting to see, when I walk by, are actions open, with your muzzles—that's the front of the gun—" Esme said, looking directly at me, "pointing downrange. Make sense? Okay.

"All our ranges adhere to a common firing line. That means no wackadoo shots. That means, boys, stay in your lanes. Someone yells ceasefire, stop; I don't want to be hearing any one-for-the-roads. Got it? I want to see guns on the table. Actions open. Muzzles facing downrange."

I tried paying attention. I did. I wanted to. But my mind kept tunnelling back to that other, earlier range. In TV and movies, a clip feeds and releases with seamless ease; but, standing in my cubicle with borrowed Beretta and fifteen-round magazine, I failed to perform even this most basic, utilitarian task. The lantern-jawed Nordic squiring me through these lessons wore a black T-shirt whose gloomy white script read CRISIS ACTOR. This man came forward and primed my weapon. And wasn't that easy? I pointed the gun down the range. "Stop," he said. CRISIS was once again at my side. "You looking to lose that thumb, guy? Keep the thumb where I told you."

Now Esme rounded the two padded tables, gliding a finger over the rail. "Next order of business," she said, her voice sounding a deep twangy note, sardonic, amused. "This here's a dry range. No booze, no drugs. I find anyone to be looking the least bit inebriated, be that inebriation of the red-eyed, sniffly, or slurring variety, I reserve the right to expel that person from these premises, toot sweet, no exceptions."

Had I been sober when I shot or failed to shoot with CRISIS? I couldn't remember. But somehow I suspected not. Well, I was sober, or sober enough, now.

"So before we start you on the range, I'm a need each of you to take a minute and review the following rules and regulations and fill out this brief questionnaire. The purpose of this questionnaire," Esme said, "is to assess your experience and suitability for adoption."

My father breezed through the questionnaire with unnerving surety. He handed his tablet back to Esme and stooped over the padded weapons tables, gaging cartridges, rounds. I hadn't bothered reviewing the preliminary safety material Willis had forwarded me and it showed. I had to retake the multiple-choice component multiple times.

When we were finished, Esme collected our tablets, wiped down their screens with disinfectant, and returned them to the bin. From the table we selected goggles and earplugs, and Esme assigned each of us a rifle. Then we followed her onto the range. My rifle—a Weatherby Vanguard—was only slightly worse than everyone else's. It was a simple bolt-action rifle with a rugged black stock, pistol grip, stainless steel barrel with a bead-blasted finish (apparently good for reducing glare), and scope. It felt reasonably light but substantial, and Willis assured me that it was a great gun for the price.

"Can't go wrong with a Weatherby," he said. "I bought a 257 a few years back. Tricked her out with a fixed scope ring system and a nice Zeiss optic with a 30mm objective. You know it's funny but just zeroing with factory ammo I was setting down groups under .75 MOA. It's a good gun. Fucking great gun, really, for the price."

"I don't know what any of that means," I said.

The gallery housed eight partitioned stations, and each station was equipped with a low metal stand propped up by vintage milk crates. Targets and towered blinds circuited in jute rigging filled the middle distance. The targets bore no resemblance to the willowy hominids I'd repeatedly failed to penetrate for CRISIS; these were hoofed baddies, bullet-plinked, perforated, burst Xmas deer.

We took turns firing down our lanes. The sound was uproarious, awful. Isaac, one stall over, fed a short magazine into his receiver well, and eased back the bolt. He neared his right eye over his sight's lens. The front of his rifle sat atop a wide nylon sack. He trailed the thumb of his shooting hand across the blued finish of his sight. His lips were still, his shoulders firm and relaxed. Breathing, his finger shifted from guard to trigger, as, releasing the breath, he squeezed. Willis, with folded arms, observed his progress, rocking on his heels.

"That's good, that's good," he said. "But now remember you don't need to let go so quickly. You were like this—" Willis lifted his empty arms and pantomimed a shot. "See that finger? See how it's snapping? You don't want that. When we shoot, think squeeze and release. Squeeze and release."

My own father shot everything he could. He tried multiple rifles and, though we wouldn't be using shotguns, a shotgun. "Very cool," he said, placing the shotgun on his stand and running his fingers over its smooth walnut stock.

I tried mimicking Isaac, but my hands were jerky and slick. My pulse thrummed. The kick wasn't bad, just a dull lurching weight collapsing inside my shoulder. I bade my eyes open, aimed down the sight, squeezed the trigger, felt the stock edge into the fat of my shoulder like a slipped crutch, missed.

No matter how I implored myself, every time I went to shoot, I closed my eyes, and every time I closed my eyes, I thought about my students. I couldn't help it. I dreaded—even before Travis I dreaded— the arrival of an active shooter on campus. This strikes me as a common enough anxiety among those of us who've spent the better part of this century in a classroom. Perhaps these fears were more trenchant for someone like me, whose imaginative flights of atrocity flourish on very little oxygen. That said, I identified a stark escalation in my bearing in the months after Holbrook, when I began noting—catching myself noting—emergency exits, theoretical fortifications, ad hoc arsenals (binder, phone, Arden Shakespeare). Among my students, I silently sought out allies, mesomorphic gym rats and jocks, kids who, in the face of an impending massacre, might rise to the occasion, set some furry, carbine-wielding beta on his ass.

And now I remembered a moment—a Sunday afternoon, a few months after Travis's death—standing inside my office, staring out my window, and feeling an overwhelming sense of displacement, as though I were observing myself in the third-person, from without. The room smelled (not unpleasantly) of decaying apples, cruciform clementine peels that came apart in my fingers like crackers. In all the years I'd spent in this office, I'd never once bothered turning down the blinds, and the books and papers cluttering my desk were stiff and faded with sun.

Spirals of steam drew off the stacks of the Foothills hospital. I could see the mountains, their peaks, massifs, winding ridges, and all of this collared in snow. Campus was quiet, and I seemed to govern over this stillness as out of an eyrie.

Before me: a tall window, with a thick sturdy ledge you could probably walk across. It didn't open, but I wondered, if it did, if I might jump, tumble from this height like a bag full of loose pieces. Below me was Swann Mall. Snow had gathered in the brown grassless folds between the trees. I collected the overdue library books whose acquisition and return had impelled my trip to campus on a Sunday, and placed them in my tote.

I'm not sure what came over me that afternoon. Possibly I admitted the idea because I couldn't open the window. I wanted to jump because I couldn't jump.

I didn't feel exactly suicidal, if that's even the word. The thought that I might jump out a ten-storey window passed over me like a tiredness, and I reflected that one feels this longing, this incremental descent, always. Always but by degrees. I didn't want to die; I just didn't want to be entirely alive at that moment.

Years ago I'd read an account of dozens of dairy cows discovered dead at the base of a steep cliff in the Alps. But cows travel in herds. Perhaps the leading cow had wrongly glimpsed grass? Anyway, I wasn't suicidal, I kept telling myself, not at all. I was more like the third or fourth cow back—I didn't know what was going on.

And then something happened. Maybe a door slammed, or an engine backfired. They'd been tearing up the lot out back of Scurfield Hall, and so it's possible, yes, it is entirely possible, that what I heard that afternoon were simply the big metal teeth of a digger stamping down on a slab of obdurate asphalt. In any case, the sound sounded like what it sounded like: a shot.

I walked to the other side of my desk and sat down. I was terrified. My throat throbbed. There again was that taste of metal, of lost linty coins furled in couch dust, and the taste coated everything. My gums, teeth, my roving tongue. I tried to swallow. I tried naming five things I could see, four things I could feel, three things I could hear, two I could smell, and one I could taste. Floaters sparkled in my left eye but not in my right. I gripped the unadjustable arms of my chair, and spoke the word "vegetables," very slowly, twice. There was a broken bit of shoelace on the floor with a squashed aglet. The aglet was clear and slitting. I didn't feel safe. The expanse of my desk resembled that Alex

116   HIDES

Colville painting with the framing of window, waves, table, and gun. Though, of course, there wasn't a gun. I closed my eyes and focused on my breathing, which helped until it didn't. "This is still a chair," I said, standing. And then, for some reason, I immediately called my father.

"What's up?" he said. "Hello? What's up?"

"Nothing," I said. "How are you?"

"I'm fine," he said. "What's up?"

I knew then that calling him was a mistake, that whatever I hoped to communicate, whatever distance I intended to heal, wouldn't yield.

"Nothing," I said. "I just felt like saying hello."

Back at the range, the delirious thump of rifle fire cascaded across my body like a strained nerve. The shots didn't resonate but reverberated, sparking down my spine. I sensed that I was lapsing into a bad state, one of my deep, irresolvable depressions. I set my unloaded rifle on the table before me and regarded my tremor. The pad of my right hand was fully numb. I sped this hand inside my pocket and made a fist, digging my nails into my skin. Esme stood behind my father, squaring his shoulders. Possibly this sounds absurd but I felt like I might weep. An older woman, unsmiling, peered through the classroom window, her long white hair flowing over her shoulders. She wore tinted safety goggles, ear protectors, and a grey linen shirt with black spots. The shirt was buttoned right up to her throat and its collar was very narrow. She did not seem to be looking at anyone else but me. Shots trembled around me, and ejected shells spilled to the floor. My eye itched from where I'd clamped my goggles over the sight, and I wanted to take them off. My father clapped Willis on the shoulder, and the two men— these two fathers, I should say—laughed. Isaac lined up another shot. I backed away from my station and totted up my spent casings. I'd fired my rifle a total of six times. The shells were worn, dented, and blackened along the webbed rib of their case heads. I jiggled them in my palm, and, trying for a smile, stepped fully away from my lane, and looked behind me, but the face in the window was gone.

TWELVE

DOWN THE BROAD FLAGSTONE LOBBY AND INTO A CROWDED
tray-ceilinged foyer we came, the air vibrant, briny, clanging with
glassware and chatter.

"What's all this?" Willis asked.

It was just after four. The sun, starting in on its ebb, held like a
second moon atop Herzog's orb.

Post-range, we'd hoped to pre-empt the throng of dinner rush.
But apparently we'd missed our mark. Prospective diners—preponder-
antly white and male and (one would have to presume) rich—milled in
the fading light, jostling toward a set of parted barn doors, across which
a loose velvet cordon sealed us out. My father pressed a hand over
my shoulder and raised himself up on his toes to assess our progress.
His chin reeked of the sandalwood aftershave he'd slathered all over
himself back in our room. "It doesn't look like they're letting people
in." An oniony trail of steam, of warm stainless steel, rolled over the
doors' dark wooden rails. My stomach moaned.

I was wildly underdressed, even by the standards set by our
own party, but especially standing scrunched up against my father:
double-breasted tweed, starched oxford, and tie.

"Madness," he said. "Who are all these people?"

"Conference attendees?" Willis asked.

"Researchers," Isaac said. "Linguists. I think these are the theoretical phoneticians I read about."

"Who and the what now?" my father asked.

It was true that there were many foreign voices in attendance. I discerned German amid the general ache and rabble. French voices, Japanese. A waitress inched past, wielding a tray of drinks. "Champagne?"

We—all but Isaac, anyway—accepted flutes, clinked, and drank.

"You don't own any shirts?" my father asked.

"I wasn't expecting a dress code," I said. "And besides, what's wrong with what I've got on?"

My father appraised me. They all did. My boots, black cable-knit sweater, and jeans. I was fond of this look. Close-fitting and studious, absent the boots, this was my go-to lecturing garb.

"You got feathers and shit all over your back," Willis said. He reached around my shoulder and showed me a stitch of down.

A bell clanged and we filtered through the barn doors and into the dining hall. The seating area projected over the ocean floor. You could see down into the water through a series of circular glass tiles shaped like porthole windows and fringed in brass. In the back corner a massive whale carcass or mobile of whale bones rotated above a barren bandstand festooned in fishy filigree. Hooks, nets, trawl tubs, and jiggers. Beyond the mic stand and amps and ruby-tinted drum kit were harpoons and gaffs and snaggy pikes tacked to a ropey ladder.

We pointed and gazed, and my father, shooting his cuffs, said, "You think it's real?"

"All 356 bones. A blue whale beached in Bonne Bay," said Isaac. "Am I the only one who read the literature?"

"There was literature?" my father asked.

"It's so clean," said Willis. "So polished."

"That's just sawdust and cow shit," Isaac said. "That's how they got rid of all the muktuk and blubber. Manipulate the carbon-to-nitrogen ratios to optimize humidity, and there you go."

"That easy?" my father asked.

"You'd be surprised," Isaac said.

The situation here was buffet-style: first come, first served. White linen tables, arrayed with fish, game, and starchy beige curios, glowed under arcing heat lamps. The carte du jour promised an unconventional culinary experience, with traditional local delicacies joining an anarchic, North American fare. There were baskets of shoestring, curly, and waffle-cut fries—crisped in glorious duck fat—spinach-skinned venison dumplings with sesame seed peanut dipping sauce, cod tongues, scrunchions, fiddlehead ratatouille, salt beef, chicken fingers, sausage rolls, moose sliders, peameal bacon mac and cheese, baby octopuses globed in a sake-hinted aspic, and big bleedy joints of steak. I made myself a plate of miscellaneous potato parts—at the sight of those garlicky fries my stomach started in on its basso mewl, my intestinal whale song—chicken fingers, and sliders, and ordered a gin and tonic.

We piled cutlery onto our trays and proceeded to our table.

"I think I see a fish or a squid or a jellyfish or something," my father said. He set his tray on a tiered drinks trolley and crouched over the glass. Willis peered over his shoulder. I could see myself, my obscene bumps and declivities, reflected underfoot, staring. Three bodies floated below us, snorkelled and swaying, gusting bubbles.

A man balancing a piece of cheese bread on a blue paper napkin approached us. "Please don't tap the glass," this man said.

"I wasn't," my father said.

Our dinner companions were the same couple who'd mistaken my father for Werner Herzog, and who were headed back to St. John's the following morning, Jill and Eric Lyle, an improbable mother-son duo, it transpired.

"Did you bag anything?" Willis asked.

"We killed a lot of coyotes," said Mrs. Lyle.

"Can you eat those?" my father asked. "I've always wondered." A wet bite of cod dangled from the fork he held aloft.

"You can," said Mrs. Lyle. "But people don't."

"Some do."

"Yes, Eric," his mother said. "Some do. That's right. That's very observant of you, very comprehensive. But generally people don't. Which was the point I was trying to make."

"I'm sorry. I didn't mean to make you so enraged." Eric twisted his sideburns. His black hair bore the glossy, deadish sheen of a bad dye job. He looked vaguely taxidermied.

"I'm not angry," his mother said. "I'm just trying to be realistic for once."

My father swallowed his cod and pushed his fork to the side of his plate.

"Have you met Judith?" Eric asked.

"Dr. Muir?" I took a sip of gin and considered my slider. "No," I said. "Not yet."

"You will," said Mrs. Lyle. "She's—what's the word?"

"A force," said Eric, arranging his asparagus across his plate so that their lemoned heads and spears described a near-perfect square. "A force of nature. A force to be reckoned with. A gale force wind or even a sort of Force 17, if that makes sense."

"What's this guy's problem?" my father whispered.

"No. Not a force," said Mrs. Lyle. "It's more magical than that."

"But isn't that what I'm trying to establish?" Eric asked, placing half an eggroll at the centre of his square.

"I don't think it's right, killing coyote," said Isaac. "The trickster."

"You don't need a permit," said Eric. "So, financially speaking, it makes complete sense, in terms of an investment."

"They're an invasive species," said Willis, sitting up and pressing at the bottom of his stomach with his fist.

"Sorry, but that's not a hundred percent accurate. Coyotes have been on the island for over forty years. In fact, if you think about it, they're extremely adaptable. Partly," said Isaac, setting down his spoon and facing the Lyles, "it's because they're such opportunistic carnivores. Coyotes will eat anything. Caribou, moose, carrion, hare. They'll eat fruit, berries, birds, birdseed, cats."

"They disrupt the ecosystem," Willis said.

"We disrupt the ecosystem," his son shot back.

———————

Later that night they screened *Fitzcarraldo* and Les Blank's *Burden of Dreams* in an old-timey 35mm theatre, called, for some reason, the White Library. Rows of red vintage seats descended aisles tracked out in lighted carpet. The walls were puckered in plush, bluish-grey drapes. The seats creaked, the arms were cramped, and the floors were sticky with pop; yet the sound my soles made adhering and peeling appealed. Candied popcorn and cocktails were served. A tuxedoed officiate prefaced the double bill with house rules (no talking, no whispering), a canned synopsis, and enjoined us to kick back and enjoy the show. The lights dimmed. Someone tittered, another shushed. I drank two negronis, a non-alcoholic Corona (by accident), watched up to the part in *Fitz* where Klaus Kinski's girlfriend buys him that boat, but the music (Bellini's *I puritani*) and woozy river shots were more than I could handle, and I decided to go for a walk.

I exited the White Library and followed a meandering pea gravel path down to the water, passing the domed sports complex. The smell of chloramines spurting from the building's bulky ventilation system touched off a languid longing in me. Poolside summers of onioned patties and the iodine my mother daubed on nicked knees. Masses of fog drifted in the rocky grass like scattered linens. I came to a sheltered lookout and sat down on a reclining Adirondack. Caged lanterns hung from a pressure-treated post beam, their taut, sludgy flames whipping in the breeze. I strummed the chair's slats and listened to the waves and lit a joint. Though it was dark, I could see, gazing out over the balustrade, about a metre or two into the depths, but not well. Small incandescent starfish lounged in the grainy deep.

Footsteps scuffed on the boardwalk and a face emerged by the lamplight. "Judith Muir," the face said. This was the woman from the gun range. "I didn't mean to startle you."

We shook hands. Her fingers felt cold and satiny, thickly moisturised. She wore olive joggers over tan desert boots, a roomy black fleece and scarf. Her cheeks were freckled, and her grey hair shone like the hazy white fluff of a dandelion's scatter.

"You're the bereaved?" she asked.

"Not quite," I said, shying the joint behind my back, and nicking the cherry off with a nail. "That's the other one, my friend."

"The loud one?"

"He is loud," I said.

Judith came forward, and rested her elbows on the balustrade. She acknowledged my cupped hand. "I saw that, by the way. Not that I mind."

Waves folded and swirled in densely shaded furrows, raking pebbles. I relit my joint and took a short pull. "You want some?" I asked.

Judith accepted the joint without comment, firming the filter in her lips as she dragged. "I like to walk by myself at night," she said, handing back to me. "It doesn't matter where. I think this is what I miss most about cities, busy cities, bustling at night. The anonymity of a twenty-four-hour grocery store, a certain brightness or boot squeak, the silent aisles."

"I needed to turn my mind off. Crowds," I said. "I can't do crowds."

"Solitude's underrated."

"This from a resort manager," I said. "A provocative take."

"Is that how you see me?" Judith asked. "An innkeeper?"

"I don't know you from Adam," I said. "You want more of this?"

Judith waved me away. "And what about you?" she asked. "What do you do?"

"For work, you mean?" Which was a dumb thing to say. "I'm an English professor at the University of Calgary." I often do this, with taxi drivers and barbers, I often embellish, I often lie.

"What's your focus?" Judith asked.

I toked first and said, "Irish modernism," and released the breath.

"An Irish modernist in Alberta," Judith said. "Cutting edge."

"We're a rare breed."

The surf rattled and foamed. I'd forgotten how much I missed that sound, of salt spray and whisking sediment.

"I wonder who's won," I said.

"It doesn't matter."

"The election," I clarified, gesturing, somewhat meaninglessly, at the ocean.

"It doesn't matter. One man or another. It's all the same."

"Sure," I said. "I completely agree. But you didn't vote? Because I would think that, given the, uh, the situation here—"

"I never vote. I can't remember the last time I cast a ballot." She brought her arms under her chest, burrowed her chin in her fleece. "It's not that I don't care," she said, facing me briefly, and then looking away. "That *we* don't care, I should say. We care very much."

"Because here, surely, you've got—there must be thousands of regulations, governmental strictures, permits. This isn't a Michael Crichton novel," I said.

"No? I mean it could be. Though of course I always thought the problem with *Jurassic Park* was pedagogical, a marring, misplaced idealism. You don't reanimate extinct species to study them, to make a cute little petting zoo for the children, no. The impulse is misguided, counterintuitive." Slowly, a half-smile matured on the edge of her face. "We want to kill, is my thought. Maybe we need to. Why deny ourselves that?"

"I'm sorry?" I asked.

"Well, here we let you. Here, if you wish, the violence is limitless."

I thought about this, or tried to. It dawned on me—not in a paranoid way, but in a way that might trend paranoid if I let it—that I was unbelievably stoned. "But the animals here are real," I said, carefully. "I guess they're real in *Jurassic Park*, too, with the mosquitos and the sap or the sap that traps the mosquitos whose DNA, once extracted, becomes, but—" I wasn't entirely sure where I was going with this. "But here, the animals here, they're real, they're—"

"They are. Or most of them, anyway. Of course the orange fish in the moat aren't real. And some of the cephalopods you might've seen, some, not all, are digital."

"The fish aren't real?" I pictured the cod on my father's fork. The hoary flakes and bones.

"They're real enough. A company in New Zealand, Edge, they started developing dolphins, life-sized animatronic dolphins for use in aquariums, parks, movies, TV. You've seen their work, I'm sure of it. *Flipper, Free Willy, The Life Aquatic*."

"But the animals," I said, "the coyotes."

"The mammals are as you see. The coyotes are here to stay—and a problem. They fuck like rabbits. The moose and bears we farm. We track them and keep careful quotas."

"Meaning the territory is under surveillance," I said. I tried for another toke but my ember had dwindled to a papery grey braid.

"Yes and no. We do get poachers. And so some of the pine marten—" Her eyes veered over mine. "Some of the pine marten are spies."

"Spies?"

"They look like pine marten. They scurry around and forage just like pine marten. But we've equipped them with smart cameras, sophisticated recording devices. They operate on the same AI you find in most hospitals. The pine marten gather and analyze vast swaths of data. We rely on them for forecast and deterrence. Some problem-solve."

I wasn't confident that I knew what a pine marten looked like, and I wanted, annoyingly, to Google it.

"Why do you take away our phones?"

"Do you want to use your phone?" Judith turned and faced me.

"Not really," I said.

"Well?"

We were quiet. I prized open my Altoids and pocketed my butt.

Behind us, fortressed in the high dark rolling hills, Herzog's orb hovered; from within, a green light strobed twice and went out.

"Is he here?" I asked.

"Who?"

"Herzog," I said. "Werner."

"He comes and goes." Judith smiled. The caged lantern jangled and groaned, mussing its agile flame. Judith stretched a finger across my face and glanced a nail against my cheek.

"Eyelash." She presented the lash. Short and kinked like a tiny spike of soil. It didn't look like mine.

"Make a wish," she said; so I did.

THIRTEEN

NEXT MORNING, BEFORE SETTING OFF—MY FATHER HAD roused me (sans coffee) from a deep sleep at six—we had our picture taken outside the pistol range. I suspect this backdrop was selected for its inherent rusticities, a cowpoke frontage of hay bale targets, banded in peg wood and wire. We stood smooshed together under a seedy tarpaper shack, in our dun parkas and anoraks and reflective vests, clutching our rifles, smirking, enveloped in wilted spruce. Moose antlers tenanted the shack's gravel demesne and the railing's newels were capped in stiff barky skulls. Some of these were avian, while others—to go by the snouts and nerdy overbites—I took for rodent, bucktoothed ermine or vole.

"Let's do a few more over here on the grass," our photographer said. He was a small man, tipsy, almost gnomish, in Elmer Fudd mackinaw and plaid. "Can I get you two shorter guys parked down there in front? Right. There's good. Now you two—perfect."

I squatted on a mangy sod pallet, damp mud rising through the knees of my jeans, sogging me. "You think we can speed this up?" I asked. A broad-beamed floodlight held us in an ersatz dawn.

My father slid a fist over my shoulder and noogied me, driving his knuckles over my toque's pert navy bobble. I ducked and swatted with my non-rifle hand, but elevation worked to his advantage.

"Grow up," I said.

"You first," he said back.

He had on a pair of semi-circular wraparound shades with copper-tinted lenses and a splotchy brown boonie with emerald eyelets. His bearing was confused, roguish, tumid with play. He hovered and feinted, pawing sod. With his rifle and bandolier of nipply water bottles leashed to his chest, my father presided over this scene with the despotic self-possession of a lesser Bond villain. The glasses were polarized and presumably what you wanted in the fog—levelling glare while enlivening contrast—but I didn't love how I could still see his eyes working around behind them, could still glean their puckish con game, their scheming. What was the purpose of all this? On occasion, my father, propelled by some un-developed sophomoric complex, delighted in goading and teasing me. These incitements came in all shapes and sizes. A small-scale operation might entail swapping out my preferred breakfast cereal (Cap'n Crunch's Peanut Butter Crunch) for a sleeve of sugarless bran pellets. And who could forget the night my father commissioned a pair of actors to pick me up after my grade eight (eighties-themed) prom via horse-drawn chariot? There, in the front parking lot, before me and my peers (I'd gone as Marty McFly: jean jacket, red gilet, and jeans), stood two toga-clad centurions—plumed helmets, sandals, coppery chest plates—barking my name and brandishing their wooden swords with colossal aplomb. Paul Berg, my father's longstanding ELT and sometimes scenographer, played the horse—and the horse talked.

I readjusted my toque, squaring the logo plumb over my eyes, and drove my elbow back into his shins, slipping and missing wildly.

"Hey! Let's watch where we're swinging that thing. And you," said Judith, directing a mitten at my father, "play nice."

We did a couple more group shots. Then we took turns loitering under a frail trellis arch with our rifles angling gamely off our hips—

sprezzatura douche. My stock's comb was embossed with a gridded print and where my fingers closed over the butt the molding sat scratchy and coarse.

"Let's try for a big smile," our photographer said; and then, "On second thought, let's not."

It was a cool morning, and a light, needly breeze was licking in from the east. Thin bands of sun like violet contrails diffracted across a sky here and there ribboned in cloud. Isaac's pimple hadn't quite cleared (or popped) and he wore over this cap an itchy mantle of pus, rosy and flushing.

Where we were headed was a fifty-kilometre wind through razored switchbacks, and then another fifteen-minute ferry or so via motorboat to our hunting stage proper. We took two vehicles. Judith and Isaac and my father rode in a large black company truck, hauling coolers—we'd received our pre-ordered provisions from the Castle's commissary earlier that morning: potatoes, steaks, eggs, bread, beer, and so on—and skiff, with myself and Willis bringing up the rear in an ailing Jeep Renegade with a dented fender and draggy clutch. "Don't worry if she starts bucking a little on the hills," said Judith. "That'll be pretty normal."

The road was snugger than the one we'd come down yesterday and swollen with stumps and mounds of rubbly sawdust. It'd snowed overnight and twists of white spun from the trees, as out of an hour-glass stream silent tassels of sand.

There was no argument from me over which one of us would shoulder the driving. Willis drove, balancing a plate of bran muffins he'd snagged from the continental buffet on his lap, a Ziploc of diced grapefruit pinched against the wheel. He chucked the gnawed rinds out the window, aiming for the trees. I sipped my coffee, which I held close to my lips with two hands.

"How much farther?"

"You're worse than Isaac," said Willis. "Maybe forty-five minutes, half an hour."

"That thing doesn't look like it'll hold all of us," I said. "Much less a moose."

"Trips," said Willis. "I'm thinking the plan here is trips."

"And you're sure they've got toilets at this place?" I breathed in the steam of my cup, a dwindling luxury, for all I knew.

"Outhouse."

"But no running water," I said.

"There's a tank. Six hundred gallons, they said. Which'll more than suffice."

The black truck crunched through a film of partly frozen puddle, splinters of ice tossing like a mess of protractors, as the trailer's stiff narrow tires banged over the ruts. I set my coffee in the cupholder, braced for impact. We centred our way over this divot and, facing Willis, I said, "When we get there, you guys need some space, you let me know. My dad and I, we can make ourselves scarce whenever you need."

Willis nibbled at one of his muffin stumps, which was slivered in raisins and carrot. He didn't seem so keen on talking, which was fine, but it occurred to me that, beyond the trip, I hadn't much clue what either he or Isaac intended in the way of a ceremony. Was the trip, I wondered, in itself, the thing? Or had the two of them hashed out some private remembrance? I wanted to know. More than curious, I was desiring, for my own sake, and for my father's, too, I guess, not to fuck things up.

"I'm assuming you guys have something planned?"

Willis swallowed and ran his tongue across the front of his teeth, clacking one cheek and then the other. "I don't know," he said. "Isaac, he's got all these ideas, this plan for—fuck."

"Watch the road, watch the road," I said, as we came slamming over a slight stump.

"I'm watching it, I'm watching it." Willis tilted the rear-view mirror. "Anyway," he said. "It's these books. Sky burial's what Isaac keeps calling them. The Egyptians, their, who am I thinking of, their goddess, with the vulture or griffon—"

I shook my head. "You lost me," I said.

"Well, whatever. It's Isaac's thinking that we in the west need to reconceptualize—or, no. That's not the word. The word he uses is deinstitutionalize. Fucking kid. To deinstitutionalize our associations with death." Willis balled up his muffin's cup and tossed the crumby wax pill in the back seat. "We're too glutted, too pampered. This is Isaac talking now. We like to keep everything clean and remote and hidden away." Willis brought his hand to his chest and attempted to burp. "Anyway, so whatever, I don't know, to answer your question, we've got ashes. A vial. We've each—myself, Caitlin, Pen, Isaac—got a vial of ashes. With the idea being that we each get to decide what we want to do with Travis's remains. Together but independent of each other."

"But all that sounds fine." There was a strand of meat stuck between my teeth and I worked at the peppery flap with a nail.

"You'd think so. But Isaac didn't want him cremated, see. Didn't want his brother buried either, pumped full of chemicals and sewn away in the soil with nothing, nothing of himself to give back. And he really is livid about the cremation. The buildup of greenhouse gases and whatever else, the three hours of fuel it took to burn his body. Gruesome stats. You don't want to get him going on this shit, trust me. It were up to him there wouldn't be a body. Just leave his brother rotting in that Walmart parking lot by the station, like Diogenes and his dogs or whoever the fuck, for the gulls and magpies—"

"Because Baker said—"

"Baker doesn't know shit."

"He said—"

"What did he say?"

"Well he says he's depressed. Said he just sits in his room all day, playing games."

"He's not playing games. Or I don't know." Willis scratched his stubble. The beard he could not quite commit to growing was a mistake; this was not, someone needed to tell him, a thing he could do. "There's this other aspect," he said, and paused. Broken capillaries spidered his nostrils. "I was coming downstairs to call him to dinner one night. This, maybe three, four months after Holbrook. We ceded Isaac the basement after Travis left for university. I'd hoped to convert the space to a home office, but whatever. A boy needs his space. A man. So, anyway. I come downstairs to tell him dinner's ready, whatever, but right away I can tell nobody else's around. The whole area's just pitch black except for the little glow in the corner coming off his laptop. Which was only partly folded, I should say. The screen. So I go over to it and open it up. And I know I shouldn't be doing this, okay. I've talked to my therapist, my guy, boundaries and privacy, so I don't need you starting in with the judgments."

"I'm not saying anything," I said.

"It was a manifesto. *The* manifesto," Willis said. "A PDF of the document the shooter had posted to 8chan or wherever the fuck that afternoon, hours before the attack."

"Fuck, that's—"

"Yeah."

"Did you—"

"I skimmed," Willis said.

I let this sink in. A caps-less, unpunctuated slab of malice spanning who knew how many single-spaced pages. I could understand looking, or wanting to. I could bring myself that far. But to catch your own son looking. To catch your own son in congress with the mind that left you sonless. I didn't know what to say.

"The fucked-up thing of it," Willis said, his knuckles blanching at the wheel. "And this goes back to the Unabomber, right. But it's all this climate stuff. The document he was looking at. The shooter's. The manifesto. All this stuff about—I don't know. Ecofascism. Which I read online Kaczynski incidentally decried, but whatever. This call to purge. To accelerate. Bring us white boys round to some dumb fucking ethno-state. Obviously this goes in a totally different direction than Isaac—that's not what I'm trying to say. But like what the fuck? What was he looking at this for?"

"What did you say to him?" I asked.

Willis shook his head, blinked. He brought one hand up from the wheel and closed his fingers across his mouth.

"It's okay," I said. "You alright? Here," I passed him my water bottle. "Have a drink of something. Small sips."

"No," he said, glancing in the rearview mirror. "I'm fine, okay? That's not it. It's—why are we stopping?" The black truck cut its engine and the lights on the trailer extinguished. I could see the shape of my father rustling in the front seat.

"Look," I said. "There's a cat. Like a big cougar."

"Sorry, Darwin. There're no cougars in Newfoundland."

"Well what's that then?"

"Where? Use your language for fuck sakes. I still don't see where I'm looking at."

"Over there," I said, pointing. "Between those bushes."

"I think it's a lynx," Willis said.

"There's lynxes?"

"There used to be, but the northern hare, the decimation of the northern hare—what's your dad doing?"

"Oh god."

"Where'd he get that camera?"

"He's going to scare her away."

The cat sauntered out to the edge of the road, nosing a lacy brown shrub. Its ears were heavy, with two drab tufts, like stripes of twirled caramel, perking at the tips. My father clambered across the truck's running board, one arm crooked over the roof rack, his camera panning. We waited. The lynx withdrew from the shrubs, stalked back into the woods, and flopped down on a rug of moss, its short black tail pert and thumping. The lynx considered my father, us, then licked a front paw and scrubbed its ears. A knot of something jutted inside its shoulders and the lynx slackened itself on the moss, flexed its paws, turned away from our vehicles, and—as if out of politeness—yawned. My father shrugged. He put away his camera, hopped back in the truck, and slapped the roof twice with his palm.

We rode on.

I wanted to press Willis on Isaac; and, horrible as this sounds, I wanted to know more about that manifesto, too. Was Willis certain that he hadn't located in its pages a current of ecological extremism that ran in tandem with Isaac's own thinking? Such a question now seemed unbroachable. We came down one hill and up another and on through a pallid sweep of lime-fissured rocks mounded in slant poplar and ash. The lake shimmered below us, a bilgy foam prattling the ridges like a dirty wedding train. Willis slipped the Jeep into neutral and we idled a minute while Judith backed the trailer down a paved launch ramp. My father had once again exited the vehicle. He scurried across the wharf trailing a length of braided utility rope from what I'm going to go ahead and call a bow cleat. He did not know what he was doing. As Judith released the winch and the boat slid into the water, coming to an easy, floating halt, my father widened his stance, spooling the excess rope over his forearm like a madman, as if the fate of this vessel were his alone to bear.

Willis turned off the engine. I unbuckled my seatbelt and took my coffee down to the water. Scrub grass swayed from between the rocks, grey blades bearded in frost. The clouds had thickened, grown billows, and somewhere, not far off, a loon yodelled. Crossing the beach, cold stones shifted and clattered, a sound like gritty mussels tossed in a bowl. The lake was still. Its surface flashed glassy and shallow under the low scum of fog. You could just see the other side, maybe a kilometre or two away, a spotting of rocks, blackened trees. Concrete pilings with stakes of wood nested fast in their middles descended the launch ramp and spokes of rebar showed bent and poking through the struts.

I joined my father on the dock, which was a sturdy, T-shaped promontory with rubber treads and aluminum railings. I was unsure of my footing and hovered a palm over the rails, bracing myself for wobble and pitch, but the floats clapped solidly underfoot.

It was quiet. The loon's whistle sounded lonely and glad. My father unwound his glasses and brought up a pair of binoculars, peering out across the water. Slimy, pink-orange rocks banked the shoals like an archipelago. Two kilometres might be stretching things. It didn't look too far. Or deep.

"Bet I could swim that," my father said.

"Or walk it," I said.

"It gets deep," said Judith. "There's pockets."

We came back ashore and started hauling items from the trunks and sorting all our gear onto the dock. The boat's tub was like the guts of an old empty dishwater. That creamy, nearly jaundiced white. The gunnels were unsanded and scarlet blots of paint ran off the seams which were notched. I studied our gear, our alloy-frame packs leaning higher than six-year-olds, our coolers, jugs, stoves, kettles, guns, crates of ammo. I tried volunteering a few items onto the boat but my intuition was apparently wanting. So be it. I let Willis and Judith administer priority berthing.

My father wasn't helping much either. He'd stationed himself at the base of the ramp and was whacking at the air with a scoop of driftwood he'd acquired, hooking and smashing the stick up from his knees like a cesta. His sunglasses swung from his neck, their lenses dizzying the rocks.

"Try lifting like this," he said to Isaac, dropping his stick and lowering himself into a thunderous, rugby-like squat, fishing around with his hands. "And up—up."

Isaac and Willis made the first crossing. We watched them sputter away from the beach, an irised plume of oil greasing in the wash.

"Now what?" my father said.

I roamed the beach in search of good skipping stones. I tossed a few. Traced the disks as they quavered and fled. Beyond the dock I glimpsed another loon or maybe the original loon sleuthing amid the toppled bulrushes. A sharp face, red eyes set in the feathers like cold, shaded cherries. It scooted around the reeds, dipping and shaking its beak, before secreting itself back under the water's lip in a supple gulp.

Voices, Willis's and now and then Judith's, threaded in the wind. My father stood on the dock with his back to me. He'd unrolled his sleeping bag and appeared to be emptying the contents of his backpack, refolding pants, shirts, etc. They'd be a few minutes sorting gear on the other side and I figured Judith would need to show them the trail to the cabin. I skipped another rock and wandered back over to the Jeep and got down my daypack and pulled out another of the Rugaby pinners and lit up.

When I came back down to the beach, my father had dispensed with his hat, jacket, sweater, and shirt, and was busily spreading sunscreen onto his cheeks and chest and neck. "Want some?" he called out. He lobbed the near-empty tube my way, and I squirted a watery dollop into my hands, laying the thickest daub over a brownish abrasion on my wrist I wasn't sure when I should start worrying about. In a few minutes Judith was headed back with the boat, cruising across the lake with a lightened load.

I had the right grade of high working for me this morning, a shrewd distortion, not so stoned as to go about our hunt in an enraptured haze, but just addled enough to find, amid the lap of waves and snick of wind, a renewing buoyancy. Spent shotgun shells, red hulls leanly rusting, littered the beach, along with some stray bits of tackle. I stomped an empty beer can, flattening it under the proud weight of my boot. Scattered in the rocks were small thorny crabs like annoying puzzle pieces with missing arm parts, ribbons of parched kelp, and driftwood gored over by ants. Off the side of the road was a sheltered sitting area with a few stodgy logs circled around a makeshift firepit. Etched into the seat of the plumpest log were hearted names and messages. "Dear Suzy," read one, "You were my best friend and only confidante. And now no one will ever know the sordid depths of me." "Alex hearts Fred," read another.

"You coming?" my father called out.

"What?"

Judith had docked the boat, which was, to my surprise, fully packed.

"Sorry," I said. I stubbed out my joint and put it back in my Altoids case and zipped the case away in my jacket pocket. "Sorry."

"What were you doing over there?"

"Nothing."

"Smells like it," said Judith.

I smiled, but she didn't, and my father just shook his head.

We boarded the boat. I sat on the side with the least amount of gear, a human ballast, while my father and Judith shared the back wooden bench.

"You want to drive?" Judith asked.

"I'd love to," my father said.

The wind had picked up and a gentle bulb of sun was rising further over the water and scattering the fog. Judith turned on the ignition and my father held firm the throttle which jiggled his fist. Our trucks receded from view and I sunk my hand into the water, the cold biting oddly hot on my wrist.

We passed a narrow islet of sheer gunmetal cliffs thicketed in small scrawny trees. The escarpment flowed underwater—broad as the belly of a whale. The cliffs looked almost impregnable. You could breach them but it would take some doing. And how nice would it be to lay claim to just this one brief chunk of land? To call this jagged territory, whose square-footage ran to maybe just under a fifth of my apartment (but across whose core I could see installing a tubed, single-room cabin; commission Castle staff to ferry supplies; subsist and fish), yours, and yours alone?

As we drew alongside the island, Judith switched off the ignition, and we drifted, rudderless, to shore. Judith took up a wooden paddle with a worn shaft and splintered blade with electrical tape knotted over its grip. She lifted it out of the boat and its rounded shoulder gonged on the gunnel and the light caught the water streaming off its blade like a knife and on the beach a lank, edgy-headed raven untucked a wing and stirred. The water was too shallow to work much more than the meniscus, much less pull a full sweep, but Judith engaged the paddle like a gondolier, pegging us forward by the tip. She knelt on one leg. Her white hair shone on the sides but not on top. The only sound was of the raven and the paddle's gummy end pushing against the bottom of the lake and of the skiff chopping over the waves.

A snow started. The flakes bulged, wind-fat and gliding. They listed like cartoon leaves in a slow float, dissolving on the water's surface like minced garlic in too much oil. I coaxed my tongue out to catch one but caught instead my father's eye, through tinted lenses, livid and creasing.

We scrabbled to shore and I took the joint I'd pinched off out of my pocket and lit up, but before I could take a drag, my father grabbed my weed and tossed the joint in the water.

"Sober up," he said.

FOURTEEN

OUR CABIN WAS ALL OF ONE ROOM. OR SHOULD I SAY THAT a curtain of rank muslin divided our sleeping commons from a linoleumed kitchenette across whose seamy, air-bubbled tiles an assortment of knives had been laid out on a worn gingham dish towel? The stoutest of these was a tall rosewood cleaver with three fine silver rivets arranged in its grip. Behind them, pushed up against the wall, was a small fridge, a Dutch oven, and two battered skillets, stacked one inside the other, and a can of no-name bean medley with a faded orange price tag smeared to its lid. A squat iron stove stood in the other corner, grate open and ash pan hoary with coals.

It felt far later than 9:54. I was despondent and starving. I chided myself for not re-upping on the tenders and taters, braving a venison dumpling, or bolting Eric's islanded eggroll. Or maybe this was the weed gnawing. I unwrapped one of my PowerBars and waved the stiff wiry snack under my nose. It smelled like a roomful of cardboard soused in grainy ganache. I took a bite, and a game of tug-of-war, in which metaphor, you might say, my teeth served as rope, ensued.

"Get that door shut. You'll let in the cold air." Judith crossed the room and tore down a sheet pinned up behind the stove. Wooded sunlight filtered in from a thin four-paned window serried in bird shit and dust. I'd managed to pull my first bite loose but now the real cud-work had begun.

"Is this it?" Willis asked. His eyebrows retreated as his nose quested across the rafters like a rat's.

"You were expecting what?" Judith asked. She dropped her pack. "Flat screens?"

We crowded into the foyer, stomping our boots on a worn mat, and proceeded into the main sitting area, the cabin cool, dusky, pungent with mothballs, a rank, old-tobacco-like musk. You wouldn't need a builder's level to know that the entire foundation was grossly off-kilter. The roof leaned, the steps leaned, the laths. The door's bottom rail sat askew of its jamb. I felt wickedly off-kilter myself. Low nylon cots spanned the wall opposite the kitchen, which was of unpainted drywall. I called dibs on the cot nearest the door (for ease of egress), and stowed my pack and rifle under the bed frame. The mattress was sturdier than I expected, though short and bowed near the head. At the centre of the room sat an old Ping-Pong table, absent net, a stack of black folding chairs, two bar stools, and an embroidered loveseat with an occult scroll of ducks and frothy streams repeating across its cushions and arms. I stretched out on my cot and gazed up at the rafters where tiny white mushrooms bloomed in between bands of old rotten weatherboard which were themselves eruptive with moss. Was this normal? Dangerous?

There was a thump at the door, and Isaac shouldered his way inside, carrying our last cooler of food. "Can someone help me with this?"

"Over there," Willis said. "There's room in the fridge."

My father came past my cot and sauntered into the kitchen. "Well, this is interesting," he said. He picked up one of the knives and began brushing and scraping the edge of the knife along the dry bony joint of his thumb. "This is actually pretty sharp."

"Please don't touch those," Judith said.

Adjacent the loveseat was a complicated shelving unit whose

forked trestles and sills housed many paperbacks. *The Spy Who Came in from the Cold*, José Ortega y Gasset's *Meditations on Hunting, Trees and Shrubs of Newfoundland and Labrador: Field Guide, Actual Air* by David Berman. I hopped up from my cot and pocketed the guide.

Judith and Willis intended to camp outdoors, leaving my father, Isaac, and I the cabin. I unrolled my duffel and loaded my pillow sleeve with excess sweaters and pants. Then I changed out of my jeans and pulled on my good socks and thermal underwear and turtleneck. I felt blocky and volatile in my hunting garb. I didn't feel young. The polyester rain pants I'd rented from the Castle clung to my thighs and made a weird chafing sound like a straw grabbing at a near-empty glass as I shambled around the cabin.

As I bent down to grab my Weatherby, Judith came forward with a pair of binoculars. She put a hand on my shoulder. "Why don't we stick with these for now?" she said.

"I'm not bad," I said. "Really."

Judith shook her head. "Rules are rules," she said.

We retained our earlier teams. Judith would lead Isaac and my father west of the cabin across a low river valley, while myself and Willis would head back down to the beach and canvass the shoreline.

Judith crept a finger over her map. Along her nail were horizontal white slits. "Now look, if you want, if you two start looping back around this way, say, around one-ish," she said, indicating an amoebic green splotch on the map, "we could probably link back up in here some-where, by this little bend in the river, for lunch."

"Unless we're on the trail of something, you mean?" Willis said. He made a note on our map with his carpenter pencil, which was a short flat yellow pencil with a squared lead.

"Of course," said Judith. She refolded her map and stuffed it back in her coat pocket. "We'll just play it by ear."

"Not that I expect we'll be seeing much of anything this late in the day," Willis said.

"Tomorrow, we'll start bright and early," Judith said.

I couldn't decide how best to carry my binoculars, dangling uncapped from my neck or bundled away in my bag. They were bulkier than I might've liked and painted a splintery tan. As we scooped along the trail, I knelt where Willis knelt, surveying trees, miscellaneous networks of branches I kept misconstruing for antlers. Willis endured these errors and the eagerness with which I summoned them with placid frustration.

"That's just a big rock," he'd say. Or, "Those are birches," and so on.

We swerved off the main trail and spent an hour or so crouching around a slippery, stump-addled path adjacent the shoreline, descending sleek rocky crevices, passing much lichen and moss and tidy nubbles of excrement, the freshest of which Willis dutifully studied and massaged.

"Moose?"

"Naw. That's caribou shit. Moose poop's bigger and oval. A caribou's shit's smaller, pelleted, more like a Raisinet. But see how shiny this is? I don't even need to touch it," he said, touching it. "Like this is really fresh. And a big dump, too."

I studied the shit, unsure if I accepted the analogy.

We continued to the water in silence. I ate another PowerBar and drank most of a lemon Gatorade I'd found in the fridge. I could hear the lake stirring to one side of us and a joyous brook bending coolly through the trees. A few of the trees were scarred blonde and bands of bloodied antler velvet swung in the broken bushes like a pitcher plant's drifted slipper. By now my spotting was proving so ineffectual that I hoped to resist the urge to name those things that Willis might shoot, for fear of reprimand. In any case, it was hard enough just keeping my footing. My fingers were tacky with sap-muck and blisters welled on my heels. As the sound of running water grew nearer, we slowed to a stop. Willis pointed first at the ground, which was imprinted with round, crescent-shaped tracks, and then to his forehead, before squatting behind a rock and raising his binoculars. I squatted also. Below us, through a mass of leaning firs, snuffling at a ghostly spray of lichen, stood a large brown shape with hard shiny antlers and a white rump—a caribou, I guessed. The antlers were short, reddish, and remarkably symmetrical; coved, four tines to a brow.

"Is that a bull?" I asked.

"Do you see a penis sheath?"

"You mean like a foreskin?" I adjusted the finder on my binoculars, and queried the blurry brown mass.

"Foreskins hood glans. An ungulate's dick's passive, gets burrowed, retracted all the way up. So what you're left with is a preputial sheath. Are you registering any preputial sheath?"

"No," I said. "And please stop saying preputial."

"So what does that tell you?"

"But I thought only bulls have antlers," I said, and felt very dumb indeed.

"Tell me where you're seeing this penis sheath?"

"So it's a woman?"

"A cow," said Willis, raising himself up from behind our rock.

"Meaning we can't kill it?"

"That's right."

We waited for the cow to move on before breaking clear of the treeline and stumbled toward the beach. I'd always prided myself on my sense of direction, my ability to compass the obscurest circuits and cityscapes, but it occurred to me that I had no idea where we stood in relation to our cabin, or where—gazing down the beach, admiring its spiny issuings and swirls—we'd docked. This minor disorientation asserted a strange terror over me. It was akin to the episodes of sleep paralysis I experienced with disturbing frequency as a boy—immobile, encradled in the thick paralysis of REM sleep, my mind utterly awake to its imprisonment. In the darkness of those nights faces formed in my room. I would see a tall laughing man with a skinny black moustache who would look at me and, the instant our eyes locked, suddenly stop laughing; or else a dark shape that somewhat resembled my grandmother: the stern bulk of her skull feeling its way over my blanket, across my chest, the weight of its breath, or my own, hissing. I would try to speak, to ward these apparitions away from my unshifting limbs, but my lips wouldn't summon a word. Time, it seemed, was my only salve. But there would be no apparitions here, no delusive visitors. Now, on the beach, as I faced away from the wind and regarded the water, across which a few lusterless, slag-bellied clouds stood reflected, I tried to resign myself to this disorientation, this spell. I rubbed my hands and listened to the sound of Willis wading through the water. It was a good sound, and the sturdy break of waves chucking upon the rocks soothed me. I sat down and nestled myself up against a stack of brown rugged stones. I hadn't looked at my phone in nearly twenty-four hours, and I wondered, again, if they'd called the election. My thumbs, so accustomed to clicking, scrolling, dragging, grabbing, liking, unliking, enjoyed an odd flexibility, full of clumsy potential, even if I didn't really know what to do with them. Tracing the adjustable eyecups of the binoculars, twiddling the finely grooved wheel, I remembered the weight of my phone, its chipped case and soiled inner slip, which I missed like a dead mechanism, a phantom limb.

"What, we napping now?" Willis asked.

"No," I said. "Just resting."

I accepted the hand Willis offered me and sprung up onto my feet with stunning facility. Willis brushed the silt from my shoulders, and suffered me what felt like a fatherly glare. "Take some water," he said.

Around noon, we started back up the streambed and into the woods. Willis had given up on spotting through the trees and we tottered swiftly along the banks locating our party in a small grove, a metropolis of nodding alders and aspen.

I'm not sure what Willis expected, but for ten grand a pop he seemed pretty chagrined by the offerings. Perhaps he envisioned too-English scenes awash in wool foulards and hounds—a parliament of green gabardines. I could see it now. With our bowlers and brogues and buckskin gloves, we'd reassemble, mid-hunt, for champagne cocktails abreast one of those lavish Rolls-Royces with the boxy wooden gun troughs and leathered cases snuggled over the mudguards.

Hardened footmen and their idiot understudies would top up our cocktails and serve us flat silver trays of cucumber sandwiches, fish-finger toasties—whatever else these imperial sportsmen of old imbibed.

As it was, our prepackaged fried bologna sandwiches and veggie wraps were about on par with your prevailing airplane catering. The falafels were scanty and stale, the hummus runny. Willis hadn't touched his and I couldn't tell what he intended to communicate by way of this hunger strike.

Isaac had brought along a tiny stove he'd constructed out of pop can bottoms looted from the blue bins behind the Castle's dining hall. Who knew where (or by what means) he'd acquired the black film canister of white gas which he decanted into the base of his stove and lit with a strike and ferro rod. It took him less than ten minutes to boil a pot of water which he poured over a biodegradable satchel of ramen. When he was finished he made everyone pour-over coffee.

"Anyone for milk?" Isaac asked. He held up a bag of white powder.

"Thanks, no," my father said. "The nighted colour denotes me truly."

"What'd you use to make these perforations?" Judith asked.

"Scratch awl. Guess you could probably get away with a screw or even a screwdriver if you wanted."

After lunch, we traipsed back down to the stream, following a dark, sluggish current, banked in torn sallow foam. We picked our way along its edges in stealthy subterfuge. Pond striders skated across the water's slow glassy surface, their long middle legs whipping back and forth like oars. As we continued along the stream, I noted that the water now seemed to be rising steadily over the banks.

"Are we splitting up?" Willis asked. "The day's not young, but—"

"Something stinks," my father said.

He wasn't wrong. The air had taken on a definite fecal spice— of sweltering sewers bricked in urinous crotch rot, of marshy, long-festering stool. I hiked my shirt over my nose and availed myself of a sharp sour dose of my own design. A hump of stone sprawled in the stream's middle and along its edges the water forked fast and spumy.

"Fuck," Willis said. "Not again."

"What is that?" I asked.

We neared the obstruction. Swatches of bloat shone on the broad clay-coloured frame. Judith set her rifle on a banked gravel bar and started into the stream. She did not seem in the least bothered by the cold as the water treaded up past the knees of her waders.

"Caribou?" my father asked.

"Moose," Judith said.

I stalked upstream to get a sense of the front. It hadn't a head.

"Looks like poachers made off with the antlers," Willis said. He pointed to a ragged, slantwise laceration starting back from the spine. Maggots rutted in the unwanted chuck. "How long you think it's been here?" he asked.

"Hard to say," Judith said, scooching around the carcass. She unzipped her jacket and fished out a digital camera and snapped some pictures. "You can tell there've been ravens at it, but the hide's too tough and cold for them to break all the way through."

"Man," Willis said, leaning in. "What'd they use on the head? Imagine lemon zesters make cleaner cuts than this. Christ. There's bones and chips and shit all over the goddamn place."

"I'm not seeing any bullet holes," Judith said.

"The ribs are all poked up on the side here," Willis said.

"Crazy how preserved things can get just in water," my father observed.

Isaac edged past me, his gait stiff, soldiery. "When it comes to freezing," he said, "what we want to concern ourselves with are gross melts." He slipped a hand into his coat pocket and hauled out a thin spiral notebook and pen. "I'm talking anthrax in permafrost in the Siberian tundra. Microbial breakdown. Adaptable pathogens."

"Siberian anthrax," my father said. "I'm listening."

"Because if you want to look at vectors of contagion, revived bacterium, then—"

Willis shushed him. Judith steadied herself in the water and shimmied along the back half of the corpse. "Pass me a stick, would you?"

I rummaged around in the brambles for a decent stick. The best I could drum up was a blistered log with a bulbed, faintly sceptred end.

"Come on," she said. "Toss it over."

I entered the stream and flung the stick toward her, upwind of the current. Judith caught the stick and flipped it around, prodding at the underside of the moose with the cudgelled end, tilting her head away from the smell. "Looks like it's latched on there pretty good," she said.

She splashed ashore and handed me the stick. The whole thing was mucked over in slime.

"Thanks," I said.

Judith squatted on the gravel bar and unbuckled her pack. She withdrew a coil of coated manila rope and a yellow strap with two metal biners lashed to either end. Water riffled from the backs of her waders onto the gritty stones. On the side of her pack was a small hatchet and a short cabled tool with a red crank—a sort of winch or pulley or what Willis kept calling a "come-along." Judith unhooked this device and gathered the rope and strap and clumped up the bank. She stopped at the base of a broad birch, and rocked her shoulders against its trunk.

It didn't budge.

"Can I ask what difference it makes hauling him out of the water or is that a dumb question?" my father wanted to know.

"It's not a major problem," Judith said, belting the yellow strap around the base of the trunk and tugging in the slack. "But I'd sooner have him sunning above ground for the coyotes and ravens than freezing his ass off underneath." She released a catch on the winch and paid out a line of cable, which she dragged back down to the water.

"You want me to work the lever?" Willis asked.

"Sure," Judith said. "Just make sure the line is tight." She looked at me, Isaac, my father. "Okay. Now you two," she said, meaning, I assumed, my father and I, "it's time to get wet."

My father thrashed into the water with galling enthusiasm. Judith tossed him an end of rope. Together they squirmed the rope under the lodged carcass, drawing the line up over the forelegs and shredded neck.

"I'm not much for knots," my father said, considering the two ends of rope.

"Please just do it for him," I said, waving my stick. I stood partway in the stream. Water lapped at the tops of my boots. It wasn't clear to me what my role was, but, as self-appointed overseer or project manager, I felt it a duty incumbent on me to shore up efficiencies.

"I can figure it out," my father said, a little injured.

Judith snatched the rope from my father and, applying a few mysterious twists and loops, knotted the ends together and fastened the spiralled noose to the cable's hook. "Easy-peasy," she said; and then, turning up the bank to Willis, "Okay. Grab in that slack."

Willis, kicked out at the base of the birch, one-armed the lever and the moose jerked forward. I plotted my stick underneath the back legs and jimmied away the rocks. Helping or hindering—who could say? As the moose snaked onto dry berm I thought I heard something crack.

"Hang on," I said. "I think it's hooked on something back here." I stepped my left foot forward. The stream was much deeper than I'd thought. Now I could feel the water rushing coolly through my boots.

"You okay?" Judith asked.

"It's slippery," I said.

"Careful," she said. "Just be careful."

Willis cranked the winch and the stick broke apart in my hands. I burst forward, teetering suspensefully on my back foot, and fell face-first into the stream.

A bad feeling followed.

My mind blanked, as great gulps of raw muddy water greeted my nose and throat and lungs. I swam and spat. My head surged briefly above water, but my boots, my beautiful new boots, had gotten snared on a rock or subaqueous root system. I couldn't stand up, and I soon found myself fully submerged. Had I lodged myself in a pocket of squelchy quicksand? Was quicksand even endemic to the island? I held a leg. There were bumps on the leg. And I thought: Why are there bumps? All along the bone of its shin ran a label of these little, like, spherical corms or boils. And I thought: Why am I touching them? Firm as frigid gummy bears.

I opened my eyes, tried dragging myself up the tumorous leg and onto a more significant aspect of moose. This too was not a happy feeling. I felt like I was searching through a loaf of curdled tofu. There really wasn't much there. Above me a disturbed world faltered and swung. So this is how it ends, I thought, just as hands—Willis's—swooped down and grabbed me, fetching me up onto shore, a heaving, spitting thing.

How much of this does one describe? How much am I better off suppressing? Rivulets of sludge issued from my chin. A milky gruel passed from my lips like battery acid. The smell was no longer an external entity but an internal one, and I, its reeking locus.

"I thought I felt something biting on my line," Willis said, hysterical with laughter.

All but Isaac attended me. Judith handed me water, Willis—with much effort—worked off my boots and wrung out my socks, while my father helped me out of my sweater and draped his own coat over my shoulders. As an undergrad, I'd once witnessed, mid-class, a prof break down before us in the throes of an epileptic event. One minute he pondered the board, dawdling, chalk in hand, and the next thing I knew he was down on the floor stricken with alien convulsions. I hadn't known what to do then and so remained in my seat. I watched as others, braver and bolder than I, rushed to the fallen man, loosening his shirt and tie, gliding a soft spongy binder under his head.

So, as I sat there, drinking water, shivering, I knew, or like to think I knew, where Isaac was coming from, keeping his distance, sitting apart, with his notebook and pen, grimly, or so it seemed to me, recording all.

FIFTEEN

MY CASTLE PANTS DANGLED FROM THE RAFTERS, MY MERINO
underthings, my socks.

Judith had fired up the stove for me (and, I assumed, for supper)
as soon as we stepped back into the cabin, and a single log burned
over the coals. Beads of moisture slid from my pants, bubbling on
the stove plate like sizzled spit. Everyone insisted on pampering me,
and I welcomed the indulgences. The hot mug of tea, the towels and
blankets and borrowed socks, the bowl of corn chips and homespun
salsa verde, the moose jerky Willis had wanted to save for tomorrow
but was willing to part with, partly, he said, because one whiff of me
had—and I quote—"ruined moose." Judith even let me smoke indoors.

But before any of this, the shower Judith required I take was the
crudest and worst of my life—and by some distance. Nudely I squatted
(or was made to squat) on a sage-green tarp inside a low-pitched
vanity dome Judith had rigged up out of mosquito netting and tent poles.
A gap in the dome admitted a soft rubber catheter through which a jerky
spray of water resembling a camel's gleek dribbled onto my person via
a hyperactive bladder my father and Judith took turns milking from
above. The experience was about how I imagine getting peed on in the

woods in mid-October at the behest of an exacting but encouraging stranger ("Make sure you squirt behind your ears!") and giggling father might feel, only colder and lonelier and worse.

Now I sat in the cabin—assigned an indoor task—on the love seat, enshrouded in towels, cubing potatoes—binning sprouts, skins, suspect blotches of chlorophyll. A black mop bucket served as a receptacle. I was trying to avoid landing too many scraps in the wringer, but my hands were still freezing and one can only be so diligent. Anyway, my work was impatient, brash. There were two bottles of red open on the table and I drank, democratically, from both. I worried at the state of our cutting board, which was oniony and dull, worn funky with cuts.

Willis chopped wood. I could hear the steady chuck of his axe as the logs drew cleanly away. Isaac and Judith had set up shop at one of the picnic tables just outside the cabin under a marquee of canted aluminum and were prepping the rest of our dinner by lamplight, readying salads and patting our thick fatty T-bones with salt. My father was nominally in charge of amassing kindling for the stove, ferreting Willis's chopped logs to the firewood rack at the back of the cabin. He sifted in the pricklier thickets for scrolls of burnable birchbark, jabbing at the tangles of red elderberry with a poker.

We ate inside. The light was fast vanishing but the fire and mantle lanterns admitted a hospitable glow. I set the table, arraying two folding chairs apiece along each of the sidelines, reserving a place for Judith at the head of the Ping-Pong table, amid faded end centre line. Judith fried our potatoes with whole mushrooms and onions on a skillet smeared in gluey bear grease rendered from the fat of a black boar—"That's a boy bear," Willis clarified for me—she'd killed earlier that year; the grease was apparently great for pastries, and could double as a preventative tonic, she said, not naming names but indicating my scalp with a fork, for baldness.

After dinner, I helped clear away the dishes. Outside there were three rubber sinks on a separate picnic table and we filled each of these with cooling, boiled water. One for scrubbing, one for rinsing, and one (into which Judith dissolved a Steramine tablet) for sanitizing. We dried the utensils by hand and left the dishes to drip on a collapsible wire rack inside the cabin. The grey water Willis hurled in the woods.

I'd purchased a bottle of Laphroaig Quarter Cask from the commissary's reasonably priced and admirably stocked liquor store, my lone financial contribution, and once we were all settled back in the cabin, I poured out some glasses.

"Isaac," I said. "You're sure?"

He shook his head. "Marshmallows work for me."

We brought our chairs in front of the stove and opened the grate.

Willis, to my horror, tipped an entire can of Coke into his Scotch, Judith stuck to wine, and my father accepted a small mustard glass with water. We clinked glasses and watched the open throat of the stove. My father relaxed his iron poker against his knee. A smear of ash grimed his right cheek. Judith outlined the game plan for our morning hunt and we agreed to an early night. I felt contented, full, drunk, finally warm, and maybe even excited. My father squatted on a tomato-red blanket, mopping coals with his poker, as the smoke swung over his eyes.

"Do you want to tell us something about your brother?" my father asked.

We looked at Isaac, and then, disturbed by his silence, averted our gaze.

"I remember how he used to build robots," Isaac said, and picked up a marshmallow stick, capering the sculpted end in the fire.

"In the garage," said Willis, nodding.

"They had no specific function, but they looked so cool. He'd hammer down these odd pieces of wood," Isaac said, whacking a rock with his stick, "and get them all stuck together with random wires, old calculator parts, buttons and widgets and green circuit boards, with their transistors, those buggy microchips and little cream-coloured diodes with the red bands round them."

"They were complex," Willis said.

"And he used to face oncoming traffic, I guess. That was another thing. Whenever we walked somewhere together, like Churchill Square or St. Pat's, he didn't like me standing near the edge. Though you know sometimes I'd try to trick him. I'd stop to fix a shoelace and then step to the other side, but he'd always find a way of shifting it. So if something bad were to happen, like if a car were all of a sudden to leap up over the curb, it'd be him that got hit, and not me."

I topped off my Scotch and pulled my hoodie up over my hat. I stretched out my legs and listened for my knees, trying to distinguish their cracking cartilage from the snap and seethe of logs.

"I remember the first year he won the Tely," said Willis.

"This was the year he finally beat Colin?" my father asked.

"Colin was older. Past his prime."

"Still," my father said. "That was the year, wasn't it? And he was what? Sixteen? Seventeen?"

"He'd just turned seventeen," said Isaac.

"It's incredible," my father said.

"46:59," said Willis. "He took McCloy's record by just a hair. McCloy was twenty-two when he set that."

Isaac reached into his pocket and took out a small wooden box with a polished lid.

"What are you doing?" Willis asked.

"I'm just looking," said Isaac.

He set his thumb in the lid's groove, drew back the top, and peered inside.

"What's that?" Judith asked.

"Ashes," said Willis.

"It's more than that," Isaac started, and then he stopped, and didn't say anything. He shut the lid and tucked the little box back in his pocket. "Do you remember the year he wanted us to celebrate his birthday by only watching movies and listening to music from the year he was born?"

"I can't remember what we watched."

A log cracked and my father prodded the fire. Judith refilled her wine. I was trying to remember what year Travis was born, what movies came out when, but, phoneless, these details fluttered just out of reach, faint shapes traipsing in a misty scrim of fog.

"He ate yogurt with a fork," Willis said.

"And never stirred it. Liked to keep his fruit tucked away in the bottom, a treat, a sort of dessert. It made me sick," Isaac said.

"Peaches. For years he claimed he was allergic. I kept telling him we're having cobbler, it's good, and your mother and I we wouldn't poison you, but he never touched it."

"Why was he so stubborn?"

"It drove me insane," Willis said. He reached past the fire and fed in another log. Embers trembled and glowed. "With the peaches. You couldn't reason with him."

"People forget, because of his athleticism, because he was such an athlete, but people think he wasn't self-conscious, like he didn't have all these fucked-up inner feelings and stuff," Isaac said. "But he could be very sensitive. Part of the reason, growing up, he always had long hair, was he had this birthmark," he continued, shaping a nickel-sized oval with his thumb and index finger, "just over his ear, and I know he was self-conscious about that, didn't want people asking him about it, even though you could still sort of see it. Like the hair covered it up okay, but the part with the mark was just ever so slightly darker. If you knew what you were looking for, you could definitely like—"

"He used to love making sandwiches."

"And Mom, whenever she made pie, she would sometimes leave him these scraps of dough and he'd fold them over these big blobs of jam or sugared apples, throw them in the oven, and voila! Pastries."

"Those were delicious." Willis swilled his drink, shuddered, sipped, shuddered again.

"You remember when we took that trip to England?" Isaac asked.

"The three of us. Your mother had, I can't remember, some conference, but Travis, I guess he might've been in spring training, but he wasn't with us, it was just us three."

"Before Pen was even born."

"That's right. And you were pretty young, too."

"But I still remember it. All those museums. St. Paul's. The Whispering Gallery. I remember I got lost in the Tate Modern."

"You had your mother and I scared shitless," Willis said.

Isaac let go a quick laugh. "I didn't mean to," he said.

"I know," said Willis. "I know you didn't."

"I guess I don't know what happened, but I got all turned around, and I found myself in this room, this big old lonely white room full of trees. Or not trees, I guess. But dead trees. Dead trees done up to look like living ones."

Isaac trailed his stick over the fire, toasting the sides in the ashpit.

"It's funny," he said, "because I've been thinking about that room an awful lot lately. Not about getting lost in the museum. But the trees. Penone's the name of the artist, the guy who built them. I can't remember his first name. And how he did it," Isaac said, backing his stick out of the fire, "was he had all these pieces of, like, industrial larch, okay. And he broke these big pieces down into smaller pieces so that by carving them up he could show or discover the shape of a young tree. Like a sapling exhumed."

Isaac shook his head. "I think the point of it," he went on, "was to show how we are all of us in the modern world so divorced from nature that we forget, when we look at a big block of wood, that this was once just this tiny little tree and so on. But, you know, for me, that's not what sticks out in my mind." He paused, and it occurred to me that, in all the time he'd been speaking, Isaac had not once taken his eyes off the fire. "When I think about getting lost in the museum, and I remember those trees, honestly, all I can think about is Travis."

"Isaac," Willis said. His voice sounded sharp but only at first. The timbre here was pleading, needful. He reached out and touched his son's leg, gently, almost hovering. I couldn't imagine what Willis might be thinking, where he worried this story might go.

"It's okay, Dad. I'm fine," Isaac said. "Honest. I want to tell it."

Willis removed his hand and stroked his beard.

"When I think about those small trees, I recognize that they're dead, okay. Like I said: just these dead blocks of wood. But because of their shape I also can't help but think about what they might become: trees. Which is the same thing, of course, as saying what they once were: trees. I know I'm not putting this well," he said. "But the little trees give off an illusion of growth. They're like budding fossils, somehow. Dead things notionally stripped of death. And I think that I'm most intrigued by this image. Or idea. My mind's ability to see two things at once, two shapes evolving new memories in each other, two shapes in which the other is always found. And when I think about Travis, that's what I think about, I guess. Him, me, us. We are young, old, dead, alive. One whittled, the other whittling." Isaac closed his eyes and drew in a breath. "I feel like the little tree, the fossil that suggests his memory."

Nobody spoke. We stared into the fire. I admired the lick of the embers, and the way the flames seemed to comb out a certain groove, tracing uncharted avenues.

"And what about you?" Judith said.

"Me?" It'd taken me a moment to register the direction of her question.

"Why not?" said Willis.

I readjusted myself in my chair, set my Scotch down at my feet. Willis stared at me, the whites of his eyes steady and pearled.

"He was a nice kid," I said. "Confident, brave. Whatever you want to call it. Generous, I think." I stopped, passed my palms over the fire. "I see a lot of young people, a lot of students, but Travis, well, he always struck me as something of an old soul, like, even remembering times when he was younger, when you and Caitlin just had him, there was always this seriousness about him, a gravity, I guess, that set him apart. Most of the students I see, they're just names. Names I see for a while in my inbox. Even the ones who do well, who work hard, engage with the material, and with whom I form I guess you could say a sort of connection, I forget them, their faces, with remarkable speed, their names, it's all lost. But Travis, I don't know. I mean I didn't know him as a student, that's not what I'm trying to say. But for me, I guess, he left an impression. He said something to me once. It was just after the Olympic Trials in Calgary. He said he felt relieved. Relieved that he didn't make it. And I thought—I remember thinking at the time—how that seemed like a remarkably adult thing to say. To know."

"He didn't mean that," Willis said. "I know for a fact he was devastated. He worked his ass off."

"I'm not saying he didn't," I said.

"There are certain windows in running. You wouldn't understand. Marathoners, yes, sure, you'll find elite runners in their thirties, maybe into their forties. Maybe. But on the track?" Willis scraped his heel along the soiled floor. "You don't know the first thing about it."

"Of course I don't," I said. "I completely agree with you. I haven't got a fucking clue. But I'm just telling you what he told me."

"Are you now?" Willis said.

"Word for word," I said, and wanted to say more but stopped. All day I sensed Willis regretted telling me about the manifesto, about Isaac. The snide comments and snappish rebuttals—it made sense. This (I think) is the problem with secrets, with sharing. Willis hated himself for confiding, but he hated me even more because I listened.

We were silent. Judith took a small wooden pipe from her cardigan pocket and a leather pouch of tobacco. She spread a small pinch over the bowl, tapping loose strands over the screen. Her pipe had a weathered, academic quality, which, somewhat ironically, robbed it of pretentiousness. With Isaac's marshmallow stick she drew an ember from the fire and lit up. Her chin was mottled with creases but the skin on her cheeks and under her eyes was smooth and youthful, utterly lineless. We were all just watching her now, waiting. She firmed her cheeks and released the smoke, barely opening her lips, and the cloud she blew was even and heavy.

My father turned to her. "And so what about you, then?" he said. "What's your story?"

SIXTEEN

"MY STORY. WHERE TO START? THERE'S THE STORY OF HOW
I got here and there's the story about what that here became."

Judith stood and paced, patrolling the slabbed stonework that
circuited the back half of the cabin. She sucked her pipe. A thorned
shadow feathered her throat. We waited. An eccentric reverence
animated the subdued status of our waiting, serene and worshipful,
an avid calm.

"I was driving across the province," Judith said. "This was late
April, the week of the BP oil spill, and the roads, for some reason, were
clotted with campers. I had just left or begun the interminable process
of leaving my second husband and I wanted—no—needed away from
the city, from my work, and fast. I'd booked a crossing at Port-aux-
Basques and allotted two days for driving. The drive is doable in a day
solo with the right music or radio programming and an IV drip of coffee
flowing through your system but I thought to space it out over two.

"I said to myself, Listen.

"The drive is the thing.

"The road, the fog, this incomprehensible convoy of campers.

"I spent the night in Corner Brook, in a hotel off the highway, barely inside the city. I turned on the TV and searched out images of the disaster because all day long on CBC that's what I'd listened to, disasters. Unending updates and reports.

"It was refreshing, in a sense, to finally see water, rig and waves topped in flame. It was as yet too early for the pictures of beaches and birds, those poor loggerheads, scutes basted in petrol, but my mind went there. It had to.

"Pelicans, gannets, egrets. I love gannets. For years I studied them. Predation memory habits—that was my beat. Probably I love gannets more than most people."

Judith drew on her pipe, admiring the bowl's tight scarlet gleam.

"You might know more about this than me," Judith said, indicating yours truly with her pipe.

The face I constructed for her aspired to bewilderment. I had no idea where she was going with this.

"Did you know that the first mention of a gannet in written English occurs in Old English, in *Beowulf*, where the narrator or speaker likens the sea to a ganotes bæth?"

I didn't. Of course I didn't.

"Gander, gans, from the Latin anser. Solus goose. Morus bassanus. Morus is Latin for mulberry while bassanus refers to Bass Rock. North Berwick. Home to the largest colony in the world. Spanish dictionaries give gannet as Alcatraz. The French opt for Le Fou de Bassan.

"Jugged hare, what the French call civet de lièvre, where you stew the rabbit in red wine and juniper, and serve the little bunny foo foo up in a fountain of its own blood, looks very like an oiled-over bird, incidentally. In oozing outline, baked.

"But let's skip ahead. Let's just for once assume fire and mutilated birds and roiling oceans turbid with hydrocarbons, and move on."

The smoke coming off her pipe smelled of moist cloves and cinnamon. I could differentiate between the fire and pipe smoke and the nose of my Scotch—a medicinal citrus leathered in burned grass and rain; or, per Willis, "This tastes exactly how a wet dog smells—

with maybe a hint of rotten mandarin?" I sipped at intervals, listening to Judith—her clean, limber sentences, their liquid soothe and swerve, reminded me of my earliest professors, that selfsame narcotic lull—collating the slow progress of char on my tongue.

"So I was alone," Judith said.

"I was alone, and I thought: Something needs to change here or I do. The idea lodged itself in my mind with an awesome intensity.

"The following morning I woke up early and drove the rest of the way to the ferry, waited in the queue by the terminal, before an announcement was made and we, all the many, many campers, and I, began inching our way onto the boat. The vehicle deck. I didn't have a cabin and I'd brought the wrong book. *The Last Happiness* or *In the Valley of the Wood* or *The Arborist's Daughter* and yet somehow utterly off. Almost inside of a sentence, I knew. So I set it aside and wandered around the boat. We hadn't even left the harbour—you could still see the terminal, the navy stacks insigniated with the Marine Atlantic's white wavy logo—and I had nothing to read, no cabin, no one to talk to, and the only movies on offer were cartoons or cartoonish adult opiates on the order of *Forrest Gump* and *Field of Dreams*—which and I'm sorry but no.

"So I walked and walked. Past the cafeteria, past the bar, which was open, the VLTs already buzzing with patrons (it was maybe nine in the morning), and past the video arcade room where children of all ages were gravely assembled, the Pong blips and FINISH HIMs lingering on my skin like aerosol, and into the gift shop where the only books available were those provincial ghost story anthologies and nonsense word searches, which I glanced at and abandoned, feeling at the tags of the stuffed lobsters and moose, reading the tartan magnets with the names printed on them, touching the pens and whittled whale art, perusing the expensive local candies and chocolates and rum and butter kisses and I thought—we still hadn't left the harbour—I hate men, I really hate men, all men, all the men, present company included," Judith said. "No offence."

Isaac tensed. He looked into his father's face for a response, some frenzied rejoinder, but Willis's expression returned little more than a relentless tranquility, as if the words had sifted right through him.

"I came out of the store and continued onto the deck," Judith said, a puff of smoke wreathing her cheeks, rising up over unwinking eyes, "and—well, there we go, we were finally pulling away. But what was I doing here? Where was I going? I had no plans on the continent. Literally no plans. I have family in Nova Scotia, good friends or former good friends in New Brunswick, Quebec, etc., but what I wanted was total anonymity, to separate myself from everyone, including myself, and I could see—I was almost smiling—that I'd more or less obtained that, on the ship, looking out at the gush of water finally billowing behind us and thinking every so often about the oil lurching out of the Gulf and how whatever was coming out of there would be coming out here, too, how the two places were joined, or—more specifically, and perhaps this to your point, Isaac—how there were never two, that two was not entirely accurate, that there was only and always ever one."

Isaac was nodding now, his gaze sober and rapt. Branches bandied about the cabin's scoured cladding. My father stoked the fire and cracked his toes. He'd taken off his boots and socks, and the tops of his feet were hairless and pale.

"My rage, which is not the word I want," Judith said, "was located in precisely two places: my husband, my ex-husband, about whom I will say no more; and the spill. The spill was man-made, was male. All spills, all wars, are."

Again Willis appeared unmoved. Had all the trolling and rage-baiting he experienced at Østlig finally chastened him? Maybe therapy had awakened a meditative resilience. Or maybe he was just beaten down from the hunt. Or non-hunt.

"I was on sabbatical—technically, just starting my sabbatical—and yet I had no real intention of carrying on with my research. I was tired of teaching and wanted out of the academy. Wanting to apply myself to more radical interests. No more meetings, no more supervisory committees, no more mind-numbing invigilations. No more cap and gown. I needed out. And I thought here maybe was my chance, my out.

"This will sound manic but when, after seven or eight sleepless hours, we finally arrived in North Sydney, here's what I did: I rushed into the Marine Atlantic terminal and purchased a ticket for the next ferry going back to Port-aux-Basques, and within what felt like mere minutes to me—but which of course wasn't—found myself back on the very same boat I'd come across on. And I felt calmed. Stable.

"At 10 p.m. I went to the bar and ordered a plate of prawns and chips. Sat down and read my book. And the book—the same book—was fantastic! It kept me up all night. The blurbs weren't lying. *In the Valley of the Wood* or whatever was compulsively readable and, by turns, unflinchingly brave.

"So I was going home. Finally. Finally I was headed in the right direction.

"Or was I? The next morning, getting off the ferry for the second time in as many days, I pulled into an Irving Big Stop and consulted my map. I was roughly seven hundred kilometres away from L'Anse aux Meadows, which, appropriately provisioned, I could manage. I'd always intended to visit L'Anse aux Meadows, the Norse hovels and grassy smelters and so forth, but, in all my years on the island—we arrived fall of '72—somehow I'd never managed to find the time.

"Which I know, I know: horrible.

"I popped into the Irving and procured supplies. Jam Jams, Pringles, trail mix. Two single brown bananas and a bag of apples with the dull yellow flesh and the red skin you just know will leave your lips all tingled and puffy and I bought a crossword puzzle and a book about ghosts and shipwrecks and a cheap pair of sunglasses which I asked the attendant if he wouldn't mind snipping the little black plastic band or whatever from the frame (which, incidentally, is how I met my third husband, Doug) so that I could wear them out of the store. I got back in the car, turned on the radio, and headed west.

"My phone was dead. I'd forgotten to charge it on the boat, both times. This didn't bother me as, recall, this was of an era when we didn't feel so umbilically fettered to our technology, our devices.

"So I drove west, this time ignoring the news, and listened to music exclusively. And the station—I don't know what station I was listening to—but every song that came on I knew by heart.

"I guess that I was so wrapped up in this music, singing along, drumming my hands on the steering wheel, that I somehow managed to take a wrong turn. Which sounds impossible on a highway, but I was completely shut of the main nerve. And, as I was trying to get myself back on track, pulling into a chained-off logging road to zip myself back around, I saw a FOR SALE sign. What's this? Land?

"I got out of the car to investigate. It was then much as it is today, rocks, trees—I had, as yet, no idea of the size, the expanse. The sign was just one of those dinky red placards with a phone number scrawled inside a rectangle.

"This felt (and perhaps sounds) cloyingly serendipitous but here's what I did: I jotted down the number in one of my crosswords and drove all the way back to the Irving Big Stop and asked the man who'd clipped my glasses, Doug, if I could possibly plug my phone into an outlet and, in the meantime, were there any pay phones? Yes, he said, very kindly. There was one out front, he said, and then he gave me a quarter. My first investor.

"I placed a call and inquired. Stood outside under the station's lighted roof, which was crammed in between a stack of washer fluid and a cage of propane tanks. The window was coated with posters. Lotto Max, Lotto 6/49, three-for-seven Powerade. The air smelled of cordwood and oil.

"I spoke to a voice and conveyed my eagerness to see this Land. The voice on the phone named a number that was shockingly reasonable—or, with help, with some little assistance, reasonably within reach.

"I hung up the phone. In the bushes, waddling at the edges of the

Irving parking lot, was a small cat-like creature. There is something distinctly kittenish about pine marten, their skittish tails and arching backs, but the slight thickness of their arms and the way they lumber around remind me of bear cubs. This one stopped at the edge of the lot and raised itself up on its hind legs and seemed, for a moment, to study me.

"Apropos that call. I can't—legally I can't—get into specifics here, but I'll say this: Between my savings and inheritance and what I stood to gain in alimony, which included a sizable cash-out refinance (my ex kept the house), and with, crucially, the capital contributions of two silent partners (about whom, sorry, mum's the word), the offer cleared.

"So now I had this Land. I wasn't sure what I wanted to do with it. I only knew that this was exactly where I needed to be. So I hired contractors, a land surveyor, a property developer, etc., and, over the next couple years, built a little house for myself, and another, and some other, more essential facilities. Researchers and students joined me— our summers were initially a sort of tent city—and, eventually, when the time was right, when I'd secured the right backing, I stepped down from the university and moved out here permanently.

"The Castle is a scientific and artistic commune. Open to writers, painters, musicians, documentary filmmakers. But research remains our staff of life. We've got a team experimenting on a moose meat-based salmon feed for offshore fish farms in the hopes of preventing algae blooms. Last summer we had a group of horticulturists from the University of Dresden design a potato-turnip hybrid fortified in vitamin D—known colloquially as a 'potatobega.' We get geologists, linguists, anthropologists. The infrared scanning of road-top temperatures for the purpose of salting areas more prone to freezing—that started here, I'm happy to say.

"And this is fine, okay. This is all well and good. But it still didn't solve my problem—with my problem, in a word, being men."

Judith paused. Isaac crept an ember away from the grate with his stick. Willis, decanting Coke into his empty Scotch glass, watched him.

The ember Isaac tamped out split and the insides came away caked in greying veins. In the corner, set partly in shadow, the raftered mushrooms hung monstrous and bulged and rigidly goitred.

"My aim for this facility, and I am speaking specifically about the hunting," Judith said, "hinges on masculine indulgence. By submersing you in a world without politics, without news, in a world stripped of ambience, or in a world made up exclusively of older ambience, we harness the male ego, its deepest wills, its desire to conquer, kill, quest, and juxtapose these wills against nature. And nature, Mother Nature—"

Judith stopped. She examined her pipe and tapped the bowl's residues into the fire.

"There is nothing, no election here, no politics. The absence is itself political, obviously. But this is not a heavy absence, not a weight.

"It's the absence of men's power, that's the thing. A refuge from all those patriarchal manacles.

"I've been called fringe, a political depressive, a zombie, an eco-nihilist, an eco-fascist, a defeatist, a doomer, a human futilitarian, and worse. I prefer to think of myself as a pragmatist, an opportunistic pessimist, a recluse, a last capitalist. We are self-contained and unexceptional. Our deep winter greenhouses generate produce year-round. Our systems run on hydroelectricity and wind. We provide the illusion and, if you wish, the reality of going off-grid. Our staff are committed. Free to leave whenever they want. Not conscripts. Not serfs bound to this frozen soil. Their freedom is everywhere and they choose here. This is home. This is the place we've all created for ourselves. A place where we all might transform."

Willis yawned. He bottomed his Coke and placed his empty glass on the table and turned up his hood. "Well," he said, rousing himself from the loveseat. "I think it's high time this man turned himself in."

Judith stowed her pipe back in its worn leather pouch. My father retrieved his socks. All was quiet. Beyond us, beyond the one window and writhing trees, rose a bald pewter scalp of moon.

SEVENTEEN

IT RAINED ALL NIGHT. A COLD HEAVY RAIN DRIVING ON THE
warped battens and laths. My sleep was fleeting and dreamless. Pine
cones pelleted the gutters and damp branches frisked at the eaves. My
father snored moistly in the cot opposite me. His snores had a battered,
amphibious quality—beached capelin, I thought, krill-fat, wriggling,
gills crispy with air.

Isaac, cocooned inside a weighted sleeping bag, slept with a
pillowed eye mask full of icy blue beads tensed over his face. "It's for
my circulation," he'd said, dimming his lantern, and creasing the nose
of his mask. "Which is incredibly unstable."

Now—now more than ever, perhaps—I could well understand
Judith's not wanting to sleep in a one-windowed bachelor with three
drunk, grieving men, but Willis's determination to remain outdoors
struck me as so much spartan showmanship. How to square these
minor, survivalist affectations of his? For all his talk, I knew Willis for
a softer, more citied touch. Was this not the same man who, on the
subject of his combed cotton bedsheets (for instance) or the Bavarian
goose-down comforter with its soaring thread count and fill power,
heaped untiring tributes of wistful reverence and praise? True, as a

feral upstart, he'd managed his fair share of bay-bred self-sufficiency, traipsing around in the near wilderness west of Goobies with his uncles, gutting brook trout and salmon, flaying rabbits, but the money had muddled all that, obscured such *Iron John* origin stories as his ancestors had passed on to him; and I'll confess that I sometimes caught myself wondering which of these Willises was cosplaying whom.

The rain let up by first light. And I do mean first light. My father balanced a mug of coffee on the narrow wooden stool beside my cot. I unzipped my bag and fetched inside my pillow for a pair of fresh socks.

"You were talking in your sleep," my father said, striding behind the embroidered love seat, dawdling his palm across its worn, sunken back. "You sat right up in your cot there and you started speaking, waving your hand around like this." My father demonstrated, describing a hasty rectangle. "Wonder you didn't wake Isaac."

I cleared my throat and swung myself over the cot, resting my feet on the shoddy barnboard. "Say anything that warrants canonization?" I asked.

"Nothing of consequence," my father said. "Only you kept saying *It's happening.*"

I snorted and swiped the crud from my eyes with a very cold thumb. I hadn't taken any water with me to bed and dried saliva lined my lips like flaked wax. "*What's* happening?"

"You weren't getting into specifics," my father said.

I sipped my coffee, smoothing the bitter drink across my lips like gloss.

"Anyway," my father said, "it's time you got up and get your shit in order. Willis's fixing breakfast."

A trace of drizzle lingered in the air, and a smell of wood, full of sap sweet and the resinous underneath of bark, carried over the fumes fanning off the cabin's green Coleman stove which Judith had spaced out on one of the picnic tables. Isaac sat before a thin smoky fire. I said my good mornings and took my coffee and my Gerald Murnane to the fireside.

For breakfast Willis fried loose-ground sausage, the leftover onions and mushrooms, alongside a thermos of pre-cracked eggs, which he poured into a squared skillet and scrambled, for some reason, with a twig. We had a package of whole-wheat pitas and peanut butter to go with the eggs and a stack of wan oval lunch meat belted in gelatin and some apples and pears that my father cut up with a pocket knife. He arranged the fruit on a blue plate with a few thick slices of cheddar. Judith produced a bottle of green Tabasco which made the eggs, soggier than I might've liked, palatable.

Isaac stuck to oatmeal and fruit. He crumbled walnuts and raisins into his pouch, stirring his oatmeal with the serrated edge of a stainless steel spoon.

"Not sure I'm seeing the sustainability in all this packaging," said Willis.

"They're omnidegradable," Isaac said. "Paper-based bags layered in organic additives." He tilted the pouch and read along its bulged seam. "The additives react with microbes to create an enzyme that can break the long-chain molecules in plastic."

"So you can compost them?" my father asked.

"Yes and no. Honestly there's no real sense my using these, I guess. Most compost facilities only accept materials that decompose in like eight to twelve weeks. These take a little longer," he said, spooning his slop. "Like you can't just toss them away in your blue bin and hope for the best. Industrial composting, that's the idea."

It was after eight. We were off to a much later start than we'd planned, but nobody seemed bothered in the least. As the morning warmed, the air grew fragrant with mud and a ragged fog floated over the groggy, still-dripping trees. My gear had pretty well dried from the day before but my good socks, which I wore over a pair of thinner ones, were crunchy and tight.

Judith again paired me with Willis. And this was my preference. I was, without question, the weakest link of our party, and I wanted to keep any further evidence of my ineptitude as far away from Judith as I could. The keenness of her judgments—and perhaps, if I'm attempting honesty here, of my father's and maybe even Isaac's, too—intimidated me. Willis, in a sense, was my safest witness. When one considered the mishaps and fuck-ups and depraved confessions that marked our decades-long friendship, what more could I possibly offer up in the way of embarrassments and deficiencies, at this stage, to offend, or even, truly, surprise him? We'd endured each other at our very worst. Through break-ups, bad grades, binges, lost jobs, lost mother, lost father, in Willis's case, lost son.

Not to say, for all this, that Willis made for an obliging playmate. But then Willis would've minded anyone, begrudged the silent, loyal company of a hardened bloodhound, a veteran scenter with gored boars to its name. Still, I could tell from his sighs and the stiffening span of his shoulders and the two firm folds of skin pulsing down the middle of his brow as we readied our gear that he regarded me as an appendage, a primitive imbecile, at best.

He wasn't wrong.

Even my gun—my Weatherby—was patently ridiculous; and in a sense, almost linguistically so. When I looked at my case, its blocky, slab-serifed script encrusted in gold, all I could see was language, all I could see was its homophone: Mr. Weatherbee. That poor embattled pedagogue from the *Archie Comics*, with his rimless pince-nez perched atop that fingerling potato–like nose, perennially assailed by a gaggle of horny, ungrowing teens. And didn't Mr. Weatherbee somewhat resemble Dick Cheney? And hadn't Dick Cheney—to barb the edge still further—shot an elderly lawyer in the face while quail hunting in Texas? Of course he had.

Anyway, I was happy to put some distance between my father and I. It'd taken time to percolate, but as expected, Judith's soliloquy (lecture?) had agitated a welter of follow-ups. Over breakfast and dishes, I could hear my father droning on, pestering. "Wasn't it Corexit they used after Valdez?" "Did you ever meet the initial seller?" "Do you mind if I ask you who you contracted for the masonry?" And I wanted away from his probing.

"We all set there, Lucky Jim?" Willis pointed at my Weatherby. "Don't forget that."

I gathered my rifle and once again trailed Willis at what I judged a close but humble distance, idling a few metres back of his heels, giving him plenty of room to feel at one with nature, if that's what he needed to feel, while ensuring I didn't get lost. My stomach was a jumble of ground sausage and Scotch. The apple slices I'd washed down with my coffee had yet to loosen a stool. One whiff of the outhouse's bottomless black hellpond had settled it. I'd hold out as long as I could.

Willis's daypack sat high and snug on his shoulders. He clambered over the mucked trail with an assurance that bugged me, picking his way through the scrub, a staunch sylvan titan. I tried to keep my head up and eyes forward, to focus—on the scenery, the glistening trees, my breathing, my bowels—but I was having a hard time not staring at my feet, absorbing their dull, leery progress, as I negotiated roots and stones that Willis forded with ease.

In the woods, all around us, was quiet. The wind and rain had knocked down the last of the birch leaves and the forest floor was tinselled in yellow. We didn't speak. The quiet was ethereal, elastic, as of a thrilling, geopolitical détente. I registered the scuff and champ of our boots, the occasional crow, the odious click of my canteen bumping on my ass, the shuffle of our moisture-wicking pants, as so many aural dislocations. This didn't feel real, but replicated, sourced. And yes, I'm aware of how stoned that sounds, thank you; but walking—and gauging, as I walked, the sensory thresholds of roots on rubber, rubber on sock, sock on heel—I seemed to notice more and more the granular crevices in between these vibrations, as though my body (or mind) were operating on some very basic haptic technology. This wasn't nature, I wanted to remind Willis, but information.

At long last, our perch came into view. A dank, boulder-pocked meadow of undulant marsh and hardened marl. The boulders were the coarse taupe of whalebone and networked with lichen. The lichen was black with green kinks sprouting nearer the soil. The meadow called to mind an amateurish staging of *Godot* I'd seen in Calgary years before. Beckett gives Estragon and Vladimir a single tree with which to hang themselves. Here I counted six dead trees and one thicket. Did they look anything like Isaac's trees? The thicket was dead also—just a cage of tangly white thorns. There were no birds, no moose, no caribou, no coyotes.

Willis unhooked his rifle and shook off his pack.

"Now what?" I tried to catch my breath.

"Now we wait."

I unbuckled my pack and tucked it next to Willis's. He watched me do this, and then moved his own a little further down the line. "You don't always need to be so close to me," he said.

We studied the meadow. I sunk down on a rock. The air smelled better down here, anyway, nearer the cold sodden earth. There were three mirrors of standing water and one thin unrunning creek topped in water lily and sedge. Subtleties of colour ingratiated themselves on the soak. Cotton grass, blueberry, bog myrtle. The cinnamon ferns had turned, and their plumes' tall shallow fronds flamed a brilliant auburn, a stunning colour, like the breast of an orchard oriole. Patches of olive-brown lichen expanded out from the base of the rocks. I sipped water. I'd transferred what was left of the Laphroaig into a hip flask. I uncapped the stopper and swigged.

Willis watched me, and the lines on his forehead creased. "Little early, no?"

"It seemed fitting," I said, handing him the flask, and indicating our surrounds. "Bog, boggy. Get it?"

Willis placed his binoculars on the ledge and tilted the flask to his lips. "I don't know how you tolerate this stuff," he said.

A short tawny bird with cupped wings and a timid black tail scurried out from the ferns.

"Grouse," I said.

"Willow ptarmigan," said Willis.

Willis corked the flask and leaned the bottle on the rocks. He picked up his binoculars, propped himself up on both elbows, and peered out over the bog. "It was some speech you made," he said.

"Speech?"

"Seemed like a nice kid. Confident, brave, a certain vividness—whatever the fuck that means." Willis removed the binoculars from his face. Sweat pilled on his brow. The red of his cheeks—all those ruptured blood vessels—dimmed just short of his eyes, where the skin was crinkly and sagged. These bags were nothing new, though their colour had maybe deepened. Willis sniffled and wiped his brow, resting his binoculars over their green Velcro case.

"I guess what I'm wondering," he said, "is would it absolutely kill you—" He stopped. "You come out all this way, spend all this money, my money, just to booze it up and mope. You never think to ask how anyone else is doing, how—"

"Aren't I doing that now? Aren't we having those conversations here?" Willis was silent. He picked up a small rock and cast it into the meadow.

"You're upset with me about Travis, that I didn't, what—couldn't extemporize a spot eulogy? I'm sorry for what I said about his race. You're right I don't know what I'm talking about, but look, like I said, I was just telling you, trying to tell you what—"

"That's enough."

"Wasn't my idea to drag myself across the country to come sit in this fucking swamp."

"Swamps are coastal wetlands, fuckhead," Willis said. "This is a bog, or very possibly a fen."

"I mean you want to talk about commitment, we're all here, all of us, Isaac, too, because of you. These ludicrous war games—and Baker."

"You don't know the first thing about Baker," Willis said, his voice sharpened.

"What's that supposed to mean?"

"You know he's been trying to stay sober? That's right. And you come crashing back into town and suddenly it's Fear and Loathing in fucking Karaoke Kops."

"We didn't get to Karaoke Kops," I said. "And what's this about sobriety? We were shot for shot the entire night and he didn't say fuck all to me."

"How could he?" Willis studied me, my flask. "You and your boozing. You can't stand sitting in a room with anyone, with any of us anymore, without that shroud glazing you over. You fucking lush."

"High-functioning lush," I said.

"This is high functioning?" What started out as a snigger burst into a sour full-throated laugh.

"Whatever," I said. "Baker has something he wants to say to me—he wants to talk, talk. He wants a water, stick to water."

Willis turned away from me and wiggled his jaw. He took off his gloves and cupped his hands to his lips and blew into them. Then he cracked his knuckles, squeezing his fists and easing down on the fat of his thumbs.

"One minute you're upset with me about Travis, how I didn't say the right thing, and now we're off on some Baker tangent." I uncapped my flask and took a long drink. It tasted awful, but the gesture seemed, in that moment, the most violent, least loving thing I could do. "Which, speaking of Travis," I said, gulping back a peaty wet burp, "if you really want to get into it, wasn't I the one you called the morning after? It wasn't Baker you called, wasn't Baker you told about the document, the shooter's manifesto, the—"

"Alright now," Willis said, raising a hand. "Alright."

"Yes. Of course. That's how we like it, isn't it." I shook my head. "You know, when my mother, when—look at me—when my mother died. Where were you? Sitting here lecturing me. Where were any of you?"

"Fucking raising a family. Working a full-time job. Watching Netflix. What do you think? You think you're the only of us who's lost a parent? What kind of shit is that? Where the fuck were you, you morbid twat, when my dad—you called, sure, but, I don't know." Willis went quiet. "I'm sorry for your mother," he said.

"I'm not asking you to say sorry for my mother. I'm asking that you make an accounting to me."

Willis seemed to think about this. "Oh, fuck off," he said. "How's your life? How's your work? How's your fucking mother? Who gives a shit? You?" He was facing me again, and the whites of his eyes had grown shockingly bright. "You couldn't call? Couldn't ask how I was doing? How any of us were holding up?"

"I know," I said. We'd taken it too far. I wanted to put a hand on his shoulder, to slow everything back down, retreat and rewind, but tenderness seemed ill-advised. "I'm sorry," I said.

"Stop saying sorry."

"I will," I said. "I'm sorry."

We were both standing now. It'd happened so quickly.

"Where were you?" Willis asked. "I mean it. Like where the fuck were you?"

"I don't know. I was away. Alone. I didn't know what was required of me."

"Required?" Willis asked. His arms were shaking. "Required?"

"That's not the right word."

"There's something sinister in you." He looked away from me. "I don't know when you got like this but for fuck sakes. My son. You used to be, there once was a time—"

"I'm sorry. Willis," I said, "I'm sorry."

And with that he hit me. The punch, a brawler's loft, evolved inexpertly—all arm, no back—levelling me before I quite registered its impact. I tumbled over a tough stringy bush. I was not getting up. I shut my eyes, assumed more hurt than I immediately felt. I nudged around in my mouth for blood but could only sense its edging, the faintest trickle on my lips. Willis stepped over me and picked up his pack. I opened my eyes and rolled over, traced his progress as he skulked back down the trail with his rifle and bag, shaking his arms, fuming, plainly livid. I faced the sky and clenched at the cold silky dirt. I reached for my flask, and drank, landing the liquid away from my plump, searing lips. Then I rolled over onto my stomach and vomited. There wasn't much in it. A dreary grey bile. Just like everything else.

EIGHTEEN

WE CALLED IT GOING CHURCH.

As undergrads, Willis and I, and sometimes Baker, would meet up for coffee and cigarettes in the parking lot of the Seventh-day Adventist Church off Aldershot, which overlooked a decommissioned soccer field and the backyards of the strawberry-box bungalows lining Calver and Howley, faded, baby-blue clapboards with stiff metal fences veiled in polyethylene screens. The church—a tan A-frame with sturdy white gables plotted on soft ruddy brick—had belonged to the Pentecostals before the Adventists moved in; and, for us, the space afforded certain advantages of privacy and proximity to campus (though what impelled us to secrecy remains a mystery to me). Our sessions, as we called them, were short and quiet, abruptly courteous. Such worshippers as we sometimes encountered never gave us much grief.

The last time we'd all gathered together there, the last time the three of us went Going Church—the awkward interlacing of the phrase remains (to my ears) one of its abiding pleasures—we talked, in a way that shames me to remember now, about the future, and our respective plans going forward. This would've been 1999. A year I needn't Google. This was a year that seared. *The Sixth Sense, Fight Club, The Phantom*

Menace. Columbine. "High School Massacre," the headline read, above a graphic of blue-ruled paper, hole-punched with exit wounds, two golden casings etched over the words like a child's distracted doodles, like so much fearful symmetry.

It was a late afternoon in mid-June, a Friday, and we—Willis and I, at any rate; Baker, if I'm not mistaken, had requested a leave of absence—were in the throes of spring finals. The talk precipitated over multiple cigarettes and much caffeine, a sweet, balmy breeze easing through the rabid goutweed and Joe Pye. The lot was empty. Mowers droned in the lawns below us.

Willis, pacing the shadowed cornices, outlined his minimalistic studying strategies and expectations with an unworried sureness I detested. "There's literally nothing I can do now that'll make any difference tomorrow. No sense stressing myself out for no reason. Better to go in with a clear head." Which was easy for Willis to say. Already he'd accepted an offer in applied mathematics at the University of Toronto. I had one more semester left to me but no more prospective designs beyond finishing.

Baker, who'd part-timed the Dominion off Torbay to pay his own way through three directionless years at MUN, was heading to BC for the summer to link up with a reforestation outfit based in Prince George. After that, he didn't know. Maybe he'd re-enroll. More than anything, he wanted to travel. He had a cousin in California who taught at an outdoor education centre nested in the Lake Arrowhead and San Bernardino mountains who'd promised him a job tending kitchen in the fall if he could manage the airfare as far as San Diego.

"And I've thought about enlisting," he said.

Willis, with popped collar, with distressed jeans bootcut on checkered Vans, stopped pacing. "You serious?" he asked.

"I am." Baker, gamely hoodied, hauled back on the last of his draw, and sent his butt sparking down the lot. "I set up a meeting with a recruitment officer at the CAF in Quidi Vidi for next week."

Willis stiffened. The French inhales he executed with casual apathy betrayed a dash of early-Jack Nicholson seediness that felt studied. A fang of smoke hopped from lips to nostrils, and—and here came your *Cuckoo's Nest*—out again. "You're fucked," he said to Baker.

I don't remember if Baker responded to this, or how much of what he said that afternoon amounted to mere bullshit or boast. In a sense, whether or not Baker ended up meeting with a recruitment officer is immaterial. I know that he never went through with an enlistment and that he never broached the subject again. But the moment resonated with me—and resonates with me still—broadening inside my mind like a rogue portal. I could see Baker in Basic, in Saint-Jean-sur-Richelieu, off-ramping onto some alternate history, gliding his way through that mirrory screen.

Two years later and I'm in my first year of grad school, Willis is gearing up for his master's defence, and Baker's started in at the Pen. I remember, on what would've been, maybe, the first Monday after the attacks, sitting in on Dr. Bennet's Reading and Writing about World Literatures class, myself and three other TAs, listening to this one bruising, bed-headed undergrad sound off on Israel and the Mossad. "And what about the 4,000 Jews?" he'd asked. "The dancing Israelis?" He wore a Roots sweatshirt with torn tatty sleeves, the faded effigy of a Canadian flag scabbing on his back. "You're telling me you don't think it's the least bit suspicious, a call comes in, telling all these guys to stay the fuck home from work?"

Now, when I think back to that time, to those conversations, those attacks, I see, not collapsing towers, not bodies tumbling shoeless in a folded smolder of glass, not bewildered businessmen worrying their briefcases, bald pates rained in blood, not the white wall of missing outside Bellevue Hospital, not the former president reading *The Pet Goat* to a classroom of Black children in an elementary school in Sarasota (READING MAKES A COUNTRY GREAT!), not the former mayor striding alongside the former first lady, not even, really, the city, adumbrated in ash; certainly I'm not seeing Newfoundland in any of this, not Gander, with its hangar of dogs and cats and that Bonobo ape en route to a zoo in Ohio, en route to Broadway, ground zero, en route to a sold-out theatre venue near you—no.

What I'm seeing here is this: steely fighter jets taxiing on a carrier runway, visored ground personnel in earmuffs and reflective vests batting blurred neon wands. It's embedded troops in Charbaran and $28 million of green American money on dark-green Canadian-made camo for a nation whose forested corridors span less than three percent of their war-hammered land.

Baker figures in this, invariably. A speculative remembrance. Never a living friend but always, by degrees, a dead one. Sniper-plinked or riding a soft-skinned Humvee over a shattering IED, ball bearings and nails and smoldering copper rods ripping up through the grille and panelled chassis, a bouquet of gore expanding in gibs, in a pixel-like mist derivative of the first-person shooters we'd mastered.

Days we'd Go Church and only take one car, after our smokes, we'd drive the city, our coffees sloshing from cupholders packed tipsy with napkins and trash, a dimwitted soundtrack pulsing over us like a wasp in a jar. K-ROCK 97.5, Saturday in Big Tom's Shed, the All Request Nooner. We'd make the rounds of downtown, New Gower, Duckworth, Water, then up through Shea Heights, past Freshwater, Blackhead, Stopperside, Petty Harbour-Maddox Cove, before looping through the Goulds and carving our way back into the city by way of Paradise.

Part of the fun of it, I always thought, hinged on shirking the touristy hotspots.

Drive all the way out to Cape Spear, with its squat, neoclassical lighthouse, WWII-era dugouts and corroded coastal batteries, only to pull a Uey—not even bother stepping out of the car. Weekdays, when it was generally quieter, not empty, maybe, but absent the eager, sea-pining hoards, we might slink around the tunnels and bunkers, peruse the graffiti, the waves, nothing but waves and waves, frolicsome and grey, until you met Ireland.

Going Church or driving around the coast was where we solved the world's problems, where we called each other out on our shit, confided, and complained; Going Church was the medium through which certain intimacies, be they personal or political, gained valence. But it was Baker, absent from this trip, and often absent for these sessions, who authenticated the more enduring withdrawals; Baker, who saw in Going Church what I was maybe seeing now, nothing but bullshit, bullshit, bullshit.

As I lay on my back amid the minty morning rays, with my aching jaw and a concerning waggle lurking in one tooth, possibly still bleeding, I wondered at Baker's defection. It occurred to me that I might've been had. I assumed that embarrassment and shame at getting picked up by the harbour police, of spending the night gallowed away in the drunk tank or lockup, had stayed Baker's attendance, but then what *had* I seen? Sure, I'd witnessed, with my own two drunken eyes, Baker lurching aboard a boat. I'd watched men with flashlights, harbour police, maybe RNC, pursue him up the gangplank. But then what? And what sort of conversation, assuming even a recriminating one, might've occurred between two white harbour cops and one former prison guard? Had Baker leveraged this mild altercation (if altercation there had even been) as a means of avoiding the trip? Me?

"There's something sinister in you," Willis had said; I wasn't sure I disagreed.

It's true that I'd outgrown or grown bored of our confessional modes. Willis, too, had evolved, though I sensed, more than me, that he missed this, missed the incontinent tête-à-têtes of our undergraduate salons.

And I'd hardened, grown steadily more cynical and remote. On this Willis wasn't wrong. Where once I infused a sense of calm, soothing feuds and mending frayed feelings, now I seemed a perilous agent of chaos, an agitator of abject brawling, silence, and spite. What'd happened to me? What'd happened to the man who, hearing from Baker of his own parents' divorce, had dropped everything, driven across the city and picked him up from work, listened to him, without judgement, as he railed and wept?

As regards Travis, obviously my silence tracked callous. How could it not? But I didn't know what more I could say. Talk was unsuited to Willis's loss. And I was so tired. So very tired of talking, listening. It seemed gruesome to pretend otherwise. Perhaps I resented him, resented the perfect predictability of his career, its elemental ascendancy—philosophy, math, weather, oil, wind—his family, his money, his house. Even Travis's death, the public and political converging on the personal in violent abrogation of the self. Losing a son, and rebutting that loss with this insipid hunting trip, was not just absurd, categorically wrongheaded, and fucked, but—but what? What was I striving at here?

And then there was the matter of Baker's supposed sobriety, his difficulties with alcohol, which I couldn't help but read as indictment of my own—the pleasureless hours I spent contemplating my first drink (or, drinking, drink in hand, my next), imploring those in my warmest orbit to follow suit. I was the real problem, obviously. A bullying booze-fiend whose unbridled dependencies came at the cost of eroding relations among family and friends. Sure, I felt shitty about this (wouldn't you?), though maybe not for the right reasons. I wanted to say that, as Baker's friend, as someone who loved—or could still remember what it once felt like to love—him, I was worried for his well-being and health; but, if I'm aiming to provide the fullest account of my innermost feelings that morning, I'd better admit that it was the attention surrounding me, the consensus about my own character and conduct, that irked. I didn't want others to experience pain as a result of my behaviour (who does?), but, more than anything, I didn't want anyone to notice me, my hurt.

"How do I fix this?" I wanted to ask Willis, Baker, my father, my dead mother. "How do you fix me?"

I bit down on the left side of my mouth. The outside of my cheek and jaw, where the two were knitted, chafed. My teeth felt very present in my mouth, present but displaced, as though sitting in unassigned seats. It hurt to yawn. The air coming in and out of me sounded like our motorboat. Tugged, gassy, and snapping. Floaters danced in my left eye and my right. Maybe I needed to get myself into a program, read *The Big Book*, Go Church for real. I sat up. There was something scurrying at my feet. A slender, cat-like creature with round weighty ears and a bushy tail. It had a slightly tipped face, pointy, vulpine. Latched to its neck was a silver lanyard, from which a tiny red light blinkered. The creature regarded me with fearless longevity. I stood up, upending my drink. And then it moved on again.

NINETEEN

MY FATHER SAID, "WHAT HAPPENED TO YOUR FACE?"

I ignored him.

It was nearing noon. The sun, fattening in from the south, glinted over our pallid cabin in brilliant earnest, reviving its ailing bargeboards and mossed-over eaves. Judith stooped before the firepit, bracing a cast iron grate across the coals.

My father, propped over the fire, clasping his poker like a shepherd's mean crook, considered me. "It looks like you tried to fellate a jellyfish," he said.

"Jellyfish don't have penises," said Isaac. He sat on the rock I considered mine—the rock on which, hours before, I'd corralled wet eggs and loose-ground chorizo past my as-yet-unswollen lips—tinkering with the grooves of his stove.

"They don't have vaginas either," Judith said.

"What do they have?" my father asked with genuine interest.

"Depends on the jelly," Judith said. "Comb jellies pitch and catch. With cnidarians, anemones, and corals, it's often simpler if we think in terms of polyps and spermal mists."

"Polyps," my father said.

"And spermal mists," said Judith.

Isaac had his notebook open and appeared to be recording minutes.

"Where's Willis?" I asked.

"He came looking for you and went off again," my father said. He glanced at my face. "You should put ice on that."

"Noted," I said. I took a seat on the rock opposite Isaac. Judith rested an enamel percolator over the grate. Behind her, clamped underneath three stones, lay a strip of blue plastic sheeting, upon which a wooden salad bowl and mesh laundry bag were centred.

"What's all this?" I asked.

"Red squirrel," my father said. "We shot a whole bunch of them. Or, well, Judith did."

"The most dangerous game," I said.

Judith unfastened her pocket knife and retrieved a squirrel from the mesh bag. It was a good-sized squirrel, as far as squirrels went. Papules of coagulated blood stippled its pink little chin. The eyes were large and black as balsamic vinegar, the teeth bucked and chipper. Judith hoisted the squirrel up by the tail and flopped it belly-down on a stump, switched open her blade, and described two shallow incisions across the tailbone, broadening but not deepening the wound. Then she placed her knife on the blue mat. Gripping the squirrel by the hind legs, she brought a foot down on the tail, and pulled.

The hide flayed away like a sock.

She balled the matted fur aside, and worked away the clinging white fat with her thumbs. The feet she cut off with her knife—"Think chop, not saw," Judith said—and the head she twisted off in her fist. "Anyone want to try?" She slid the dim jam-coloured meat into the salad bowl.

"Sure," Isaac said. "But how come you don't just use a knife on the heads?"

"You can use a knife on the heads. But personally I find it a little easier breaking these guys up by hand. You start mucking around with a knife, you risk bursting the thorax and getting all those tidbits of bone stuck in your meat. You don't want that."

"Wait," I said. "So the plan is to eat these?"

"What did you think we were going to do with them?" Judith asked.

"Your blood too noble to break rodent with us commoners?" my father said.

"I don't know how to respond to that."

Isaac cozied one of the squirrels Judith had stumped to his chest. "So I just break it off?" he asked.

"Pretend you're opening a bottle of champagne," Judith said. "You ever open a bottle of champagne?"

"No."

"Well, what you want is to grip it tight, and then, just as you're about to pull, give it a final, quick little twist."

"Like a screw?" he asked. Isaac brandished the degraded creature by the tail in his left hand, miming the desired action in his right.

"Yes, but firmer. Think: Push. Then twist."

"Push then twist," Isaac said. "Push. *Then* twist." He joined his lips together in a pensive sulk and brought his hand over the squirrel's head. Closing his fingers around the animal's throat, Isaac cranked his grip down and to the right.

"Try again," Judith said.

From my vantage point, the action better behooved the appreciable frustrations one experiences wrenching open a child-proof bottle of Aspirin. But then who's to say what's what when it comes to metaphors? Far be it from me to malign the applicability of Judith's Demi-Sec. (I have not nor do I ever intend to decapitate a squirrel, pelted or unrobed to the bone.)

Isaac twisted and winced.

"That's it," Judith said. "Almost there."

There followed a disturbing crunch as the head broke clear of the throat and Isaac steered the gristly brain-helmet away from the last of its fibrous tissues and bones.

"I think I'm going to be sick," I said.

"You did it," my father said, clapping Isaac on the back.

"Okay," Isaac said, releasing a chuckled breath. "That was satisfying."

"See," Judith said. She took his squirrel and placed it in the salad bowl with the others. "Not so hard as all that."

The percolator emitted a nasally hiss, and a thin colour of coffee twirled across its windowed lid. My father removed the percolator from the fire. "Who fancies a cup?"

Willis approached the fire from behind the cabin. He handed me a can of beer, which I accepted and cradled to my throbbing jaw. "How's the face?" he asked.

"Hurts," I said.

"I think you'll live." He ruffled Isaac's hair and peered down at the squirrels, which Judith had salted and skewered and was now dusting with Old Bay. Willis faced me. "Let's take a walk," he said.

I grabbed another three beers from the cooler and stuffed them in my jacket, and followed Willis to the beach. The wind had fallen, and the sun stood at our backs as we filed down the worn grimy path. We walked right down to the water's edge and sat on a pair of flat stones. I could almost make out the beach where we'd left our cars, the gravel ramp and pilings.

"Me first," I said. "I'm sorry for what I said. What I didn't say."

"It's forgiven," Willis said. "I'm sorry I hit you. I'm not sorry I called you a twat."

"Non-apology accepted," I said. "*Did* you call me a twat?"

"Well, if I didn't, let's say the sentiment was implied." Willis opened a can of beer and took a deep pull. "It's not fair me putting this shit on you, on anyone," he said.

"No," I said. "I should've reached out. It's my fault for not saying anything. I can't imagine what you, Caitlin, Isaac—"

I let myself trail off. Speaking was unpleasant. I stroked my face, attempting a tentative palpation of my jaw. The lower left side was swollen and far sorer than the right. When I slung open my mouth, and swished everything around, a strange pain radiated in my ears. So that wasn't great.

"You know what they called it?" Willis asked.

"Who?"

"What the authorities, what everyone, even the Prime Minister." Willis gulped joylessly at his beer. "Caitlin and I, we get this call, okay. A day or two after. One of those No Caller ID numbers where you know you're just better off not answering. Heroism. That's what Our Fearless Leader called it. On behalf of the entire nation, I want to extend my heartfelt condolences. For his unflinching bravery. His steadfast resolve. I could hardly listen. I was so mad. We stood at the kitchen counter. Had the call on speaker. Caitlin's leaning over the phone, holding her head in her hands. I can't tell if she's crying or what. Meanwhile it's just this litany of stock phrases and civic clichés. It felt like a stump speech. I wanted to hang up the phone."

"But he was that," I said. "Travis. They said on the news that, without him, if he hadn't done what he did when he did. If he hadn't intervened, that—"

"Sure," Willis said. "I mean, I guess. But that's not really the point, is it?"

"The point of what?" I asked. Pond muck buffeted the motor-boat's worn wooden hull. The unopened can of beer I held to my face had lost most of its cool. I removed a fresher one from my pocket and relaxed the bottom half against my lip.

"Reducing him to a word," Willis said. "An idea." He wedged his beer can down in the craggy sand. "I miss him. I miss him so bad it's hard to care about what he did one way or another. I wish he'd been on another car. It sounds so fucking trite, but heroism doesn't bring my son back."

A bubble splashed in the water. Maybe the fish were biting. Willis put a hand over his eyes.

"That morning on the phone with you, I feel like I came to a realization. That I couldn't ever love myself or anyone fully, without him in the world. It was just like this gigantic void suddenly opened up. Taking over everything. Like all the good parts of me had gotten swallowed away somewhere I couldn't reach. And all that was left of me was trivial. This degraded vacantness."

Willis's face wore an expression of pained resignation. He fiddled with the lid of his beached lager, paring the brittle blue tab off its rivet.

"I see it in Caitlin. This vacantness. I see it in Isaac. I don't see it in Pen. Which thank fuck for that. In Pen, honestly, all I see is him. Which is funny because she's so much younger. Like they hardly knew each other. Travis was practically in university, heading out west, when we had her. But the way Pen looks sometimes. The way she squints down her eyes and lightens up a touch before doing something silly. Travis had that. A little coyness, a kind of brightening."

I said, "That's a beautiful thing. That's something you need to hold on to."

"I know," Willis said. He shot out a leg, whisking at the loose shale with his heel. "I fucking know it."

A gull plunged out over the water, trailing a wriggling white fish.

"What's hardest for me are the memories. Rising up out of the recesses of my subconscious or whatever. Memories of happier moments, sensory impressions, and these, maybe even more than the rest, these kill me, because partly I don't know what'll set them going. Something innocuous. The smell of bread, the Manna's honey oat loaves he'd gobble up by the bagful. And then I'll remember how he wouldn't eat peanut butter except cooked on toast, how he scowled at the sight of me with a spoon of it, stirring a big chunk into my oatmeal, how that specifically made him retch. And now I can't turn that off. Like his retching is there with me forever, a thing I just live with.

"When I close my eyes, and really think hard, I can see him running. The soft fall of his feet, the long stride. It was such an elegant stride. You've seen it. Probably nothing pleased me more than those mornings he asked me down to the track with him, to ferry him around to one practice or track meet or another. Best were the days when he just wanted me there with him, to clock his intervals, watch him run. The last time I drove him to the experimental farm off Brookfield Road, he wanted me to stick around and call out his splits. It was late summer. I stood at the top of the hill beside this big concrete block where he'd left his gear. He'd lent me his yellow stopwatch. 'Pick it up. Pick it up,' I hollered. How was I supposed to know this would be the last time?"

"Willis." I grabbed his arm, as if to render the seriousness, the totality of my listening in flesh. "I'm right here," I said. "I'm not going anywhere."

Willis studied me in silence. He nodded his head and his mouth became very small.

"When he was little, just a little boy," he said, "we'd bathe him in the tub. I used to love giving him these baths. Set out his toys. His fishes and duckies and floating boats. But there were some mornings, when he was old enough to stand, where I'd let him shower with me. And I remember the feel of his skin, my son's skin, his cold bare skin, and the odd little bones, and that big round bulb of his head, which made me so tremendously nervous to look at, especially for some reason when he slept." Willis covered his mouth. A single tear sped down his cheek. "And standing in the shower with me, we'd take turns, shifting positions, in and out of the wetness, and I remember thinking how I could feel his body by what it deflected. With him standing under the water, and me waiting for my turn at the front of the tub, I knew where he was."

Willis stopped. His voice had started to break, and the tears came steadily now, his and mine. I brought my arm over his shoulder and held him. Willis bowed his head. "And a few mornings after he died," he said, opening his eyes and peering out over the water, "I was showering, and I stood—I caught myself standing—just like I used to, at the opposite end of the tub. Waiting for my turn to step under the shower. Trying to find that bodily wall through which nothing, nothing but heat, warm radiant steam washing over me, would fall, but there was nothing. No wall. The water landed dully on my legs, and I knew, as I stepped back, and let myself pass through what was no longer there, that he was gone."

TWENTY

THE INTERMENT ISAAC PREPARED WAS SEDATE AND RESPECTFUL.
Early, on our last morning of camp, before setting off on a final hunt, we
gathered round a shallow trench Isaac had hollowed out in the woods, not
far from the cabin.

Above us in the close naked white trees a blue jay jeered once and
was gone. I followed its crest as it flashed through the wooded alleys,
a blurred and leaden shape. The air was redolent with stale leaves that
crisped pleasantly underfoot. The best of these were the ones with
snaps of brittle deadfall beneath them. You crunched, and then you
crunched some more. I swished my hands and stamped my feet. It
was just shy of eight, our coldest morning yet. We waited for Isaac to
speak; Isaac, in turn, seemed to wait for a single, sallow yolk of sun to
ripple through the slatted trees. He kneeled. And so we all kneeled, and
our collective breath fogged the depression he'd channeled out for his
brother. My father brought his hands together in a clasp and, bowing
his head, rested his elbows on the one raised knee. I alone of our
party opted for a full-on, double-kneed genuflection, an inadvertent
embellishment I felt too self-conscious to correct.

Isaac had packed along a clear plastic packet of his brother's rusty running cleats, a shoe, the shabby black sole greyed over with mud, a stuffed dog, its middle so worn and frazzled an old Duracell battery sparkled bronzely through the patches of snuggled fur, a book about the American runner Steve Prefontaine ("He also died young," Isaac said), the yellow stopwatch, and placed each of these items inside a tubbed PVC capsule of metallic maroon, and secreted this vessel in the ground.

I half expected Willis to hone in here on the biodegradability of these chattels, but he didn't. He kept his eyes closed and head slung low. Isaac read a poem. For the life of me, I can't remember which one. But, for present purposes, we might enlist Emily Dickinson's "I felt a Funeral, in my Brain"; or, better still, the poem read topside of Dickinson's own grave, the Brontë, "No Coward Soul Is Mine."

When Isaac was finished, he removed the wooden box of ashes from his pocket, glided open the lid and distributed its contents, gingerly, into his trench. Their colour was browner than I expected, and their consistency, the way the ashes clung and clumped, not really drifting, not quite, reminded me of the protein powders one mixes in with milk. Then he cupped the trench in soil, scattering his thumbprints with leaves. It was all very simple, intimate, almost childish, despite whatever concerns Willis might've had about Isaac's sepulchral fixations. Isaac knelt down and kissed the soil he'd patted with his hands and stepped away from the grave. We stood up. My father cried quietly. His shoulders shook, his brow furrowed, and he pinched the swollen, upper bridge of his nose. I came around the mound and drew my father into my chest. Above us a crow let out a raucous caw. I petted his back. "It's okay," I said. "It's okay."

After the ceremony, we gave Isaac and Willis some space. Judith was heading back to the cabin to take down her tent and begin lugging our gear back to the boat, leaving my father and I on our own.

"You're sure we can't help?" my father asked.

"Positive," Judith said.

We coursed the same knotted switchbacks I'd taken with Willis the morning before. The trails were mucky, the shrub trees and woody patches of sheep laurel and mountain holly shingled in frost. Broad clouds, dark as jet stone, flourished in the wiry canopy, threatening snow. The sun was still there, but barely, a diminished flint. I wore a lavender toque and my fingerless smoker's mitts and yellow raincoat— any aspiration toward invisibility all but dissolved. I leaned the barrel of my Weatherby over my left shoulder, stock in palm. I thought of toy soldiers, tin Hussars moored in felt, and of crouching, basil-green grunts. My arms were heavy and tired, and the bruise on my face— I hadn't bothered looking in a mirror—more purple than blue, according to my father, and apparently jaundicing.

"I should've put ice on it."

"Just keep drinking lots of water," my father said.

I wrenched my jaws, recalling the advice of a dental hygienist, who once asked if I gritted my teeth at night. "How would I know?" I asked back. "Try resting your tongue on your palate," she'd said. "Like this." She opened her mouth and demonstrated with her own tongue. I lay on a reclining dental engine, in sunglasses, DayGlo aviators, and bib, basted in bold, noisy light, practising. "That's it," she said. "Just like that. Now do that every night." I couldn't remember the last time I'd gone in for a check-up. I had no coverage (of course), no health benefits. But the truth is, irrespective of finances and institutional subsidies, I'd let it slide like so much else.

The sight of my father weeping beside Travis's grave—and I will call it that—had dismantled me, disabused me of my adolescent rancour. As I pulled him into my arms, feeling the sudden thinness of his body, the points of his bones, and the soft, sobbing weight of his head, I wondered where any of this ill will might've come from.

I sometimes wished that I had known him as a child; not as a father, then, but as a son. We do ourselves a disservice when we suppress all innocence from the present. To want to see the whole of a person, to seek accordance with all that is messy and rambling and mysteriously unadorned, seems, to me, a fairly desirable if not outright procurable ethos, a very basic way of moving forward in the world. Could I extend this want of sight (for lack of a better term) to my own father? Permit myself to fathom him as a child, consumed by some magnetic triviality, trailing a short stick across a white picket fence, kicking loose stones down an old dusty road?

Well?

I'd never expressed much interest in my father's work; which work, even when I myself was a child, I thought grievously unserious. Through high school and university, I performed in my share of musicals, plays, and nonsense comedies—hoping, I suppose, to impress him, to show him that I, too, possessed a certain sensitivity to the finely rendered line. I had decent range, projection, an easy affinity for memorization, timing, and a peculiar habit of narrowing my features when I wasn't speaking, which I'm told yielded terrifying results (in a good way). I manifested a steep inner turmoil, what my mother, who preferred movies, once called a "captivating lowness," and frequently played cuckolds, jackleg salesman, conniving brothers and sons. But I won't embellish my talent.

My father supported this pastime (his word), but regarded acting as categorically subsidiary to *his* art—a diminished enterprise, a platonic debauching of forms. Pressed, he might concede that he believed in casting.

I remember my last performance. An amateur matinee, a Sunday nothing. The play was Chekhov's *Cherry Orchard*, and I played the old manservant, FIRS, whom the Ranevsky clan abandons (spoiler!) to the soon-to-be-demolished cherry orchard in the final minutes of the play.

Within the world of the play, the reality of the stage, my time was done, but I didn't return for curtain call. I was twenty-three. I descended the wing stairs, made my way through the backstage corridors to the dressing room, slunk out of my costume (black waist-coat and weird Santa beard), and walked over to Burton's Pond and sat down on a concrete bench. It was winter. The pond was only partly frozen; a single gull, with a red dot on its beak and slightly drooping wing, strutted in the goopy ice.

Later that night, back at the house, standing by the kitchen sink, my mother said, "Where did you go?" I didn't know what to answer, but wanted to say, "Did he see me? Was my father there?"

My father was not in the room when my mother died, but I was.

This—the moment of her passing, I mean—occurred on a cold Friday morning in late February, at the Miller Centre, where my mother was receiving palliative—what neither my father nor I could quite bring ourselves to call end-of-life—care. I'd flown into St. John's on the last flight out of Calgary the evening before, my carry-on a mad scramble of random boxers and socks. "Things aren't so good," my father had told me over the phone. I'd just finished teaching, and I stood outside my classroom in the basement of Science B, beside a broken water fountain shrouded in hazard tape, as a cortege of students filed past me. I pressed a finger to my ear. "What?" I said. "I didn't catch that. Can you say again?" My father sighed, and this was a sigh I could fully visualize, lidded and drawn. "You still there?" I asked. "If you're coming," my father said, that slight snarl of frustration fading from his voice, "I think you'd better come now."

My father collected me at the airport. He looked, as I'm sure I did, terrible: bagged eyes glassy and creased; the hair, worn longer then, a thatch of matted greys. It was 1:00 a.m. (my time) and, in fairness, obviously later for him than me. He had no updates, no new information to relate, and we drove in what amounts to silence in my mind directly to the Miller Centre. Down Kings Bridge and onto Empire, a quick hop onto Forest Road. I felt restless and dizzy. My father had the defrost cranked to its driest rung and a stale breeze pungent with must gusted over me. I thought that if I could just focus on the streets, on the patter of slush knocking on the wheel wells, I might submerse myself inside a kind of calmed noticing. But the city was having none of it—no, at this hour, the city impressed itself upon me with the parodic volatility of a dream. There was the lake, the Dominion, the Anglican Cemetery, and there, right across from the hospice, grated in mesh wire and bars, stood Her Majesty's Penitentiary, where Baker, for all I knew, might well have been working—things had happened so fast (I told myself) that I hadn't bothered letting him or Willis know I was headed home.

We pulled up to the entrance of the Miller Centre, and my father slipped the car into neutral. "Okay," he said, easing up the handbrake, the engine still rattling away.

"You're not coming in?" I asked. I unbuckled my seatbelt and opened the door. A short skyway linked the hospice to the Veterans Pavilion.

My father kept one hand on the steering wheel, the other tensed over the gear stick. He peered over the dash. "I'm exhausted," he said. "It's what? Almost five. I need to try for a few hours' sleep."

"You're sure?" I asked. Only then did it dawn on me how badly afraid I was. I wanted him with me, I wanted him by my side. Was that so much to ask? I didn't know what the next hours might hold but knew that I couldn't endure them on my own.

My father said, "If you need me, if anything changes." He wiggled the gear stick, tapped his boot off the clutch. I reached into the back seat and hauled out my duffel and stepped out of the car. "My ringer's on," he said. He lowered the brake but was still staring at the dash.

"I'll call you," I said. I shut the door and, as soon as I did, he was gone.

My mother's room was small but private. They let you bring in your own bedding, and I recognized the grey mohair that swaddled her legs and the two shiny brown pillows like a pair of tall satin yams leaning against the headboard. On the mantel underneath a mounted flat screen were pictures of my father and I and of my mother's parents and of her brother, my ghost uncle, Samuel, who'd died in a motorcycle accident the year before I was born. A black mini fridge hummed in the corner. Atop the fridge a mylar balloon—rubber balloons, the receptionist had told me (with an insistence I found confusing), which might contain latex, were a no-go—rose up off a wavy white-ribboned tether. The balloon was grape-backed with my mother's name spelled out in silver glitter on the front. The room was unbelievably quiet. There were no whirring machines or clicking instruments, and there would be no overburdened doctors hastily making the rounds. The medications my mother received from the nurse who ministered her (and her alone; each patient had their own personal minder) were for pain and symptom-management exclusively. I sat on an amply cushioned couch to the right of her bed. The smells were about on par with any other ward. Antiseptic, starchy. A sulphurous, spoiled-egg-like reek flowed in from the hallway. The nurse who'd led me to her room, noting my disgust, identified this as a lingering melena—more blood than stool. Such a pretty word for such an abject thing.

So I sat and held my mother's hand while she slept—first, in the near dark; then by the gliding, half-square of light the room's one, east-facing window admitted. Her hair was short and combed neatly to the side. Brownish spots mottled her forehead. Her eyes were closed and the folded lids carried a slight protuberance like the throat of a toad. It took me some minutes to get used to her breathing, damp and crackling, with poignant interludes of utter silence broken apart by a moist snort. The stubs of her knuckles were badly arthritic. I rubbed their bulbs, their webbing, passed my fingers over the wide blue veins and the pale. The medical bracelet she wore over her left wrist looked like a baggy circle of glue with a fainter circuit of itself threaded inside it. I wanted to read to her but I'd not brought a book and the only books by her bedside were a leather-bound King James that'd belonged to her mother and a copy of Tom Clancy's *Ghost Recon: Choke Point* as written by Peter Telep, providence unknown.

Around nine in the morning, my mother's nurse came wheeling in with a trolley, hoping to record temperature and take blood pressure, but, as my mother was still sleeping, she decided to hold off.

"Is this normal?" I asked. "This sleeping?" In all the hours I'd sat beside her, my mother hadn't budged her eyes open once.

"Oh yeah," the nurse said. "That'll be the Lorazepam. Knock you right out. But then that's also just how a body gets." She rolled up her navy blood-pressure cuff and placed it back on her trolley. "You want I bring you a cup of coffee, love?" she asked.

"I'm good," I said. "But thank you."

I rearranged the pillows and stretched out on the couch. Another hour passed. I flipped through my phone and read around in James's Job and Telep's Clancy. Hard to say who fared worse. Poor boil-clad Job or Captain Andrew Ross, out there in the shit with his blinkering HUD, brooking rebel flak. I returned the books to the table and wandered over to the window.

The Old General Hospital, many decades abandoned, wasn't far from here. The building, which was of the same vintage as the penitentiary (slate shingles over ye olde parged English brick), had served as a military hospital before the redcoats decamped and handed the facilities over to what would not then have been called the provincial government. I remember sneaking onto the grounds with Baker and Willis to scout locations for a horror short Willis hoped to direct for a film class he was taking as an elective. Somewhere there exists a camcorder recording of the ten minutes we spent panning our flashlights around those jilted corridors before the very real eeriness of the place—cast iron beds prismed in cobwebs, shattered glass, cultish graffiti, and dangling wires (to say nothing of the startled pigeons and scampering wharf rats quartering in the rafters and walls)— overwhelmed whatever chilling conceit Willis had envisioned for us, and we came booking right out of there.

It annoyed me that, with my mother beside me, these were the memories my mind ripened. It seemed that the harder I tried to replay some vital scene, the more trivial and subsidiary these landscapes became. The best I could do was remember the afternoon she picked me up from school when I called home sick, took one look at me, palmed my forehead, and drove us directly to the Ziggy PeelGood's in Churchill Square for Pepsi and fries. "Don't tell your father," she'd said.

I came back to the bed and held my mother's hand. I immediately registered an incongruity. It is not enough to say that the hand had grown cold, thought it had, very cold, in fact, but the veins themselves, the gentle throb of blood coursing across her papery, liver-spotted skin, seemed depreciated—flattened. I released her and rushed into the hall. "Nurse," I called. "Nurse. Can someone help me?" She'd introduced herself in the waiting area hours ago but I couldn't remember her name. She came padding down the hall. "Something's changed," I said. "Her hands, they—" The nurse flowed past me and I followed her into my mother's room. She checked her pulse. She lowered her stethoscope and listened to her heart and lungs.

Another nurse appeared in the doorway. "Call Peter," the first nurse said. "And get Lanny in here."

Now the small room became faintly crowded and I retreated from the bed. The physician, Peter, leaned over my mother and repeated the same diagnostics, feeling her pulse, listening to her heart and lungs, and tried initiating a pupillary response, shining a small penlight into the eyes whose lids he held open. He clicked off his light and looked at his watch. I assume that an official pronouncement was then made but I have no memory of how this transpired.

I sat on the couch. A younger man wearing a straw-yellow sweater and a very dark goatee that looked like it'd been powdered in Vantablack took a seat next to me. He introduced himself as Lanny, the chaplain, and asked me if I wanted to pray. I didn't want to pray. All I wanted was to hold my mother's hand. I remembered a video I'd seen of a whale in BC, an orca, who, for weeks, cruising all across the northwestern Pacific, wouldn't let go of her dead calf. That's the kind of prayer I wanted. I wanted to hold my mother's hand as though it were my own hand, which it was, and I never wanted to let go.

"Can I touch her?" I asked.

"Of course," the chaplain said.

We stood up. The physician and attending nurses parted, and the chaplain escorted me to my mother's side. Her jaw had slackened, and her temples, as well as the lines under her lips, were sternly grooved. I fell to my knees and the chaplain joined me. I held her hand. I caressed the folded skin above her thumb. The chaplain rested his hand on my back. The window's half-square of light had widened. I hadn't eaten in maybe a day and, though my stomach growled, I felt bloated, dizzily full. At some point, another body—not my father's, not the chaplain's, not the doctor's, and not my mother's nurse—was suddenly beside me. Beth. She came into the room and sat down on the empty olive chair next to me. We were silent for many minutes. My mother's hand had stiffened. I did not realize that I had been trying in some strange way to warm or revive it. I kept running my fingers over her hand, pinching around at the undersides of her nails, which someone had trimmed. Beth edged her chair closer to the bed, reached out her own hand and placed it over mine. Her palm was miraculous. She lifted my fingers gently off my mother's, and I set my empty, useless hands on my knees.

"Come now," Beth said. "Let's get you home."

———————

The rock on which my father and I now perched was rimmed with crusty black nubbins of orchil. The ledge was not steep, and branches of quartz tinted its lower furrows. I worried my nose across the sleeve of my coat and itched under my chin. My father had put on his navy hat, which brought out the softer blue of his eyes and their whites, too. A slim stream, bordered in crowberry and birch, meandered below us. I half-heartedly tracked the line of it with my rifle. On either side of the water I noted a brown grass Judith had identified as scotch lovage. The way the birch was tilted, jutting out over the stream but not touching it, reminded me of a cowcatcher.

My father handed me his binoculars. So much of hunting is waiting, biding your time in gumptious expectancy. I find it discomfiting, the avidity, the moronic ardor. But within a few minutes of our arrival, my father detected movement in the trees, a shrug of bushes, and a moose lumbered onto the grass, craning its great reddish head over the stream.

About that head. The immensity of those antlers amazed me, their breadth and spread. To describe them (as guidebooks and wikis are wont to do) as either palmate or lobed seems sorely inadequate. These were giant wooden wings, Daedalian in their sweep, bolted to the moose's brow mid-soar. Icarus should have been so lucky. I counted nine tines per palm, with the longest of these curling up from the base of each paddle. It'd shed its velvet and the antlers' wood resembled that of a darkened, European yew. The growth, the very emanation or trajectory of these antlers as out of the head—and not, like a costume, merely on top of it—was inconceivable. "How?" I wanted to say, and then did, "How?"

My father ignored me. The moose, rooted in the soggy brown grass, ducked its head into the stream, and commenced lapping at the water with its inquisitive, camel-like snout. My father unzipped his green canvas bag, took out his rifle, and opened the scope. I adjusted the finder.

Needless to say, it was a beautiful animal.

The moose's front legs were longer than its back ones, and wobbled comically as it shrunk away from the stream. I remembered that the droop of skin under its throat was called a dewlap. I tried to locate the workings of the face. I wondered if the teeth were like a horse's where they extended out of the lips but they weren't. It was all lips and the colour of the lips was like wet muddy rubber. The eyes were black. I hadn't realized it was snowing until I saw the flakes landing and melting on the fur. A pair of ravens descended on the stream, perching themselves atop the tangle of protruding birch. One of them croaked but the moose took no notice. They sat there a minute, shifting their wings. I sniffled. My fingers were sore and cramped. There was a spot cresting the moose's humped shoulder like a birthmark. A near blondish patch, fuzzier than the rest. My father chambered a round and eased back the bolt, a resonant click. There was no wind. I noticed a smear of paler fur just under its snout, too. The face— I could assemble it now—was silly and intelligent. I followed its breaths, the softly swaying ribs. It wandered over to one of the crow-berry bushes and started gnawing on the bunches of withered red fruit. I placed the binoculars carefully on the ledge and wiped my nose. My father looked up from his scope, his gaze smarting over the iron sights. He set his rifle on the rock and sat up. He plucked an orange needle off the tree closest him and he chewed on this branch and he watched. I took a long breath. The lichen was giving off something sweet and jungly, like a poignant black handful of soil. After a while the moose twitched up its neck and moved on. We clambered down our little blind and walked along the streambed and studied the bushes and ground where it'd stood. The snow had stopped but the morning air was still cold and the sun was far away. My father put his rifle back in its case and slung it over his shoulder and we proceeded a while through the woods, following diverse paths, not talking, and not caring very much that we weren't.

Later that morning, veering back to the cabin, we spotted, just west of the beach, in a sweep of open barrens corrugated in glinting grey rock, Willis and Judith stooped over a brown corpse—a caribou, that Isaac had apparently taken, cleanly, at a distance of maybe 150 to 200 yards, according to his father, in one shot.

The bull had good size and the bullet hadn't splintered the bone. They'd dragged him up onto the level grass, flipped him over onto a large black tarp, and Judith, working a fixed skinning knife, was now tracing a swift, ring-like cut around the anus. "We'll leave the scrotum," she said, swabbing her brow with her non-knife-wielding hand. "Proof of sex."

I kept my distance, and so did Isaac. He sat on a low mossy rock with his rifle resting between his knees. He sucked in his cheeks and his gaze seemed to steady out over the distant bluffs, at the crimps of cloud bunching like frisky intimates on the horizon.

Willis was elated. "This is great," he kept saying. "Isn't this great? This is so great. I wish you could've seen it. It was like—wow."

The caribou dressed, we decided to head back to the Castle right away. While Judith and Willis finished bundling away the meat, my father, Isaac, and I loaded up our coolers, and began carting all our remaining gear back down to the beach. I had dreaded this moment, imagining some protracted departure, but our leaving took no time at all.

———————

Our return to the Castle was without incident. We delivered our meat to the on-site butcher, stepped into our rooms, showered, packed, received a warm meal, a night's rest, and the following morning proceeded to the main lobby, where Esme reunited us with our devices. A van would be coming for us shortly and driving us to the airport. The butcher had packaged up Willis's meat in hard-walled coolers, which we—my father and Willis, that is—would divvy up back in St. John's. Judith had come to say her goodbyes.

"You should consider coming back," she said to Isaac. "We could use someone like you to liaise with researchers."

"You hear that?" Willis said. "Structure, purpose, gainful employment. Who'd have thought!"

A young bald man, with a face so conspicuously flared at the brow that his profile seemed to suggest something faintly Palaeolithic, an early hominid, I thought, a missing link, approached my father.

"Sorry to bother you," this man said. "But you're him, aren't you?"

My father nodded at the solemn, big-headed boy. "In the flesh," he said. His German accent was impeccable.

"It's okay if I ask you for an autograph?" The man reached into his pocket and handed my father a crumpled trail map and pen. "I've seen almost half your movies," he said, awarding my father a quick, nagging smile. "I think *Fata Morgana* is totally underrated. In fact, I have this theory about the ending, *Das Goldene Zeitalter*—"

I resisted the urge to check my phone, to begin scrolling, for as long as I could. It seemed crucial that I do so, and I was managing alright until Isaac announced that they'd called the election. Then we all began checking our phones.

"This is just what this country needs," my father said, his accent fading on the *vhat.*

"Deserves," said Willis.

Judith rolled her eyes. She shook our hands and disappeared back inside the main lobby.

I didn't know what to say. I wandered outside. A single pistol tittered in the distance. There were many emails in my inbox and I realized, then, with a small, sinking horror, that I'd completely forgotten to cancel my classes, that while I was here, they were there, without me, unknowing.

My father came out of the lobby and stood next to me. "Miss anything?" he asked.

TWENTY-ONE

ON THE TUESDAY, FOLLOWING MY SECOND SKIPPED CLASS,
a pair of concerned students—one from each of my sections—notified the
undergraduate program director of my absence, which communication
initiated a torrent of departmental enquiry. The tenor of these emails
spanned a salad of bureaucratic emotion. Affable concern dwindled
to piqued diplomacy as the CC field bristled with names, epithets
faded to honorifics, best wishes and bests became thank you for your
understanding and thank you—full stop.

I was relieved that my colleagues had pegged me for a mere truant,
if mildly horrified that none had thought to call hospitals, police, or
solicit information from an emergency contact (if such a registry
existed for sessional instructors, which I somehow doubted it did).

In a sense, this was good news, though perhaps the only bit of
good news coming my way.

I sat in a lean conference room in Glacier Hall with the undergraduate program director, the acting head, and four other institutional
envoys not known to me by name. I apologized profusely (but not too
profusely) and—when asked to account for my disappearance, my
dereliction of email—pleaded delirium, fogginess, fever, chills, flu-like

symptoms made all the more aberrant by a bad reaction to an antiviral medication whose expiration date I had, in my reduced capacity, ignored.

The acting head abided my bullshit with the benumbed cynicism of one on whom thirty years of student entreaty had left its mark. "Okay," was all he said.

I expected a dismissal. Or no: maybe it's fairer to say I desired one. A solidifying outcome, a defining fall. But the department couldn't quite afford to get rid of me; and, as they hadn't the funds to enlist an impoverished medievalist or grant-spurned creative writing PhD to assume my courses mid-term—and because no self-respecting tenured or salaried professor would deign pick up the slack—my fall contracts, such as they were, remained unassailable, intact.

Still, I was given to understand, "in no uncertain terms," that serious conversations re my conduct and prospects of future employment at the university had occurred (my precarity had grown even more precarious). Effective the end of term, I would surrender my keys to Marit's office—and that's what they called it, too; not my office, finally, but hers—and vacate my burrow once and for all.

"But I can just give them back to you now," I said. "The keys."

"No, no," the head said. "That won't be necessary. Not now. But at the end of term. We're reconfiguring our allocation of offices, some of which, you may remember, we're ceding to Communications. All our sessional instructors, adjuncts, TAs, marking and research assistants, as well as those ABD candidates with temporary teaching appointments, will be sharing the old lunch room on ten starting in January. We of course recognize this is not an ideal situation for everyone—or really anyone, possibly—but we're all having, or some of us, anyway, to pinch."

I expressed my understanding with a nod, deferential, glad to be of use, and on the third Wednesday of December I arrived on campus early, before seven, before the small, family-run bodega on the first floor of Social Sciences unfurled its grated shutters, and began emptying out my office. This didn't take long. I made short work of the recyclables, shredded uncollected essays and exams. I jettisoned dry pens and leadless pencils, bagged away old, unbending energy bars, masks. I scanned the shelves and made two stacks of books, one for selling, one for home, and the rest I abandoned under a lilac sticky note marked "free."

It felt good, doing this. I felt good. I'd managed to stay mostly sober for just over a month and, though I didn't expect—or even truly intend—to abstain through the holidays, I found myself in the grips of an intimate renewal. Sobriety had awakened a nascent sweet tooth. I craved cookies and pastries, ornate cupcakes gilded in bright butter cream. By day I guzzled key lime LaCroix and açai smoothies with raspberries and chia seeds and crumpled walnuts strewn on top; by night, I consumed obscene quantities of herbal tea.

Over reading week I had met Marit for a coffee and walk around Prince's Island Park. We'd made the mistake of rendezvousing at lunchtime, and the trails were bustling with joggers and laggard pensioners power-moseying along the slabbed sidewalks, oblivious to incoming traffic, the bikers and skateboarders and heedless e-scooterists. A crew of city workers were flooding the lagoon north of Eau Claire in advance of the winter freeze, bracketing its bouldered shoreline in canvas yard tarp. We took our coffees to a park bench made of recycled plastic whose bolted slats and jarring armrests impeded sleeping (impeded with extreme prejudice!), and listened to the men in reflective vests warble and nag as they marshalled their bloated hose from one icy ledge to the next.

"So you're not teaching, you're not researching. You've got no background in educational development, and less than no interest, I'm guessing, in the private sector. So what *are* you doing? Or sorry," Marit said, tapping me on the knee, a wry smile gliding across her lips. "Is that one of those questions I'm better off not asking?"

"Well I've still got my two classes. I intend to finish up the term," I said. "But after that?"

"You ever think about going back home?"

"Home as in Newfoundland? Home as in home-home?"

"Sure," Marit said. "Why not?"

"I don't know," I said. "I do think about it." And this was true—true insofar as I'd started trawling job sites, scanning rentals, perusing floorplans, imagining myself the contended boarder of a two-bedroom, non-smoking, pet-friendly basement flat off Cavell, utilities not included.

"I mention it partly because if you're interested, I have a friend, retired now, a former colleague. Used to teach at York. She's looking to hire someone to help her outline a book project. A sort of history or biography. Something to do with this botanist, an amateur linguist from St. John's. You might've heard of him. Aloe, a l'oeil—"

"Aloysius," I said. "Aly O'Brien. His family ran the Mount Scio farm off Oxen Pond." I could see the wooded hills trailing over Pippy Park, the brilliant white clapboards and olive trim of Thimble Cottage. My mother used to send me packets of Mount Scio Savory come holidays—and how well the smell of minted marjoram and thyme coated whatever else she happened to bundle away for me in her care package, a sparkled card, a new notebook, a medley of zany wool socks. The last of these packages I received included three slate coasters. The accompanying card told of the rock from which they'd come, quarried in Burgoyne's Cove. "Don't ever forget where you're from," she'd written.

"So I have no idea what the pay might be like," Marit said, "but the work can be from anywhere. I think she's still based in Toronto. If you're interested, I'd be happy to put you in touch."

"Sure," I said. "Why not?"

My relationship with Willis seemed improved. I'd anticipated some awkwardness, a probationary period marked by austere reticence and mild indignation, but I was now receiving regular updates, nonsense gifs, and calls. Penelope had landed a part as Tiny Tim in her preschool's adaptation of *A Christmas Carol*. "She wants us to make her a crutch. Which is fine. I can manage a crutch. But there's this whole controversy at her school. Some of the teachers and parents are wanting to cut the God out her one line, 'God bless us, every one,' and they've come up with a shortlist of secular alternatives. 'Is this a real goose?' and 'Yum! Looks good!' So we'll see what comes of that." Isaac, meanwhile, had joined a conservation outfit, and in the new year would be travelling to Iceland to take part in a reforestation project in Úlfljótsvatn (Ugly Wolf Lake), about an hour east of Reykjavik. "I don't know. Whole thing sounds frankly batshit to me. Aren't there trees over here that need planting? But what can I say? Caitlin feels a change of scenery might be good for him. We think maybe he's met someone. Caitlin thinks he's fallen in love."

I'd messaged Baker as soon as I got back to Calgary and we'd started Zooming every couple weeks. He was easing back on the boozing and smokes, managing alright at work. I told him that I was sorry, sorry for everything—he hadn't been lying about the drunk tank—and that I wanted to see him in person again soon. In November, just after Remembrance Day, his beloved boxer, Brad, suffered a seizure. "He was so old," Baker said. "It wasn't really a surprise. But it was still hard. I drove him to the veterinary clinic on Topsail. I'd called over in advance and someone came and met me at the door. I went into this room and I just sat there with him. I held him. I petted his ears. I wanted him to hear my voice. I was still holding him, still talking to him, when they pulled the needle out."

We talked about our struggles with alcohol. I told him about my one-monthish achievement—no, I don't love that word either— that things were very new and strange (and, full disclosure, often freakishly boring), that I didn't have much to relate as yet, but hopefully one day, hopefully soon. Baker told me that he'd been sneaking vodka on the job, wet-lunching his way through happy hour, running a full-court press on his chequing account come weekends. His blackouts were commonplace, swaths of consciousness lost to a harrowing fog.

He woke up in unfamiliar beds with nameless companions, mysterious cuts on his fingers, bruises and scuffs. "I got used to the way people look at you when they've seen you all fucked up. I got used to smiling." He felt that his own dependencies owed something to the years he spent working at the Pen. "That place did a number on me. I don't even think I fully understood it at the time. That guy they shanked. I was there that day. I was one of the first ones who broke that shit up." At the recommendation of his family doctor Baker attended a PTSD support group but this hadn't panned out. "I went to a few sessions, okay. But these were guys, vets mostly, guys who'd served overseas, in Afghanistan, like well over a decade ago, and it's been, I don't know. I think about everything that's been going on now and how fucked up it must be for them. They were, every one of them, real welcoming and supportive and all that, but, I don't know, my being there, it didn't sit right. I used to always like to think that it could've been me right there with them, but it wasn't. It really wasn't, man." After he lost Brad, Baker signed up as a volunteer with the SPCA. Twice a week he drove down to the animal shelter off Higgins Line to walk dogs. "They kept getting after me to foster, so I finally told them, I said, Yes, alright, I will. And you know who they've got me paired with? You won't believe this. They've got me partnered up with a cat. Two cats, in fact. Kittens. A brother and sister—absolute terrors," Baker said, "both of them."

Campus was quiet and few students pestered the halls. As I packed up the last of my books and unfastened my nameplate, I imagined tourists straining behind a velvet barricade, gazing into my office, a guide saying, "And this is where they worked, or purported to. On the floor, here, where you see this purple yoga mat next to the outlet with the yellowed iPhone charger still plugged in, and the stacks of unreturned library books with the brown Noodle & Grill Express napkins tented over them like a pillow, is where this un-unionized sessional instructor with no medical benefits in all likelihood napped. And, over here, inside his desk, is where he kept his pills and deodorants and stored or collected for reasons having to do possibly with worship empty bottles of mouthwash."

I could hear our department's most prolific Elizabethanist, Bill True—a fount of irrepressible Britishisms, True could tell you everything you might ever want to know about Ben Jonson and Robert Devereux but were *rather* too bored to ask—with whom I shared a wall, unlocking his office, stamping his feet on the bristly doormat he kept to the side of his desk, clearing his throat as he unwound his scarf, hung up his jacket, and slipped out of his winter boots and into the clean, squeaky sneakers he wore indoors. I waited for him to settle in at his desk, flip open his laptop—that inaugural chord—before scurrying out of my office, past the washrooms, and up the back staircase, where, at this hour, it was unlikely I'd bump into anyone, and on past the break room and printer room and windowless alcove where they used to make you write your candidacy exams, to the department office, where I placed my keys—Marit had given me two—on the desk of our academic programs specialist. I didn't say goodbye to anyone. My final grades were submitted, the last of my clerical doldrums dissolved. I had no outstanding engagements and no forthcoming classes—I'd decided not to re-up for winter positions—so there were no forms that needed signing, no syllabi pending approval, no reason, beyond politeness, or good citizenship, I suppose, to tell anyone where I was going, or why.

It was not yet nine when I stepped out of Social Sciences. My father and Beth were visiting for the holidays. They'd arrived on Sunday night. It was my father's first trip out west since convocation, however many years ago. I'd volunteered to put them up at my place—I had room enough in my own basement to accommodate guests (barely)—but, as they intended to rent a car and spend a good deal of time in the mountains, they opted for an Airbnb. Fine by me. We were heading to Canmore later that morning, and I was supposed to message my father as soon as I finished clearing out my office, so they could come pick me up at my apartment, but first I wanted to delete my university email. I had one message from that morning, a student wishing to discuss their final grade. My Outlook account prompted three (incrementally absurd) replies: "When is it due?" "Let me think about it." "All of it." I began thumbing out my own unthinking boilerplate—"Dear X, Thank you for your email. While I appreciate your concerns, unfortunately (and in fairness to other students), I am unable to"—and then I deleted what I had written, and, with a perfunctory flick, disappeared the icon from my phone.

I hurried across campus at a brisk but bated lope, past the pillared Donor Wall with its glassy, arctic-blue halo wedged alongside the university's motto—an abridged Gaelic psalm, mistakenly etched in Irish: Mo shúile tógam suas (note to sculptor: those accents slant the wrong way)—past Admin and the Internal Attention Lab and Bio Sci, across Campus Drive, and along the icy, unshovelled walkway shadowed in high hulking oaks. Faceted red bulbs studded the rails of the pedestrian bridge feeding onto the LRT station and the morning light lapsed stiffly through them. Below me, southbound traffic thrummed over Crowchild. Spindrifts whipped in the crushed gravel tracks. My early-AM transit pass was expired, so I purchased a second ticket, descended the steps, and wandered to the far side of the platform.

It occurred to me that my father and Beth might bump into Jerry while they waited for me. The possibilities of such an interaction amused me; we had recently grown somewhat neighbourly, he and I. One morning, about a week or two after my trip, with a bin of recyclables clamped against my chest, I'd found him curled up in the backyard next to his plinth, clutching what looked like a baroque, multi-headed duck. I dropped my recycling and called an ambulance. Stroked out? Dead? I rushed into my apartment and came spilling back down the steps with pillow and blankets. I checked his pulse—there was one. So that was good. I listened inside his robe for breaths, and here they came, a whistly pant and rattle. I bandaged him in blankets and disentangled the duck beast from his talons. We sat in this way for nearly an hour, beside his plinth, waiting on EMS. Later Jerry told me that pressure in his carotid arteries had precipitated the fall. "Doctor says they're going to suit me up with a pacemaker," he said. "Look. So, anyway, I just wanted to say thanks." He handed me the duck.

The train funnelled to a stop. I took a window seat and faced away from my reflection, my backpack and satchel of books stashed at my feet. I stepped off at Sunnyside, but, instead of waiting for the number 3 bus on Kensington, I walked across the 10th Street Bridge, admiring the slabs of ice shifting in the sluggish current like comet shards, like fallen omelets of moon. I continued along the river pathway and up Barclay, south of the Weston, toward Stephen Ave., where—it happened so quickly, I hadn't even bothered registering the colour of the line—a westbound train stopped and, readjusting my bags, I got on. Blue would bring me near enough my apartment that I could probably walk home, while the Red line would send me right back across the river for Kensington. As we rustled through the downtown core—bankrupt bars and eateries and boxy high-rises, the abandoned office buildings still broadcasting a ghostly fluorescence—the river tilted away from view, in a blur of frosted balsams, and I began to relax, let myself blank. I popped my earbuds in and keyed up my phone. It was only then, my thumb hovering, that I realized what I had done, registered what train I was on. I looked for a seat but there were none around me. I put my earbuds back in my pocket. I regarded the passengers. How would you ever know who among them was it?

We swept over Bow Trail, the Centennial Planetarium, the Mewata, the skatepark, the Staples, and up over the 14th Street Bridge, the dealerships and showrooms and forsaken scrapyards (made to look like dingy Minnesotan cash drops in that season of *Fargo* where the resurrected junkie from *Trainspotting* plays both brothers) trembling below us, as we slowed to a blurry stop, coming up on Sunalta. I felt trapped, or worse than trapped, walled in from within, confined to the silt-strewn floors sparkly with boot salt, and confined to (or perhaps merely confounded by) the irons of my own anxiety, the blood grab and dance of an animal panic. I gripped the handrail. I could manage that much. I closed my fingers around the cold silver beam as a queasy squeeze ran up my throat. I swung back on one heel, shifted my grip, and let my weight slack. To my right, coursing in the south, were shuttered tenements and row-houses, roofs candied with snow. On some of these were painted placards:

SAY NO TO MASS IMMIGRATION!
CANADA IS BLEEDING.
KEEP CALM AND ROLL COAL!
I ♥ OIL & GAS!
LIFE TRUMPS DEATH!
PROTECT OUR CHILDREN!

I wasn't ready for this. I looked down at my phone, a text from my father ("We're out front. Where you at?"). The train started again and we sloped over West Scarboro and into Shaganappi Point Station. I thought to get off. I thought to step off the train and call my father, ask him to come pick me up. But I didn't. The doors opened and closed and we rode on. Up ahead the tracks dropped down into a tight swerving tunnel and the sounds of the train became chambered, oceanic and coarse. I took a deep breath, as though I were entering water myself, and tried to calm my pulse, lower its throb to a more manageable level. I hadn't been underground—hadn't traveled this far, on this line—since Travis's death. Our next stop was Holbrook Station.

In the tunnel, all around me, fiery white lights swarmed the faces of my fellow travellers. Some stood gripping handrails and bars, while others braved the rolls and jolts from a more tranquil vantage. The train's accordion inter-car diaphragm flexed, an empty coffee cup with a chewed lid rolled down the aisle, leaking cream, a woman looked up from her book to watch it roll, and a man sitting with an armful of bags folded across his chest cupped a yawn. A smell of bitter perspiration hung in the air.

A surviving passenger said the first bullet sounded like one of those snap firecrackers you flick at the ground, but that the second one, and all the ones that came after, sounded denser. The nine victims ranged from eight to fifty-one years old. Not counting the shooter, Travis was the last victim, though the first shots to strike him were not likely immediately lethal, according to the coroner's report, as he continued forward, on.

I confess that I have often wondered about this moment. The inner logistics of it, the will. Did he speak to the shooter? Had he tensed himself, primed his fists, charged, readied his body for a fight? "He'd just been crouching behind one of those little like glass barriers," one of the survivors later told reporters. "There were a bunch of us there, huddled, trying to duck underneath the seats, and then the next thing we know, he's stood up."

And what might've happened if he'd stayed put? Or ducked? Did he and the shooter lock eyes? And what difference might it have made if they had? Why was he on this train and not an earlier one? And what little lifely hiccup—a bathroom break, a loose shoelace—might've rerouted him?

As we passed into Holbrook, a voice rendered itself belatedly over the PA system, announcing our next stop. I blurred my eyes down to slits and listened to the burst and click of contact wires gusting overhead, an eager iron hum. I felt compelled or compelled myself to feel calmer, to seek out amid the clamour and violent white light strobing over me a stillness that might be sustained. I thought of Travis running and of Caitlin and I sitting in the stands waiting for him to run, the slathered sunscreen and sweat and nasally scrape of traffic riffling in the distance—what seemed to me then (and seems to me now) the special wellspring of a late-summer day. We watched the runners assemble and deform, execute the last of their high knees and tuck jumps, their quirky shoulder writhes and jiggles. A man with a wide orange cuff on his arm came forward and readied his pistol. Travis, in plum singlet and shorts, leaned up to the line. When the gun goes and the smoke clears, you'll want to find him, amid the rabble, but it can't be done. The oneness of it can't be sustained. There is too much speed in what follows. Too many bodies. The gun goes and the feet surge in a single alien gallop.

I opened my eyes. The train doors parted with a sullen jolt. I gathered my bags and stepped off the train and followed my fellow passengers up the station steps. Pigeons cooed and flapped in the sallow rafters, a kid said to another kid "I don't like to play those games," and a sleeping man with a sign accepted my change. I was nearing the top of the steps when my phone rang.

"Where are you?" my father asked. "Were you able to see any of my texts?"

It was sunny. I pushed open the station doors, and wandered back out into the day, the sky bright, warm, a touch of wind keening in the east.

"I'm just getting off the train," I told him. "I'm coming home."

Acknowledgements

Thank you to the entire Breakwater Books team: Rhonda Molloy, Claire Wilkshire, Rebecca Rose, Carola Kern, Nicole Haldoupis, and George Murray. Thank you to my wonderful editors, Shelley Egan and Brock Peters. Many sources went into the formation and thinking of *Hides*, including: *The Iambics of Newfoundland* by Robert Finch, *Hiking the East Coast Trail* by Peter Gard and Libby Creelman, *The Gannet: A Bird with a History* by J.H. Gurney, *Life Everlasting* by Bernd Heinrich, "Retreat" by Wells Tower, and *The Uninhabitable Earth* by David Wallace-Wells.

Thank you to Mark Anthony Jarman, Suzette Mayr, Tamas Dobozy, Brecken Hancock, Navtej Singh Dhillon, Charlie Lee, Harry Vandervlist, Rick Moody, Ajay Singh Chaudhary, Greg Gerke, Daniel Davis Wood, Emily Donaldson, and Deborah Willis.

Thank you to Jenessa Drebnisky, Elyse Bouvier, Ross Moore, Matt Grant, Steve Woolridge, Michael King, Jeremy Shannon, Richard Young, Jaci Carter, Alex Grill-Donovan, Michael G. Khmelnitsky, Lucia M. Polis, Mel Hamilton, Hollie Adams, Brian Jansen, Peter Forestell, Ed Griffiths, Jim McEwen, Sarah Neville, and Majors Luke, Kevin, and Anne.

This book wouldn't exist without the love and support of my family. I am grateful to the Nicol family, and to my parents, Dale and Penny. Thank you Justin and Pam and little Harrison (this one's as much for you as for your dad).

Jess Nicol and Martin Schauss endured more iterations of this book than they may reasonably care to remember, and for this, and for so much more, thank you. Finally, to Jess and Five, with all my love.

Author Photo: Elyse Bouvier

ROD MOODY-CORBETT is an award-winning writer from Newfoundland. His writing has appeared in *Socrates on the Beach*, *The Drift*, *The Paris Review Daily*, and *Fiddlehead*, among other publications. He is the recipient of the 2022 Howard O'Hagan Award for Short Story, a Newfoundland and Labrador Arts and Letters Award for Short Fiction, the University of Calgary's Kaleidoscope Prize, and the CBC Canada Writes Short Story Prize (People's Choice Award). He serves as a contributing editor for *Canadian Notes and Queries*.